The Babe and the Baron

THE BABE AND THE BARON

CAROLA DUNN

THORNDIKE
CHIVERS

This Large Print edition is published by Thorndike Press, Waterville, Maine, USA and by AudioGO Ltd, Bath, England.
Thorndike Press, a part of Gale, Cengage Learning.
Copyright © 1997 by Carola Dunn.
The moral right of the author has been asserted.

LIBRARY OF CONGRESS CATALOGING-IN-PUBLICATION DATA

Dunn, Carola.
    The babe and the baron / by Carola Dunn. — Large print ed.
       p. cm. — (Thorndike Press large print gentle romance)
    ISBN-13: 978-1-4104-3975-8 (hardcover)
    ISBN-10: 1-4104-3975-5 (hardcover)
    1. Large type books. I. Title.
PR6054.U537B33 2011
823'.914—dc22   2011017752

BRITISH LIBRARY CATALOGUING-IN-PUBLICATION DATA AVAILABLE

Published in 2011 in the U.S. by arrangement with Carola Dunn.
Published in 2012 in the U.K. by arrangement with the author.

U.K. Hardcover: 978 1 445 83816 8 (Chivers Large Print)
U.K. Softcover: 978 1 445 83817 5 (Camden Large Print)

Printed in the United States of America
1 2 3 4 5 6 7 15 14 13 12 11

THE BABE AND THE BARON

PROLOGUE

"Halloo, Laura!"

Freddie? Startled, Laura pricked her finger with the needle and quickly put it in her mouth before the welling drop of blood stained Lady Denham's shawl. Despite her husband's unusually long absence from home, she had not really expected to see him till next month — he would not miss the first Newmarket race meeting of the year.

Through the window, open on this unusually balmy March afternoon, came the sound of several pairs of boots on the flagged path.

Sally burst into the tiny, shabby parlour. " 'Tis the master, madam, wi' three more gentlemen. I were upstairs dusting and I seen 'em in the lane." Pink-cheeked with excitement, the youthful maid swung round as the front door slammed open, shaking the cottage.

Freddie appeared in the parlour doorway, fair hair ruffled, a casual Belcher handkerchief knotted at his neck. At thirty he was still a good-looking man. If the blue eyes were a trifle bloodshot, the regular features blurring, the lithe figure somewhat thickened, Laura still recognized the handsome, dashing buck who had once captivated her.

Sally bobbed a curtsy and giggled as he set his dusty beaver atop her mob cap and thrust gloves and whip into her hands.

He turned to Laura, grinning. "Well, old girl, I've something for you." Reaching into the pocket of his multi-caped greatcoat, he pulled out a heavy leather sack, plunged his hand in, and dropped a handful of gold guineas in her lap.

"Oh, Freddie, just a minute." The familiar feeling of mingled fondness and exasperation crept over her. "Lady Denham's shawl —"

"To the devil with Lady Denham's shawl." He plucked the offending garment from her hands and tossed it on the floor. "You'll have no need to take in embroidery for a while, m'dear. I've had a run of luck."

"Picked three nags in a row that didn't fall over their own feet," confirmed the plump, dandified young man who had followed him into the room. "How d'ye do, ma'am?" He bowed.

"Hello, Sir John." She had no time for more as Freddie upended the sack and deluged her with a clinking shower of gold. With a gasp she tried to contain it in her skirts, hoping the worn grey calico would not split. A few coins escaped to glint on the canvas-work rug at her feet.

"Not bad, eh?" Freddie beamed at her astonishment. "Buy yourself a new dress. Grey don't suit you. Tell you what, you can come with us into Newmarket tomorrow. We're going to tour the stables, check the form."

Cambridge had better shops, but Newmarket was cheaper. Laura expressed proper gratitude, then asked, "Shall you stay home for a while, Freddie?"

"Damned if I know. You're not going to start nagging, are you?"

"Oh no, but I have something to tell you."

"What?"

She blushed. "It's private."

"Cut line, old girl," he said, impatient. "Jack's an old friend and the others don't mind."

"Won't breathe a word," vowed Sir John Pointer. Squeezed in behind him and Freddie, the two unknown gentlemen nodded with solemn faces.

Arguing with Freddie was utterly fruitless, and now his curiosity was aroused, he would badger her until she told him. Since he insisted, let him have it plain, without roundaboutation or polite euphemisms. "I'm pregnant," she said bluntly.

He stared at her for a moment, then, with a whoop, he seized her hands and pulled her up out of her chair. Gold coins rang on the brick floor, rolled under furniture and into corners as he swung her round, knocking over a small table.

Jack picked it up. "I say, congratulations, old fellow."

The strangers murmured agreement, looking uneasy.

"At last!" Freddie exclaimed. "This calls for a toast. Bring us a bottle, Sally."

"Please, sir, there's nary a drop in the house."

"You have been gone three months, Freddie," Laura reminded him. "Since December. You were on your way to a Christmas hunting party with —"

"Never mind that. We'll have to go down to the Bull and Bush to celebrate, fellows. I'll need a spot of the ready rhino." He stooped, collected half a dozen guineas, and dropped them in his pocket. "See you later, Laura." Patting her cheek, he herded his

10

friends out of the parlour. A moment later they tramped back down the path to the lane.

"Now you just sit you down, madam," said Sally. "It won't do you no good crawling on the floor in your condition." She plumped down on her knees and started gathering guineas.

Laura pushed the loosened pins back into her dark hair, and straightened her cap. She sank into her chair, then reached over the arm to retrieve the shawl. Smoothing it between restless fingers, she wondered why she had imagined her news might induce Freddie to change his way of life.

Not that she wanted him at home all the time. The cottage was too small to contain his energy. He was always bored to irritability in Swaffham Bulbeck within a week, even with Newmarket nearby.

She had built a contented life for herself in the little hamlet in the years since she insisted on buying the cottage with the proceeds of an earlier run of luck. Her neighbours, both villagers and gentry, were friendly and helpful. Lady Denham not only paid well for Laura's exquisite embroidery, she brought commissions from her acquaintances. Sally, a farmer's daughter, was honest and hardworking, glad of the chance to learn. One day the girl would seek a better position at Baldwin Manor or Swaffham Prior House; in the meantime she was cheerful company.

Freddie's infrequent visits sometimes brought welcome funds, but they disrupted the even tenor of Laura's days. However unsatisfactory his presence, when he departed he left a gaping hole that took time to paper over. Once again she would have to bear the commiserating glances, the whispers behind her back, the scarcely concealed pitying scorn of women whose husbands seldom strayed far from home.

How different things might have been if he had found her attractive! Folding her hands on her barely swelling abdomen, Laura blinked away the tears that rose to her eyes. Freddie had married her out of careless kindness and had never come to her bed sober. Small wonder it had taken five years of marriage to conceive a child.

"That's all I can find, madam. Two hundred yellow boys, near as makes no odds." The maid sat back on her heels, regarding the gleaming heap with satisfaction.

"Thank you, Sally. Take your wages for last quarter and the next, and put the rest back in the bag. Then we had best start preparing dinner in case Mr. Chamberlain brings his friends home. How fortunate that the squire brought a rabbit this morning."

Laura was not in the least surprised when Freddie failed to return to dine, with or without his friends. Nor did she wait up when ten o'clock came and he still had not put in an appearance. She had just donned her white cambric nightgown, unpinned her hair, and picked up her hairbrush when she heard a commotion in the lane.

A rush of footsteps on the path. The door-knocker's clangour beneath her window. A group of dark figures at the gate, silent now. Laura opened the casement and leaned out, holding her candle.

"What is it?"

Jack's round face turned up to her. He doffed his hat and clasped it to his chest. "Mrs. Chamberlain, there's been an accident," he panted, his words slightly slurred.

She froze. "Freddie?"

"He was dancing on the table, you see, celebrating, merry as a grig, and he took a notion to swing from the lantern hook on the ceiling. Stands to reason it wouldn't hold a grown man. Broke his neck."

When everyone had gone, Laura bowed her head in her hands and wept, not for the past, or the present, or the future, but for what might have been.

CHAPTER 1

"Damme if you shouldn't be banned from the Marriage Mart as a heartless flirt." Captain the Honourable Rupert Wyckham stretched his long legs across the width of the carriage, careful not to brush against his brother's impeccable white stockings.

"Hardly likely, when half the Ton has rushed off to Paris, leaving London thin of company." Gareth laughed, his teeth gleaming by the light of the gas lamps in the street. "Besides, the lady patronesses will never turn away a wealthy peer with an unblemished reputation, as long as he turns up in knee-breeches."

"And arrives at Almack's by eleven o'clock. But why the devil do you go, Gareth? A more insipid evening cannot be imagined. Nothing to drink stronger than ratafia; whist at sixpence a point; and the patronesses always dragging one off to stand up with some fubsy-faced chit scarce out of the schoolroom."

"Why do you accompany me?"

"There's always the chance of meeting a dashing widow." Rupert preened his blond mustache and flourishing side-whiskers. "Your mistresses are always Birds of Paradise, and you're not looking for a bride."

"It's amusing to keep Society wondering where I'll toss my handkerchief," said Gareth lazily, "even if I've no intention of getting leg-shackled."

"Aunt Sybil was asking me the other day when you mean to do your duty and provide an heir. I pointed out that you're only eight-and-twenty. Plenty of time to put your head in parson's mousetrap."

"My thanks for your defence, Rupert, but I see no need of yet another heir when I have you and Cornelius and Lance and Perry all perfectly able to succeed me. I shouldn't wonder if you each produce several sons. They seem to run in the family." He paused, and his next words were not the *non sequitur* they doubtless seemed to the captain. "Do you remember Mama?"

"Of course. I was eight when she died. I remember — well, not very much." The stalwart young Guardsman ploughed on, embarrassed but game. "Mostly just how kind and gentle she was, and loving her,

16

and Father being jolly and playing cricket with us. He never did after she died."

"No, never. Ah, here we are." Gareth picked up his chapeau-bras as the carriage turned into King Street.

Heads turned when the Wyckham brothers entered the assembly rooms. Tall, broad-shouldered, with dark blue eyes and thick, wavy fair hair, they both had the resolute Wyckham chin to save their aristocratic good looks from mere handsomeness. Rupert boasted an inch or two over his noble brother, and the scarlet and gold of his uniform coat drew every maiden eye. Gareth, elegant in sober black, was the choice of the more discerning matrons, and their husbands.

Inevitably, wealth and title counted for the greater part of that preference, but by no means for all. The baron was known as a kind-hearted gentleman who did not have to be pressed into duty to dance with unhappy wallflowers. He had a dry sense of humour lacking in the gallant captain, four years his junior. More important, he had already sown his wild oats, settled down to tend his Shropshire acres and take his seat in Parliament, with a particular interest in foreign affairs.

He must surely be ready to choose a well-bred, conformable wife to fill his nursery. Each fond mama knew with absolute certainty that her own dear daughter was the perfect bride for Gareth, Lord Wyckham of Llys.

Gareth enjoyed dancing. He raised the spirits of two shy and three homely young ladies, and the hopes of five matrons, before retiring to the supper room in search of sustenance.

Ruefully acknowledging Rupert's accurate description of the refreshments, he surveyed the buffet table. He filled a plate with thin-sliced bread and butter — the cakes were invariably stale — and stood there pondering the respective demerits of lemonade, lukewarm tea, and sickly-sweet ratafia.

"Wyckham!"

The booming voice was unmistakable. "Aunt Sybil." Sighing, he turned to greet his late father's only sister.

She sat with a crony at a small table, sipping tea and undoubtedly gossiping. Lady Frobisher prided herself on knowing everything there was to know about the Ton. A large, elderly lady with the Wyckham jaw, she was an impressive sight swathed in violet gros de Naples, the Frobisher amethysts gleaming on her ample bosom.

"Join us, Wyckham," she ordered.

"Mrs. Payne." Gareth bowed to her friend and seated himself, abandoning his bread and butter with little regret.

"We have been talking about your Cousin Frederick," said the Honourable Mrs. Payne in a thin, high voice. "Most regrettable . . ."

"Freddie Chamberlain? What has he done now?" he asked, not greatly interested in his second cousin's latest disgraceful exploit.

"He's dead," said Lady Frobisher, never one to mince words. "Swinging from a lamppost, I gather."

"Good gad, he hanged himself?"

"No, no."

"Hanged by outraged citizens, *à la lanterne, à la française?*"

"Merely foxed and up to his usual high jinks. Bound to come to grief sooner or later."

Gareth noted Mrs. Payne's gleeful expression and wished he had not voiced his unwarranted surmises. Within twenty-four hours, every tattlemonger in Town would be convinced that the ne'er-do-well Freddie had either done away with himself or been done in by revolutionaries.

"Happened a month or two ago," his aunt continued.

"There was no notice in the *Morning Post* as the Chamberlains cast him off years ago.

I daresay the widow did not care to remind anyone of her existence."

"Widow?" asked Gareth, startled. "I'd forgot he was married, I confess."

"He ran off with Medway's eldest daughter," Mrs. Payne reminded him with malicious pleasure. "She was ruined and the earl cut her off without a penny."

He frowned. "Surely Lord Medway will make her some allowance now she has lost her husband."

"Called on Lady Medway this afternoon." Lady Frobisher savoured her triumph. "Wanted to make sure she knew about her son-in-law's demise. She made it plain the girl disgraced herself beyond redemption and need not expect anything more from her family. If you ask me, there was more to the business than a simple elopement." She exchanged a significant glance with Mrs. Payne.

Whatever her misdeeds, Gareth could not help but pity the young woman. "Freddie is unlikely to have left her anything approaching a competence," he said slowly. "I had best offer her a home at Llys."

"Not respectable and not your responsibility," his aunt pointed out.

"Freddie was my cousin, and I am head of the family." When he spoke in that tone, his relatives knew better than to argue with him. "Have you any notion, ma'am, where I may find his widow?"

"Understand Sir John Pointer was with him when he died. He may know, if you can find the fellow. Another ne'er-do-well here-and-thereian, just like Freddie."

"Pointer? Ah yes, another devotee of the Turf, I believe. If he's not in Town, I shall try Newmarket."

On the way home to Albany, to the comfortable bachelor lodgings he shared with Rupert, he told his brother of his plans.

"By Jove!" Rupert groaned. "Not another female at Llys. Isn't Maria enough for you? Not to mention her devilish brood."

"Aunt Sybil didn't mention children, and she would have, the way she was ghoulishly gloating over the poor woman's misfortunes. With luck, Lady . . . Dammit, I didn't think to ask her name. With luck she will be company for Maria, take her mind off her grievances."

"Or else they'll put their heads together to plague you."

Another horrid possibility dawned on Gareth. He echoed Rupert's groan. "That would be better than having them come to cuffs! Still, no use repining. I cannot aban-

21

don her, and if I set her up in her own household, Maria will feel justified in demanding the same."

"She already does," the captain pointed out.

"In any case, you have no cause for complaint, so rarely as we see you in Shropshire."

"Now that Boney's safely put away on Elba, I've some leave coming, which I'd intended to spend at Llys." Rupert sounded injured. "I was going to try for the Long Vac, when Lance and Perry will be home."

"I hope you still will." Gareth was pleased that the swaggering young officer did not disdain the company of his younger brothers. "If you can take a day or two now, come with me to fetch her. Perhaps you will be agreeably surprised."

"Devil take it, you're right, as usual. Perhaps she'll turn out to be the dashing widow I didn't find at Almack's."

Gareth laughed, but warned, "None of your philandering while she's under my roof."

The next day, they both made enquiries as to the whereabouts of Jack Pointer. As a result, Sir John himself turned up on their doorstep that very evening.

"Heard you was looking for me?"

Rupert was on duty, and Gareth was about to leave to dine with friends at his club, but he invited the chubby young baronet in and offered him a glass of wine.

"I thought I'd have to chase you to Newmarket," he said.

"Fact is," said Sir John gloomily, swigging the best Mountain Malaga as if it were ale, "it just ain't as much fun following the nags without Freddie. Freddie Chamberlain — friend of mine."

"My second cousin."

"Oh? Expect you know he kicked the bucket, then."

"Yes, that is why I wanted to see you."

Jack Pointer looked alarmed, as if he expected to be blamed for Freddie's unconventional demise. "I told him that lantern hook wouldn't hold him, damme if I didn't. Tried to stop him swinging from it, but to tell the truth I was a trifle bosky. We all were. Stands to reason, seeing it was a celebration for Freddie's wife."

"A celebration?"

"She just gave Freddie the news. Can't tell you about that, promised her to keep mum, but Freddie was full of frisk, prime for a lark. Sobered us up pretty quick when he broke his neck, I can tell you. Nasty shock."

"I'm sure it was. May I enquire why my cousin was swinging from a lantern hook?"

"Dancing on the table, happened to see the thing. On the ceiling, you know." Jack's abbreviated style of speech reminded Gareth irresistibly of Aunt Sybil. He added earnestly, "Just a bit of fun and gig. Not an ounce of vice in Freddie."

"I daresay. However, I am more concerned with Freddie's widow."

"Not an ounce of vice in Mrs. Chamberlain, neither, assure you."

"Mrs. Chamberlain? Does she not use her title?"

"The Honourable?" Jack sounded puzzled. "No, she ain't one to ride the high horse."

"As daughter of an earl, she is entitled to call herself 'Lady'."

"Lady Laura? Well, if that don't beat the Dutch! Freddie never let on. Lay you a monkey she didn't want it known, living in that hovel."

Dismayed by the word 'hovel,' but relieved to reach the point at last, Gareth said, "So you know where she lives?"

"Little place between Cambridge and Newmarket. Dammit, what's its name? The tavern's the Bull and Bush."

"And the village?" He refilled Jack's glass, envisaging days spent scouring the Cambridgeshire countryside for a tavern called the Bull and Bush.

"Dashed odd name. Damme, it'll come to me. Begins with a P. On the tip of my tongue. P-p-p . . . or is it M? Ha, Swaffham Bulbeck. I say, you don't mean to make trouble for the lady, do you, old fellow? Because if you do, you'll have me to deal with." The belligerent expression sat ill on his round, easygoing face. "Friend of mine, Freddie."

"No trouble. I wish to assist her."

"Offered her blunt. Wouldn't take it."

"I, however, am the head of the family," Gareth pointed out with a degree of hauteur.

"Yes, right, so you are," said Jack, abashed. "Well, if all's right and tight, then, I'll be off."

Lord Wyckham had several social engagements in the next few days, and a certain amount of political and financial business to clear up before he left London. He saw little of Rupert. The captain slept in barracks, taking extra duty for friends who would cover for him for a few days leave. After accompanying his brother into Cambridgeshire, he intended to visit a friend who had sold out after Toulouse.

25

"I'll have to be back in Town at the beginning of June," he told Gareth as the brothers rode northward one bright, summery midday. "The Russian Tsar and King Frederick of Prussia are due to arrive for the victory festivities. There'll be parades, reviews, guards of honour, processions — I tell you, I'd a sight rather be fighting Boney."

"Gammon, you revel in cutting a dash for the crowds. I daresay I ought to put in at least a brief appearance in honour of Prinny's royal guests. What a bore!"

"Gammon, you revel in ton parties."

"I'd rather spend June in Shropshire. I'm glad you could get away now. I've been thinking over what Jack Pointer said, and I may need your support."

"Don't tell me she is a game widow?" said Rupert, grinning.

"I'd hardly go so far. Yet I gathered from Pointer that she was present at their drunken spree in the tavern. They were all bosky, he said, and it was a celebration on her account, for something Pointer promised her not to reveal."

"Therefore doubtless discreditable."

"It's possible," Gareth reluctantly agreed. "He did tell me she has 'not an ounce of vice' in her, but since he said the same of

Freddie, one cannot rely upon his judgement."

"I should say not! If ever there was a rakeshame —"

"Exactly. You see my dilemma. I cannot leave her destitute in a hovel, nor do I wish to introduce a woman of uncertain morals into Llys Manor."

"Lord, no. Aunt Antonia would skin you alive. I'll tell you what," he suggested with a lascivious leer, "give the jade a purse and I'll take her off your hands."

Gareth laughed. "I'll consider your generous offer. Look, the road is clear. Let's spring 'em."

Neck and neck, they galloped up the turnpike.

Meeting Gareth's travelling carriage in Cambridge, they spent the night at the Eagle, then in the morning enquired the way to Swaffham Bulbeck. As the carriage rolled between the flat green fields, Gareth began to wish he had never embarked upon his errand of mercy. If Lady Laura Chamberlain were obviously a hussy he would know what to do, but suppose she had the outward appearance of a respectable female?

Scarcely half an hour later, having asked at the Bull and Bush for Mrs. Chamberlain,

27

they pulled up before a flint and brick cottage. A pair of dormer windows peered from beneath symmetrical eyebrows of thatch. The tiny front garden, separated from the lane by a clipped beech hedge, was bright with orange pot-marigolds and purple stocks.

"No palace," said Gareth, straightening his top hat as he descended from the carriage, "but hardly a hovel."

Rupert followed him. "Methinks Sir John is given to exaggeration. I wonder to what extent he exaggerated the lady's virtue?"

"This is an unlikely setting for a confirmed doxy." He opened the white-painted gate and started up the flagstone path.

"I don't know. It's a sort of midway point between a haystack and a mirrored boudoir."

"You had best keep your mouth shut until we discover what's what," Gareth commanded severely. He knocked on the door. The mob-capped maid who opened it had a scrubbing brush in her hand. She curtsied, her dazzled gaze fixed on the glory of Rupert's scarlet and gold, behind Gareth. "I am Lord Wyckham," Gareth informed her. "I wish to speak with Mrs. Chamberlain. Is she at home?"

Sparing him a brief glance, she curtsied

again and said in a breathless voice, "Aye, my lord, in the back garden, but you can't come through for I be a-washing the kitchen floor. D'you want me to show you round the side?" she asked hopefully, addressing Rupert.

"Thank you," Gareth answered, amused, "I expect we can find our own way."

"I did ought to announce you, my lord."

"That will not be necessary." He was glad of the opportunity to take Lady Laura unawares, before she had a chance to assume an air of propriety.

The path led them round the corner of the cottage and under an arched trellis festooned with yellow laburnam. Emerging from the arbour, Rupert at his heels, Gareth saw a girl seated on a bench in the filtered sunlight under an apple tree in bloom.

He stopped, raising his hand to silence his brother while he studied her.

Her dark head, crowned by a small, simple cap but hatless, was bent over some task in her lap, about which her hands were busy. Heavy braids, neatly pinned up, emphasized a graceful neck. She wore a plain gown of black cotton, unrelieved by any touch of white, with long sleeves and a high neck. Nothing could have been more demure.

She reached into a basket at her side, a plain gold band gleaming on her finger, and Gareth realized that she was shelling broad beans. Not the sort of chore one might expect a trollop to stoop to! His doubts withered.

"Lady Laura?"

She looked up, startled, revealing a complexion as delicately pink and white as the apple blossom. As she stared, the colour fled from her cheeks and she raised one hand to her parted lips in . . . dismay? Alarm? Then she shook her head, relaxing. "Oh, foolish!" Her voice was sweet and low. "How very like Freddie you are. Lord Wyckham?"

"Yes." Disconcerted, he bowed. "How did you guess?"

"We met once." Setting aside the colander in her lap, she rose and came to meet them. Her face was pretty, if not beautiful, with particularly fine eyes of an unusual greenish grey, but her figure was over-plump and she moved awkwardly.

"I'm sorry," he said, contrite, as Rupert bowed over her hand, "I don't recall the occasion."

She chuckled wryly. "There is no need to apologize. It was during my Season, and you, like every other gentleman, had eyes only for my sister. I don't regard it."

Before Gareth, taken aback for the third time, could respond, his brother said with automatic gallantry, "Had I had the pleasure of making your acquaintance, ma'am, nothing could have driven the memory from my mind. Captain Rupert Wyckham, at your service."

Rosy lips curved in a warm smile. "How do you do, Captain. How kind of you both to call. Are you on your way to Newmarket?"

"As a matter of fact, no," said Gareth. "We came from Town especially to see you. I learned just the other day of Cousin Frederick's unfortunate accident. Allow me to present my sincere condolences."

"Thank you, my lord." Her direct gaze was a trifle skeptical. "I was under the impression that the Wyckhams, like the Chamberlains, had cast out the black sheep."

"My aunt and uncles did their best to ignore his existence, but I . . . er . . . was able to oblige him on one or two occasions."

"He touched me, too," said Rupert cheerfully.

Lady Laura flinched. "I see. If you will tell me the amounts, gentlemen, I shall repay you as soon as I am able."

"Good gad, no!"

"Jove, I should say not!" Rupert sounded as outraged as Gareth felt. As though they would dun a widow!

"You mistake us, ma'am. As head of the family, I have come to offer you a home at Llys Manor, my country seat." His duty done, he awaited her effusive gratitude for rescuing her from a life of penury, wondering whether it would last any longer than Cousin Maria's.

"You are most generous, sir," she said quietly, "but I fear I must refuse."

CHAPTER 2

Despite the unmistakable family resemblance, Laura was beginning to see how Lord Wyckham differed from Freddie.

For a start, he was impeccably dressed in a bottle-green morning coat, starched cravat of modest height, snuff-brown waistcoat and inexpressibles. His top boots shone as Freddie's had not since the day they were bought. Altogether his unostentatious elegance made his brother appear a gaudy coxcomb, and would have made Freddie look slovenly.

A year or two younger than his cousin, the baron had a mature dignity Freddie would probably never have attained. Freddie had failed to inherit that strong jaw, so obvious in both brothers as to be almost a caricature. The stubbornness it suggested, Laura's husband had possessed in full measure, however — at least where his own actions were concerned. She might go her own way, as long as she did not try to interfere with his. How much easier life had been since she realized that!

She had had enough of handsome, charming, stubborn gentlemen. "No," she reiterated, "I cannot accept your kind offer."

Lord Wyckham flushed. "It is not a matter of kindness or generosity, ma'am," he said stiffly. "I should be failing in my duty if I permitted a female relative to live alone in reduced circumstances."

"Not at all the thing," put in the captain.

"Not the thing!" Laura rounded on him, shaking with sudden anger. "Sir, I have been living virtually alone for four years without Society caring a groat. I care not a groat for Society's opinion."

"That's not what I meant," he protested and opened his mouth again to explain. His brother glared at him. He shrugged, saluted ironically, and sauntered away, whistling.

"I believe Rupert meant that my failing in my duty would be not at all the thing," Lord Wyckham said with a rueful smile that

Laura mistrusted. "Indeed, it would not. Will you be seated, ma'am, while we discuss the matter?"

Though she considered there was nothing to discuss, she was glad to return to the bench. Sinking down at one end with a sigh, she pulled the basket and colander towards her and waved an invitation to his lordship to take the other end. With the colander in her black-clad lap — the black dye had faded already, she noted — she continued to shell the beans as she spoke.

"I am sorry if your failure to persuade me will distress you, or bring censure upon you, though that I doubt. In any case, you cannot be accused of permitting me to live alone, since you have no authority over me. Indeed, I acknowledge no one's authority."

"Understandable." He nodded, and she knew he was aware that her family had rejected her as Freddie's had rejected him; that speaking of Society she thought of her mother and father, her brothers and sisters. " 'Permitted' was the wrong word," he went on, "and I am more concerned for your comfort than my reputation, or yours."

She smiled at him, noting the sensitivity of his mouth, at odds with that determined chin. "So it is kindness that brings you, not duty."

"Touché." He laughed, dark blue eyes crinkling at the corners. "I plead guilty to contradicting myself, but not to prevarication. Call it mixed motives. To which may I add that I should be very pleased to welcome you to Llys."

His charm strengthened Laura's resistance. "I am perfectly comfortable here," she said, fishing a pink apple-blossom petal out of the colander of pale green beans. "My neighbours are pleasant, obliging people. The cottage is mine. My father's lawyer sends me ten pounds every quarter day, I have a little money put away, and I earn more with my sewing."

"Sewing!" he exclaimed, shocked. "My dear Lady Laura, that is —"

"Not at all the thing?" She reached for another bean, hesitated as she saw a long-legged spider clambering over the heap of pods.

Before she could steel herself to deal with the horrid creature, Lord Wyckham whipped out his handkerchief, gently caught it, and shook it out on the ground. The simple action brought tears to her eyes. How long since anyone had protected her from a spider?

"Very well," she said in a shaky voice. "I shall come to Llys. But I will not promise to stay, and I will not sell the cottage."

He had won. Did he realize he owed his victory to a spider? More likely he supposed he had made her recognize the enormity of earning her living. What a very proper, conventional gentleman he was.

How different from Freddie!

"Excellent," he said matter-of-factly, standing up. "My carriage is at the door."

"Good gracious, sir, I cannot leave at the drop of a hat. I must pack my clothes and take leave of my friends and close up the house . . ." A dozen necessary tasks raced through her mind. "If you are in a hurry, I can travel by stage."

"I beg your pardon, I did not mean to rush you. If my coachman drives you to call on your friends, can you be ready to leave this evening, do you think? We might spend the night in Cambridge and reach London tomorrow."

"London? Where is Llys?"

"In Shropshire, on the Welsh border, due east of here but it will be quicker to go back to Town and out again by the post roads than directly cross country."

"I . . . I had rather not go to London." Papa and Mama never missed a Season in Town. She could not bear the possibility of a chance meeting.

"As you wish," he said, with an indifference belied by the understanding in his eyes.

Lord Wyckham was altogether too knowing. Had he heard the full story of her elopement? Laura faced the fact that his motives might not be half so admirable as he claimed. She must be mad to go off with a stranger to an unknown destination. In a sudden panic, she clutched the bench with both hands. She was safe here . . .

The colander slid from her lap, depositing half its contents on the carpet of pink and white petals. Setting his hat on the bench, the baron crouched to right the colander and scooped up the handful of beans.

Impossible to distrust a man who gathered spilled beans and rescued one from spiders, she decided with a silent sigh.

He bowed, smiling, as he presented the colander to her. "Your luncheon, ma'am. We shall dine in Cambridge."

She took the colander, and the hand he offered, and rose. He picked up the basket as if it were perfectly natural for a fashionable nobleman to carry such a prosaic object. They turned towards the cottage.

At the open back door, the gold braid on his scarlet coat flashing in the sun, Captain Wyckham stood flirting with Sally, invisible in the kitchen. The maid's giggles proclaimed her delighted with the attentions of the dashing young officer.

"May we interrupt?" said Lord Wyckham dryly.

His brother grinned. "I was just telling Sally she's in for a treat, ma'am. All settled is it? Sal, my girl, take off your apron. We're off to Shropshire."

"Oh no, sir, I can't do that." She appeared in the doorway, looking dismayed. "If you please, madam, Pa won't never let me go to furrin parts. He took on something dreadful when I wanted to work in Cambridge."

"Of course, Sally, I did not expect you to go with me. I shall give you a quarter's wages and you can take care of the cottage for me while I am away."

Lord Wyckham frowned. "That is all very well, but you cannot travel alone with a gentleman, ma'am."

While his insistence upon propriety re-assured her, Laura was ready to seize the excuse not to go. Captain Wyckham inter-vened.

"I'll go with you, Gareth," he offered obligingly. "Two gentlemen, both relatives, will make it quite proper, ma'am — Cousin Laura. We must be sure to call each other Cousin."

His brother agreed, though he seemed a

trifle dubious. Perhaps he guessed at Laura's second thoughts.

They arranged that the carriage was to take the gentlemen back to Cambridge for the day and then return to be at Laura's bidding. She went up to her chamber to begin packing.

Through the open window came their voices as they walked around the outside of the cottage. "I expect I could hire a maid in Cambridge," said Cousin Gareth. "You wanted to visit your friend."

"I can see old Bunjie any time. I don't mind coming with you. Cousin Laura's a Trojan, isn't she? Game as a pebble! I rather like her. She's no beauty, of course, but it's just as well, for Maria don't take kindly to competition in that department."

Laura gazed dejectedly at her meagre wardrobe of practical brown and grey cottons and worsteds, some cheaply dyed to mourning black. Not even fashionable clothes could ever turn her into a beauty. Ceci was the beauty of the family — Ceci, already the apple of her parents' eyes, who had caught the heir to a dukedom in the middle of their shared Season. If only Grandmama had not died the year before, so that Laura might have had a Season to herself instead of competing with her younger sister . . .

She shook her head vigorously. No more if only's. In her present situation, her mediocre looks were a positive advantage, she told herself with determined cheerfulness. She had been foolish to fear that Cousin Gareth had a dishonourable motive for whisking her away to his den, even if, as she suspected, he had not guessed she was pregnant. He would have no eyes for her — doubtless the loveliest ladies in the land sought his company.

Among them Maria. Who was Maria?

Laura sank down on her bed, sadly crushing the shabby gowns she had laid there. Why had it never crossed her mind that Lord Wyckham might be married?

Not that it made a great deal of difference to a five-month pregnant widow, except that Lady Wyckham might very well resent her arrival, pretty or no. She wished she had never agreed to go to Llys Manor, but she started folding her clothes for packing. She had agreed, and Freddie's cousin had gone to considerable trouble for her. For a month or two she could endure being an unwanted poor relation, then she would come home to have the baby.

"I'm going to ride the next stage," announced Rupert, as the carriage pulled into the yard of the Wheatsheaf at St. Neots. He opened the door, stepped down, then turned to address his brother. "Gareth, it's about time you warned Cousin Laura of what awaits her at Llys, and I don't want to be around when she throws her bandbox at you." With a grin, he closed the door and disappeared.

Laura glared at Gareth. Though she realized Rupert was joking, Gothick fancies traipsed through her head. "Just what does await me at Llys?" she enquired grimly.

"Nothing so dreadful," he protested, on the defensive.

"The house is falling down?"

"It's in excellent repair."

"It is set on a crag in the midst of gloomy mountains with the nearest neighbours a day's ride off?"

"It's on a gentle hillside with a superb view — admittedly of the Welsh mountains — a mile from the village and ten from Ludlow, a pleasant market town."

She tried to avoid the one question she really wanted to ask. "Your butler is a tall, cadaverous individual given to ominous predictions of imminent disaster?"

Gareth began to smile. "Lloyd is short, stout, and cheerful."

41

"The housekeeper is addicted to strong drink?"

"Mrs. Lloyd is a Methodist. They have both been with the family all their lives."

"The family . . . ?"

"The family." He grimaced. "It is to the family, of course, that Rupert referred."

"I'm afraid your wife will not be pleased —"

"My wife! I am not wed, nor like to be."

Laura's heart suddenly grew lighter. She relaxed against the luxurious olive-green velvet squabs as the carriage started off again. "So Maria is not Lady Wyckham."

"Heaven forbid! I mean, no. Maria Forbes is the daughter of one of my uncles, a widow like yourself but with three children."

Laura gathered from his gloomy voice that he was not over fond of the children. Her resolve to leave Shropshire before her baby's birth strengthened, though it had wavered when she learned that no affronted wife awaited her.

"Mrs. Forbes makes her home at Llys?" she asked.

"Unfortunately Uncle Henry, her father, is a diplomat with no fixed abode in England."

"I daresay Mrs. Forbes runs the household and acts as your hostess."

"No, my Aunt Antonia does that, my mother's sister. She brought us all up."

His mother had died when he was young, then. Laura's memories of her own mother were not such that she could sympathize, so she evaded the subject. "All? Ah, yes, Cousin Rupert mentioned another brother."

"Another three." At last he cheered up, his affection for his brothers obvious. "Cornelius is a year younger than I. He took holy orders and holds the living at Llys. Then Rupert, then Lancelot, who is up at Oxford. And Perry — he's Percival but you call him Percy at your peril — he's at Rugby."

"I look forward to meeting them." She hesitated. "You have a large family. Are you sure there is room for another?"

"Lord, yes, plenty." He laughed. "Though once appropriate, 'Manor' is misleading now."

"It is a mansion?"

"Not if you envision a Chatsworth or a Blenheim. For one thing, Llys Manor grew up over the centuries rather than being built to a unified plan. But it is large enough for most purposes. I haven't even mentioned Uncle Julius, and we usually have at least one or two guests. Not formal house parties, just friends staying for a few days. It is an informal household, to Aunt Antonia's despair but I daresay you will not mind?"

"Not at all. After my life in the cottage, an excess of ceremony would make me terrified of putting a foot wrong."

"No fear of that. I hope you will soon come to feel yourself quite at home," he said seriously.

To her surprise, Laura found herself anticipating her stay at Llys with pleasure.

As the day wore on, and the sway of the carriage on its efficient springs became faintly nauseating, niggling doubts set in. Nothing in what Gareth had told her of the people at Llys explained Rupert's insistence that he warn her. She seized the chance to find out more when the captain came to sit with her while his brother rode — they were by far too gentlemanly to leave her alone.

"Llys Manor is a large house, I collect," she opened, "since Cousin Gareth is able to accommodate so many relatives."

"Jove, yes, a positive rabbit warren, with wings sprawling in every direction. It's not too difficult to get away from each other."

"Why should you want to?"

"Aha, so Gareth was his usual discreet self. He didn't tell you, for instance, that Uncle Julius is mad as a March hare?"

"No!"

"Quite harmless," he assured her hastily,

"but definitely bats in the belfry. Aunt Antonia, on the other hand, is devilish — deuced — high in the instep. Her frown puts me in a quake, I can tell you. I'd rather face Boney any day."

Laura suspected that she, too, had rather face Boney than a straitlaced elderly lady who was bound to disapprove of her. "And the others?" she asked with a sinking feeling.

"My brothers are all right. Cornie's a bit of a wind-bag, but what can you expect of a clergyman? It's Cousin Maria and the brats you'll want to avoid."

"Why?" She hoped it was just a vigorous young man's natural impatience with small children and their doting mother. Maria ought to be her natural ally at Llys, and she was beginning to think she might need one.

Rupert shook his head. "I'll let you discover for yourself. Gareth would comb my hair with a joint stool if you turned tail now because of anything I said. You will like Llys, anyway, I promise you." He went on to expatiate upon the glories of galloping across the hills, fishing in the streams, shooting in the woods and fields.

His enthusiasm for his home was endearing, but scarcely calculated to dispel Laura's growing misgivings.

CHAPTER 3

Gareth frowned. He had hoped to reach Warwick that day. The cross-country roads slowed them more than he expected, despite being in good condition after a week of fine weather. Worse, Lady Laura had turned out to be less robust than she appeared. She had eaten almost nothing when they stopped for luncheon, and now she slumped back in the corner of the seat, pale, her eyes closed.

"Cousin?" he said, softly lest she were asleep. The grey-green eyes opened. "You are unwell, I fear."

She smiled at him with an obvious effort. "Just a little tired. It is a long while since I travelled any distance and now I am . . ." She hesitated, and seemed to change her mind. "Now I am unused to long journeys."

"We shall stop in Daventry," he decided, wondering what she had been going to say. "It is another ten miles or so but I know the Saracen's Head is a comfortable inn."

"I do not wish to be a hindrance to you, sir."

"Not at all. Rupert will be delighted. Daventry is famous for its whips and he will happily spend several hours seeking out bargains. I did not give Aunt Antonia any particular date for our arrival so she will not be looking for us. Now, why do you not put up your feet on the seat? You will find it more restful, I daresay."

"May I?"

"Of course." To spare her blushes at any unavoidable display of her limbs, he bent down to search for a cushion beneath his seat. "Here, put this behind your back."

"Perfect," she said gratefully. "I might even fall asleep, I vow."

She leaned back with eyes closed again, and he tried not to stare rudely at her dumpy outstretched figure. Her worn half-boots of cheap jean, protruding from the loose-fitting, shabby, black fustian mantle, caught his attention. It was embarrassing enough travelling with so dowdy a female; he could not let her go about in rags at Llys. Sooner or later he must provide a new wardrobe but he expected a battle over it. Unlike Maria, she was most reluctant to accept of his largesse.

On the fourth day at noon they reached Llys. Incessant drizzle obscured the grey-stone, slate-roofed village, the castle ruins, the river, and the surrounding green hills. Dank hedgerows dripped on either side as they turned up the lane towards the Manor.

"A poor welcome, alas," Gareth apologized, disappointed that Laura could not see the beauty of the countryside, nor the home he loved.

"I cannot hold you responsible for the weather, Cousin." She already drooped wanly in her corner though they had been on the road only four hours.

Her quietness seemed due to a mixture of fatigue and apprehension. The prospect of making the acquaintance of a large new family, even with Lance and Perry away, must be alarming after her isolated life in Swaffham Bulbeck. Not a word of complaint had passed her lips, yet from chance remarks Gareth had learned quite a lot about her years of virtual exile.

"I hope the sun shows its face tomorrow," growled Rupert, disgruntled after a morning confined to the carriage by the rain. "I have to leave the day after."

"I am sorry that my weakness should have curtailed your time at home," Laura said.

"Never mind, I'll be back for a month or two as soon as we get rid of the damn — dratted — Allied Monarchs. Jove, it's good to be home, whatever the weather." He let down the window and leaned out like any schoolboy released at last from his Latin and Greek. Gareth and Laura exchanged a smile.

At last the carriage stopped. Rupert jumped down and turned to help Laura as a footman appeared with a huge green umbrella. Gareth followed. He offered her his arm and she leaned on it heavily. They entered the vast Tudor hall of Llys Manor.

Gareth was eager to point out its glories, from hammerbeam ceiling to minstrels' gallery to carved stone arch over the stairs. He was not vouchsafed the opportunity. Two small, dripping whirlwinds converged on him, clung to his legs, and set up a clamour.

"Cousin Gareth, tell Mama we won't get a 'flammation of the lungs just 'cause we got wet."

"It's warm out, Cousin Gareth."

"Gareth," Maria wailed, wringing her hands in a distraught manner worthy of the stage, "my poor little boys are bound to be ill and now this wretched woman wants to beat them. She has no control over the horrid creatures whatsoever."

"How can I control them, my lord, when I am not permitted to punish them?" demanded a plain, sturdy female in a brown stuff dress. Gareth recognized her as the latest governess — governesses seldom

49

lasted longer than a few months at the Manor. "May I point out, however, that I did not suggest beating them."

"What a pity," interjected Rupert.

"I wish to give my notice, my lord," the woman continued doggedly. "I have been offered a position in —"

"You see," screeched Maria, dissolving in tears, "she has been plotting to leave me in the lurch."

"We just went for a walk, Cousin Gareth," George declared in a self-righteous tone. "We didn't do anything bad."

"Be quiet, all of you." Although he did not raise it, Gareth's voice cut through the babble and silenced it. "Maria, sit down and compose yourself." He spotted his butler hovering on the outskirts of the fray. "Lloyd, a glass of wine for Mrs. Forbes. George, Henry, go to the nursery and change your clothes, then remain there until I come. Miss . . . er . . . ma'am, you will excuse me if I do not discuss your employment at this moment. Three o'clock in my study, per-haps?"

"Certainly, my lord." Her back stiff, the governess followed the scuttling boys up the stone staircase.

"I'll get there first." George's voice echoed back as the archway hid them.

"Not fair, you're bigger."

Maria's tears had miraculously dried, leaving pale blue eyes untouched with red, golden ringlets untousled by the storm. At twenty-seven, a willowy figure in blue mull muslin, she was still beautiful, though constant petulance was beginning to etch its marks. She had a delicate version of the Wyckham chin, in her case a sign of wilfulness. She was staring at Laura.

Gareth turned to Laura. "I beg your pardon, Cousin," he said with a rueful smile. "Your welcome has not been what I would have wished."

She made a dismissive gesture, but dismay was plain on her pallid face. He was about to introduce her to Maria when his aunt came into the hall. Every inch of her tall, thin presence expressed disapproval, from tight lips to the rustle of her grey silks as she stalked across the hall. He went to greet her, gave her the expected peck on the cheek, and led her back to Laura.

"Aunt Antonia, Cousin Maria, this is Lady Laura Chamberlain, who will henceforth make her home at Llys. Cousin Laura — Miss Burleigh and Mrs. Forbes."

Maria and Aunt Antonia gave identical glacial nods.

A tinge of pink coloured Laura's cheeks,

but far from wilting, she squared her shoulders and raised her chin. "How do you do," she said evenly.

Aunt Antonia's response was automatically courteous, if cool. "How do you do, Lady Laura. Mrs. Lloyd will show you to your chamber."

The housekeeper had entered the hall with her husband, who bore a glass of wine that Maria waved away. Mrs. Lloyd curtsied to Laura. "If you'll please to come this way, my lady," she said, in the musical Welsh intonation common here in the Marches.

Knowing Laura's exhaustion, Gareth stepped forward to lend her his arm. She shook her head very slightly and plodded up the stairs after Mrs. Lloyd.

Suddenly angry, he was tempted to reproach his aunt and his cousin for their hostility, but Maria would only resent her the more and Aunt Antonia's opinion would not alter by one iota.

As they came to know Laura, he was convinced, they would soften. His own original willingness to condemn her had quickly changed to pity and admiration.

Rupert broke the momentary silence. "Hello, Aunt. I hope I see you well?"

"Very well, I thank you, Rupert. Welcome home." She favoured him with a restrained smile, no doubt holding his brother entirely to blame for the introduction into the house of the dubious widow of a distant and disreputable relative. "A cold collation will be served in the breakfast room in half an hour."

"Good. I'm hungry as a hunter."

They both departed, she with stately tread, he taking the stairs two at a time.

Maria scowled after him. "Rupert has shocking manners. He did not even greet me."

"No doubt he considered you too taken up with your own troubles to note his arrival, since you spoke neither to him nor to Lady Laura."

"I cannot imagine why you invited her to live here." She pouted. "She is only a relative by marriage. Her own family should take care of her."

Gareth was relieved that she seemed unaware of the scandal surrounding Laura and the late, unlamented Freddie. Maria was not half so interested in gossip as in her own affairs. "Cousin Laura has nowhere else to go," he said tersely. "Now, if you will excuse me, I must go and speak to George and Henry."

She hung on his arm. "Gareth, you will not beat my poor darlings!"

"No, though Rupert may be in the right of it, there."

"And you will not let Miss Coltart leave? I cannot possibly manage the little horrors without her."

She apparently saw no contradiction between her two views of her sons. Gareth made no effort to enlighten her, knowing from experience that it would be useless. "I shall endeavour to persuade Miss Coltart to stay," he promised, disentangled himself from her clutch, and headed for the nursery.

Half an hour later he met Rupert in the breakfast room. Their plates laden with cold lamb, rabbit pie, and pickled beetroot salad, they sat down, only to rise again as Aunt Antonia came in.

Quivering with outrage, she fixed Gareth with a steely glare. "Mrs. Lloyd informs me that Lady Laura is a good five months gone with child. How could you make the poor girl travel so far?"

Fear stabbed through him. He felt the blood drain from his face. "Oh my God, I didn't know," he groaned, appalled.

After luncheon on a tray — poached chicken and a custard prepared specially to tempt her appetite — and a long nap, Laura was ready to explore. She glanced at the bell-pull, but decided against calling a maid to show her the way. She would be taken to join the others, and her cold reception from the ladies of the house, though half expected, had hurt.

Mrs. Lloyd, the small, dark, neat housekeeper with the beautiful voice, had led her along endless corridors and galleries, up and down stairs, to her chamber. Every step had required a concentration that precluded noticing the route, or anything else. Discovering her own way back to the main part of the house, Laura thought, she would be able to take the time to study any items of interest she passed.

Her box had been carried up before she fell asleep, and a chambermaid had hung up her dresses. Choosing the least shabby, she tried to shake out the creases. She would have to find out where she could use a hot-iron, and where to wash her gowns, too. The home-dyed materials needed delicate care.

Donning the limp black muslin, she regarded herself in the looking-glass, without satisfaction. Mrs. Lloyd had known at once that she was pregnant. Soon altering gowns would no longer serve. She was going to have to make up new ones. Perhaps a groom might drive her to Ludlow to buy material.

Anxiously she felt under her pillow for the leather bag of guineas. There it was, very nearly as heavy as the day Freddie had emptied it into her lap. She need not stay here long, to be looked down upon by Miss Burleigh and Mrs. Forbes; just long enough not to seem too ungrateful for Gareth's kindness.

The prospect of the journey back to Cambridgeshire made her shudder, but she put it out of her mind, and set out to explore.

First she went to the window, to get her bearings. Rain still pelted down outside, dripping from the eaves of the stables two stories below. She had definitely not been put in the best guest chamber!

Sighting sideways, she saw a long stone façade punctuated by regular rows of sash windows. It ended at the main block, two stories of brick and stone topped by another two of black and white half-timbering. There the windows were smaller, casements with leaded panes. Beyond, veiled by rain, a lower wing projected at an angle. The Barons Wyckham of Llys had added to their manor as desired without the least attention to unifying the style. Laura rather liked its whimsical eccentricity.

She went out into the passage, lit by a

window at the near end and a stairwell ahead of her. The gloomy day gave just enough light to see two steps going down. A little farther on there was another, and then three rising, as if the floor level conformed to the hillside's contours, belying the even rows of windows.

Servants hurrying with hot water must hate the ups and downs. As Laura negotiated them, she made a mental note to take particular care at night, when her way would be lit by a single candle.

She passed several closed doors, presumably to bedchambers, whether tenanted or not she could not tell. On the walls between hung paintings, mostly watercolour landscapes. These were signed Sybil Wyckham and depicted, in bold outlines and rather harsh colours, local scenes such as Ludlow Castle and the River Llys. Laura wished she might see some of the sights, but riding was out of the question at present. Perhaps the river was close enough to walk to, she hoped.

At last she found her way to the Great Hall. Wandering around the huge, high-ceilinged chamber, she inspected tapestries and coats of arms, halberds and arquebuses. She was studying a vast oil painting of a naval engagement when Gareth came down the stairs.

The elaborate arch over the stairway hid her from him until he was near the bottom of the flight. He ran down the last few steps.

"Laura, what the devil are you doing here?" He looked aghast and sounded furious, and he had never used such language in her presence before.

Puzzled, she responded calmly, "Admiring your warlike family history."

"You ought to be in bed!"

"I am quite recovered, thank you. I cannot sleep forever."

"But you must rest. Come and sit down."

Aha, he had discovered her delicate condition. "In a moment. Tell me, pray, what battle is that over the fireplace?"

"Gravelines. The second baron sailed with Drake against the Spanish Armada. Do come and sit down, Cousin," he pleaded, clasping her upper arm. His deep blue eyes held a hint of desperation. "Lloyd has just taken tea into the drawing room."

Tea would certainly be welcome. Unfortunately, Miss Burleigh and Mrs. Forbes doubtless wanted some, too. Laura held back, delaying the moment when she must face their hostility. She wondered why Gareth was so frantic, but did not like to ask. "Your house is delightful," she said. "I should like to see more of it."

"Yes, yes, naturally, I shall give you a tour — one of these days. The drawing room is an excellent place to begin." He drew her irresistibly towards the stairs, then stopped and ran his fingers through his fair hair. "Dash it, you cannot climb the stairs."

"Don't be nonsensical, of course I can." She pulled away from him and started up, holding the rail and taking it at a leisurely pace. "On the way from my chamber I climbed countless stairs, both up and down."

"I know, I'm so very sorry about that. Here, lean on me." He offered his arm. She spurned it. "Aunt Antonia has already had a different chamber prepared for you, close to everything."

"That is most kind of Miss Burleigh."

"I'd have insisted had she not suggested it. I shudder to think of you walking all that way, and without help."

"Cousin Gareth, I am not an invalid," she snapped, beginning to be irritated. "Pregnancy is a natural condition, not a debilitating malady. That the journey tired me, I admit —"

"If only you had told me!"

"— but otherwise, I have never felt healthier. Indeed, the exercise of walking from my chamber has given me a healthy appetite. I hope the tea is accompanied by something to eat."

"Cakes, biscuits, perhaps sandwiches. You are eating for two, though, and you ate so little as we travelled. I shall order something more substantial. What would you like?"

Much to her annoyance, Laura felt a sudden, overpowering craving for hot-buttered toast. She could almost taste it, slightly smoky, burnt at the edges, dripping with sweet butter. At home she would have gone to the kitchen, sliced a loaf, taken down the brass toasting fork from its hook, and toasted the bread at the kitchen fire. In this grand house, as in her childhood, it was a nursery treat. Wistfully she shook her head.

Not deceived for a moment, he asked anxiously, "What is it? What do you want?"

"I know it is impossible: hot-buttered toast."

A grin of pure delight spread across his face. "What an absolutely splendid notion. I wager the toasting forks are still up in the nursery. Come and sit down, and I shall see what I can do."

Laura smiled at him, forgetting his maddeningly excessive solicitude, forgetting to mistrust his charm.

He ushered her into a high-ceilinged room

with dark linenfold wainscoting and tall lattice windows spattered with raindrops. A painted frieze ran round the walls above the panelling. At one end, a huge, intricately carved chimneypiece framed an inviting fire.

Two faces turned to observe her entrance, their expressions anything but inviting. Maria Forbes looked sullen, Antonia Burleigh stiffly disdainful. Laura clutched Gareth's sleeve.

CHAPTER 4

Gareth seated Laura by the fire, pulled up a tapestry-work footstool, and insisted that she use it. Miss Burleigh poured a cup of tea and he brought it to her, along with a plateful of tiny, triangular watercress sandwiches, trimmed of crusts.

"To keep you going," he said. "I shall be back in just a moment."

Though he left to provide for her whim, Laura felt deserted. The ladies sipped their tea in silence. Nibbling on a sandwich, she studied the fireplace, carved with wreaths of honeysuckle, bunches of grapes, arabesques, and arched niches holding vaguely Classical figures.

"Mama, who is that lady?" asked a small voice. Half hidden by Mrs. Forbes's chair, a gold-ringleted child of four or five, seated on another footstool, regarded Laura with bright-eyed interest.

"Her name is Lady Laura Chamberlain, darling."

"Why is she here? Is she a visitor?"

"She has come to live at the Manor," said Maria Forbes resentfully.

"Maria," snapped Miss Burleigh, "pray do not speak of Lady Laura as though she were not here. Present the child to her."

She pouted but obeyed. "Arabella, show Lady Laura how well you make your curtsy."

"If I do, can I have some more cake?"

"Of course, darling. You shall have your brothers' share because they were naughty and Cousin Gareth says they may not come down to tea today."

Arabella came to stand in front of Laura. She was dressed in a miniature version of her mother's high-waisted gown, white India muslin with deep flounces and co-quelicot ribbons. She performed a perfunctory curtsy and said, "Hello. Why are you wearing that horrid dress? Are you a servant?"

Laura paused a moment to allow Maria to correct her daughter's impertinence. When no lesson in good manners came, she smiled at the child, who was after all not to blame for her mother's indulgence, and said, "Hello, Arabella. No, I am not a servant. I am in mourning."

"But it's afternoon," Arabella pointed out with irrefutable logic. "You did ought to wear something pretty, like me and Mama. Do you want some cake, 'stead of those horrid sammitches wiv the green stuff in them?"

"Maria, if you cannot make the girl mind her tongue, pray send her from the room!"

"I won't go, I won't go," screeched Arabella, suddenly transformed into a small virago. "I didn't have my cake. You're a horrid old witch. I'll hold my breaff till I die." She clapped her hands to her mouth, puffed up her cheeks and began to turn crimson.

"Really, Aunt Antonia," wailed Maria, "you know what she is like. Why must you interfere? Now she will make herself ill. She's only a baby. Lady Laura did not mind. Hush, darling, you shall have your cake."

"No, she shall not," said Miss Burleigh grimly. "It is past time she was taught to behave herself."

They continued to wrangle, ignoring Arabella who was now nearly purple. Leaning forward, Laura poked the child hard in both cheeks. Her breath exited with a whoosh and she gaped dumbfounded at her assailant.

"Well done, Cousin." Gareth had come in unnoticed, bearing two toasting forks and followed by a footman with a tray. "Arabella, go to Nurse at once."

"I want my cake!"

"Little girls who throw tantrums have to make do with bread and milk," he said sternly and pointed at the door.

She began to trail out, head hanging. Maria jumped up. "You are cruel, Gareth!" She seized a plate and a piece of cake and sailed from the room, nose in the air, towing her stumbling daughter after her by the wrist.

Gareth sighed, shrugged. "How can a mere male contend against a mother's love?"

His rhetorical question drew an immediate response. "Pooh!" said his aunt, as the footman set down the tray and departed with discreet haste. "Nonsense. Maria likes to have the child about her because she was once told what a charming picture they made together. She will not trouble herself to discipline her, and any attempt to do so she takes as aimed at herself."

"I am inclined to agree," said Laura hesitantly, "as far as I can judge from what little I have seen. Mrs. Forbes was far more intent upon her quarrel with Miss Burleigh than upon Arabella's imminent suffocation. Not that I suppose for a moment that she could possibly have held her breath long enough to suffer any damage."

The elderly lady threw her a glance of surprised approval. Gareth looked doubtful. "Maria is easily offended," he admitted, and changed the subject. "Aunt Antonia, you will not mind if I make some toast at the fire for Cousin Laura?"

Miss Burleigh waved gracious permission. "Another cup of tea, Lady Laura?" she enquired.

"If you please, ma'am." Laura started to push herself out of her chair.

"Sit down!" roared Gareth.

Taken by surprise, Laura sat. Sooner or later, she thought crossly, she must make it quite plain to the dictatorial gentleman that she refused to be wrapped in cotton-wool. For the moment, there had been enough pulling of caps for one afternoon. She meekly accepted the cup he brought her.

He set Arabella's footstool before the fire and sat down. Soon the mouthwatering odour of toasting bread arose.

"Toast?" A pear-shaped gentleman of perhaps fifty summers wandered into the drawing room, sniffing the air. Narrow head with thinning grey hair, sloping shoulders, and undeveloped chest in a long labourer's smock widened to a comfortable pot-belly. Spindly legs in green satin breeches and clocked stockings seemed an unnecessary afterthought.

He peered through thick-lensed spectacles at Laura. "Have we met?" he asked uncertainly.

Gareth turned away from the fire. "My uncle, Julius Wyckham, Cousin. Uncle, this is Lady Laura Chamberlain."

"You are burning the toast, nevvie," observed Mr. Wyckham, peering now at the ascending curl of smoke.

Swinging back to his task, Gareth jolted one of the forks. The toast fell off the prongs and rapidly blackened among the dancing flames. "Sorry, Laura. I'll have another for you in a trice." He reached for a slice of bread.

Mr. Wyckham removed the fork from Gareth's hand and examined the prongs intently. "Must be a better way to do it," he muttered, and trotted out of the room again, taking it with him.

"Julius is an inventor," said Miss Burleigh with austere disapproval.

Gareth took the toast from the remaining fork, spread it lavishly with butter, and passed the plate to Laura. "You must admit,

Aunt Antonia," he said, spearing another slice, "occasionally he comes up with something useful. Remember the drying machine?"

"How could I forget. It was a large metal drum, Lady Laura, perforated with small holes. A clockwork mechanism rotated it above a charcoal brazier and it tumbled sheets and towels about, drying them quite efficiently in wet weather. Unfortunately, the clockwork broke one day. Two pair of the best sheets were badly scorched."

"Uncle Julius had lost interest by then and never repaired it," Gareth added.

"It sounds very clever," said Laura. "That reminds me, I must wash and iron my gowns, ma'am. I daresay Mrs. Lloyd will tell me where to go?"

"You will do nothing of the kind!" Gareth swung round, once again endangering the toast.

Laura opened her mouth to protest, then licked a drip of butter off her hand instead as Miss Burleigh added her shocked prohibition. "It is quite out of the question. I shall have Mrs. Lloyd direct one of the maids to wait upon you."

"Thank you, ma'am." She might have argued with Gareth, but she recognized his aunt's objection as motivated by propriety, not over-solicitude. Besides, the old lady had mellowed somewhat and she had no desire to reawaken her antagonism.

Gareth gave her another slice of toast, and then spread one for himself. He was about to take a bite when he intercepted Miss Burleigh's wistful gaze. He exchanged a glance brimful of amusement with Laura. "Aunt Antonia, do you care to sample the product of my venture into domesticity?"

"Thank you, I will take half a slice."

"Might I suggest, Cousin, that you provide Miss Burleigh with a napkin?" Laura caught another drip with the tip of her tongue.

With a rueful grin, he passed her a napkin and served his aunt. Rupert came in, his scarlet coat exchanged for an aged shooting jacket. Exclaiming indignantly that no one had told him and he had nearly missed the treat, he took over the toasting. What had started as a thoroughly disagreeable situation turned into a merry party.

The last of the loaf disappeared into the captain's bottomless pit. He bore off his brother to the stables to discuss the horses purchased since he was last at Llys. As Gareth left, he bent over Laura and asked anxiously, "Are you quite comfortable? You need not come down to dinner, of course. Aunt Antonia shall order a tray for you."

"Perfectly comfortable," she assured him with a smile, ignoring the rest of his speech.

In fact, she was still a little tired after the journey, though she would not admit it to him for the world. As soon as the door closed behind him, she said to Miss Burleigh, "If you will excuse me, ma'am, I believe I shall lie down for a while before dinner."

"Your previous accommodations were arranged before I was aware of your . . . delicate condition." Miss Burleigh stood up and went to ring the bell, a hint of pink touching her sharp cheekbones. "Mrs. Lloyd shall show you to your new chamber, and I shall ask her to arrange for your dinner to be brought to you on a tray."

A footman in brown and buff livery came in and was sent for the housekeeper. In the awkward silence that followed his departure, Laura decided that she could not live with the uneasy truce. Better to have the scandal in the open, where she could defend herself.

"I do understand, ma'am, why you wish as much as possible to exclude me from the family. My reputation was . . . sullied, through my own fault, five years ago. But I have done nothing since to deserve your contempt, unless my husband's faults be imputed to me also. Am I to suffer all my life because I was so foolish as to elope?"

"If it were only an elopement!"

Laura bit her lip. "You have heard the story, then."

"I have."

"Does Lord Wyckham know?" she asked in a strangled voice.

"I believe not. He was twenty-three at the time, a mere boy with no interest in such matters. I see no need to enlighten him."

"I thank you, ma'am, but let me tell you my side of the story. Let me explain the circumstances, I beg of you."

Mrs. Lloyd appeared in the doorway. "Madam?"

"Show Lady Laura to her chamber, if you please." Stiffly she turned to Laura. "We shall speak further at another time."

At least she was to have a chance to exonerate herself, she thought as she followed the housekeeper. Her father had refused to listen and her mother, whom she had never seen again, had not answered her letters.

Mrs. Lloyd led her by way of the minstrel's gallery above the Great Hall to a door on the same floor, at the near end of yet another wing. "The Rose Suite, my lady." Opening the door, she ushered Laura into a small sitting room. The predominant colour was blue, but carpet, curtains, and wallpaper were patterned with roses, pink and yellow, not so much faded as mellowed by time. "Your bedchamber is through here." She opened another door. "This is Myfanwy, who will be waiting on you."

A tiny, dark-haired girl with snowy starched apron and frilled cap curtsied, beaming. Laura nodded and smiled at her.

"His lordship dines at eight, my lady," the housekeeper continued, "being used to Town hours. The family gathers in the Long Gallery first. Myfanwy will show you the way."

Laura realized that nothing had been said of dinner on a tray. She was determined to dine with the family, both to prove to Gareth that she was no invalid and to defy any attempt to isolate her. That private sitting room might conceivably be due to her rank and her pregnancy, or it might be a hint that she was not welcome elsewhere.

She thanked Mrs. Lloyd, who left.

"I hung up your ladyship's gowns," Myfanwy announced. "There's glad I am to be waiting on your ladyship. Auntie said to hold my tongue, but sometimes I must talk, look you, or there's bursting I'll be."

"Of course. Is Mrs. Lloyd your auntie?"

"That she is, my lady. She's worked here

at Llys Manor since afore I were born." She pronounced Llys in the Welsh way, vastly different from the same word spoken by the English as in *fleur-de-lis.* "What will you be wearing for dinner, my lady?"

The wardrobe had not miraculously sprouted an elegant black silk evening dress. Laura picked out a calico which she had dressed up with a black velvet ribbon around the neckline. "Sponge and press it, please. Most of them need washing, and all of them ironing, as soon as you have time."

"This very day, if all night it takes," the girl vowed.

"Oh no, you must not stay up all night about it. I shall rest now and change for dinner at quarter past seven."

"I'll be here on the dot, my lady." Myfanwy rushed to fold back the blue, rose-embroidered counterpane and plump up already plump pillows. "Well aired it was this afternoon. Will you be wanting the warming pan, my lady?"

"Not now, thank you." Laura gratefully accepted her aid with buttons and hooks, and was soon tucked in beneath the covers.

She did not sleep but drowsed, drifting through the impressions of the day. One insistent question nagged at her: why was Gareth in high fidgets over her pregnancy?

He was considerate, generous, amiable, but if he insisted on guarding her from every least exertion they were going to come to cuffs sooner or later.

Myfanwy returned with hot water and the refreshed gown. She chattered as she helped Laura wash, rebraid her hair, and dress. "Mr. Cornelius is come to dinner, him as is vicar. Chapel we are, but they do say he preaches a grand sermon, with ever so many long words. Indeed to goodness, my lady, you will not be wearing this gown much longer. Already let out it is at the seams, and there's tight the body is, look you."

"I can feel it. I shall have to buy material and make up some new gowns."

"I'll help you, my lady. Even Auntie says it's good with my needle I am. That's it now, let's see." She regarded Laura with a dissatisfied look. "There's a pity you must wear black, pretty as you are, my lady. Will you be wearing a necklace?"

"Not tonight." Nor any other night. Freddie had brought her pretty trinkets now and then, all soon to be sold when his luck faltered. How long ago and far away Freddie seemed now, like a dim memory from a different life, a different world, almost as distant as her life in her parents' home.

Myfanwy showed her down a short flight of stairs to the Long Gallery, running the width of the old house beneath the drawing room and behind the Great Hall. One long wall was panelled and hung with portraits of ancestors. Opposite, a dozen floor-to-ceiling windows and French doors looked out on a terrace and dripping gardens. The rain had stopped and in the west the sun set fire to the last fleeing streamers of cloud.

As Laura entered, a gentleman turned from consulting a mahogany-cased weather-glass hanging between two windows. He was obviously one of the Wyckham brothers, with the thick blond hair and blue eyes. In him the strong jaw tended to heaviness and he was considerably shorter than both Gareth and Rupert, his figure a trifle portly.

He came to meet her. "Am I correct, ma'am, in supposing you to be, hm, Lady Laura Chamberlain? Permit me to introduce myself: I am Cornelius Wyckham. Welcome to Llys Manor."

"Thank you, Mr. Wyckham. You are the vicar of Llys, I understand?"

"I do indeed serve that function in my, hm, humble fashion. May I offer my most sincere condolences, ma'am, on your recent, hm, unhappy loss? If religion can provide any, hm, consolation, I beg you will not hesitate to call upon me."

His weighty pauses lent unwarranted significance to his words, making him sound pompous, though kindly. Laura responded to the kindness, with gratitude but careful not to suggest that she had any intention of turning to the Church for comfort. To do so would be sheer hypocrisy. She had been more comfortable since becoming a widow than ever during her marriage.

"I am, hm, glad of the opportunity to become acquainted," said the vicar. "I understood from Gareth that your, hm, delicate condition precluded your joining the family for dinner."

She suppressed a sigh but spoke through gritted teeth. "I assure you, sir, that I am perfectly well. As a clergyman, you must be aware that your female parishioners do not take to their beds only because they are breeding."

The Reverend Cornelius was saved by Mrs. Forbes's arrival. She swept into the room, looking Laura's shabby widow's weeds up and down with undisguised smugness. Her own gown was of rose crape over a white satin slip, far too grand for the country, especially for a family dinner. Laura had no objection, since Maria's smartness seemed to have put her in a high good humour that her children were not present to dispel.

"I fear mourning becomes you ill, Cousin Laura," she commiserated. "Such a trying colour, though when Mr. Forbes passed away people were kind enough to say that black enhanced my fairness."

Laura returned a civil answer and Cornelius managed a ponderous compliment to both ladies. Miss Burleigh came in, followed shortly by Rupert and Gareth.

"Uncle Julius cannot be detached from his workbench this . . . Cousin Laura!" Before Gareth could order her to sit down, or even to retire to bed, Lloyd announced that dinner was served, narrowly averting a clash she was not ready for.

Gareth contented himself with giving her his arm into the dining room next door and plying her with delicacies. Fortunately her appetite had recovered from the buttered toast. She did full justice to the delicious meal, thanking heaven that at least he did not consider her one of those invalids requiring a diet of gruel.

Rupert entertained them with tall tales of the wild exploits of his fellow Guards officers. He captured Maria's attention — no mean feat when the subject was not herself — and even succeeded in bringing a smile to his aunt's thin lips. Laura revelled in the new experience of a family at ease.

She was unprepared for the wave of panic that swept over her when Miss Burleigh rose to lead the ladies' withdrawal. Suppose she took advantage of the gentlemen's absence to demand the accounting Laura had offered?

As the dining room door closed behind them, Laura said, "If you will excuse me, ma'am, I believe I shall retire now."

She did not want Maria Forbes to learn her story. She dreaded baring her soul to Miss Burleigh and finding herself still condemned. Most of all, she could not bear to let the awful, humiliating memories loose in her own head.

CHAPTER 5

Laura ate breakfast in bed.

"His lordship ordered it, my lady," Myfanwy had said anxiously, "and for all the kindest master he is, none on us'd disobey an order, look you."

So she indulged him, and herself, and she found she enjoyed lounging against a stack of pillows with a tray of eggs and muffins on her lap, a pot of tea on the night-table. A day empty of chores awaited her, no dusting, no garden to be weeded, no marketing and no cooking. Through the open window came the fragrance of lilacs and a thrush's warble. The sun shone on the spring-green, five-fingered leaves and white candle-blossoms of a huge horse chestnut just visible from her bed.

To be cosseted for once was a pleasure, but the bright perfection of this last day of May called her out of doors. She drained the last drop of tea and threw back the covers.

Half an hour later, she was strolling down a gravel path between beds of roses sprouting new, reddish leaves and swelling green buds. Between the bushes, polyanthus vied with pansies to make the best show in a dozen brilliant colours. In the west, beyond gardens and park, fields and woods, the Welsh mountains loomed on the horizon.

An elderly gardener raking the gravel saluted her and she complimented him on the flowers. With a toothless beam, he poured forth a flood of words. His intonation was Welsh, but owing to the lack of teeth she was not sure whether he was speaking in that language or English. She smiled and nodded and strolled on.

The path ended at a steep flight of steps, patched with orange lichen, leading down to a lower level of gardens. Shaded from the morning sun, the stone was still damp from yesterday's rain. Laura hesitated. The less formal garden below was enticing, with peonies, columbine, and lily-of the valley surrounding a fountain. She had castigated Gareth for suggesting that she ought not to climb stairs. On the other hand, these were steep and looked slippery, and she had no need to tackle them.

She was about to turn away when she heard the crunch of rapid footsteps on the gravel path behind her. Before she turned, before he spoke, she knew it was Gareth.

"Cousin Laura! Don't go down there, I beg of you."

He was bare-headed, his hair shining gold in the sun. The fear on his handsome face startled her. With a flash of insight, she recognized that he was driven less by regard for her, for Laura Chamberlain, than by some urgent inner compulsion.

Her curiosity increased, but the realization made it easier to say imperatively, "My lord, I am a grown woman and I refuse to be dictated to."

"I only want to protect —"

"I know my own strength. I am accustomed to independence, to making my own decisions."

"My duty —"

"If you continue to believe that my acceptance of your hospitality makes it your duty, or your right, to lay down the law," she snapped, "I shall be obliged to return to Cambridgeshire at once."

"No," he cried, horror-stricken. "You must not attempt that journey again —"

"Must not?"

"I mean, please, Cousin, don't leave. I could not endure knowing myself responsible if any harm should come to you."

"No one could possibly hold you to blame."

"I should blame myself." He gave her a crooked, irresistible smile. "I beg your pardon for laying down the law. I shall do my best to curb the impulse, I promise you, if you will promise to forgive occasional lapses — and to take care of yourself."

"It's a bargain." Mollified, she held out her hand and he took it in both his. The warmth of his bare hands, strong and shapely, penetrated her thin, much-darned cotton gloves. It would be easy, she thought, to give up the struggle and let him take care of her. His dark blue eyes were warm, too, gazing down at her. If only his concern were for her as a person, not as a dependent, a pregnant dependent.

Feeling the warmth reach her cheeks, she pulled away her hand. "As a matter of fact, I had already decided that to have to climb back up these steps would be shatterbrained. Such a pity; the English garden is most attractive."

"I should have trusted your common sense." He grinned. "As it happens, there is a carriage drive behind those ilex bushes. If you wish, I shall help you down the steps and fetch the gig to drive you back up the hill to the house."

"That will be delightful, Cousin." She laid her hand on his arm and they descended.

The fountain featured a pink marble naiad pouring a sparkling stream of water from an urn balanced on her shoulder. As they approached, Laura noticed a marble dragonfly perched on the lip of the urn, and then she saw that the naiad held a frog nestling in her other hand. The shelving rock she stood upon was a haven for other marble creatures: otters, newts, a water-vole, a pair of nesting ducks. Behind her a swan spread wide protective wings.

"Oh, charming!" Laura exclaimed. "I have never seen its like."

"See if you can find the smallest creature."

Challenged, she knelt with one knee on the rim of the fountain and peered at the sculpture. "A snail. There by the littlest otter."

"Which would crunch it up, no doubt, were they real. But no, there is something smaller. Look next to the larger newt."

"A beetle? Oh, a water boatman, of course. The children must love this."

"We did, my brothers and I, when we were small. Maria's children are not allowed here."

She frowned. "I recall some sort of hullabaloo over her sons when we arrived but I did not properly gather the cause — yes, I admit I was tired," she added defensively. "Are they so ill-behaved they cannot be trusted in the gardens?"

"By no means. George and Henry are normal boys with a normal share of naughtiness. But Maria is convinced they will come to some dire end if they are permitted to run about."

"Surely it cannot be healthy to keep them cooped up in the house."

"They are allowed sedate walks in the shrubbery with their governess," Gareth said dryly.

"I daresay that is all the exercise Mrs. Forbes cares to take, so she cannot understand that children need more."

"Possibly. More to the point is her fear

that they might drown in the fountain —"

"In four inches of water?"

"— or break their necks climbing trees. I freely confess I have not sufficient fortitude to face Maria's hysterics should I overrule her where her darlings are concerned."

"Her darling devils. Hmm," said Laura, deep in thought, "I shall have to see what I can do."

"Don't tell me I have taken a managing female into my house!"

She laughed. "I cannot be sure. I have never had much opportunity for managing people and I may well prove an utter failure."

"I doubt it. You have by far too much force of mind to make a mull of anything you set your mind to."

Reminded of the mull she had made of her life, she shivered. Instantly Gareth whipped off his coat and draped it across her shoulders. "You are cold," he said, full of remorse. "The morning air is still chilly at this season. Here, come and sit on this bench in the sun while I fetch the gig."

He set off up the steps at a run, his shoulders broad in his white shirt, close-fitting buckskins revealing slim hips and muscular thighs above his refulgent top-boots. Gareth Wyckham was no mincing

Town Beau in need of a valet to release him from the imprisonment of a fashionably tight coat. She huddled his riding coat about her, breathing in his odour, mingled with the fragrance of peonies and lilies-of-the-valley.

Not that she was actually cold. In a gesture of revolt against her momentary weakness, she threw off the comforting garment, folding and smoothing it. With a deliberate effort, she turned her thoughts to the problems of Mrs. Forbes's children.

She had reached no solution when she heard the clop of hooves beyond the high ilex hedge. As she headed for the small white-painted wicket gate, Gareth appeared to open it for her.

Handing him his coat, she said, "I am not cold, I promise you. I hope your aunt did not see you without it."

"Not unless she happened to look out of a window at the wrong moment," he assured her, shrugging into it, "and then she might not have recognized me, at such speed did I pass. Old Daffyd was startled half out of what few wits he possesses."

"Is that the gardener?" She accepted his help to climb into the gig, a smart dark blue vehicle picked out in black, with a dapple grey between the shafts. "I spoke to him but

84

understood not a word of his reply."

"Daffyd understands English but speaks only Welsh. I know enough to communicate when necessary. Drat, I had not thought. We shall have to drive as far as the lane before I can turn." At his signal the grey started down the hill between the ilex and a hawthorn hedge bright with may blossom.

"I don't mind. It's a beautiful day for a drive. Only, I fear your surveillance of me is keeping you from your usual pursuits."

"I have an appointment with my steward this afternoon, but no particular business until then. Rupert went out at dawn with the dogs and a gun, as if he had not enough of guns in the army. Aunt Antonia spends her mornings conferring with Mrs. Lloyd and Cook, and writing letters. Uncle Julius is still in his workshop, having slept there, I collect. I trust he remembered to eat. And Maria never appears below stairs before noon. I am quite free to keep you under surveillance for an hour or two yet."

"Then could we possibly drive into the village?"

"Of course. Do you wish to make some purchases? I hope you will not be disappointed — there is only one small shop."

Laura shook her head. "No, I'd just like to see the place now, but . . . Oh, but we cannot go. You have no hat!"

Surprised, he touched the top of his head. "So I have not. I forgot. When I saw you in the garden from my window, I did not stop for hat and gloves."

"How fortunate that you were otherwise fully dressed!"

Gareth laughed. "I'll have you know I rose and went for a gallop while you were still abed."

"Only because I ate breakfast in bed, to spare my maid the horrid fate of those who disobey you," she retorted.

"I am not such a tyrant!"

"Merely a dictator. No, Myfanwy said you are the kindest of masters." She observed his flush with amusement. "What is more, I enjoyed breakfast in bed and shall probably make a habit of it, for the present."

"Splendid." He fell silent as they reached the lane and he neatly executed the tricky business of turning the gig in the narrow space. As they started back towards the house, he said, "Any time you wish to go to the village, one of the grooms will drive you if I am not available. Do you ride?"

"Yes, or I was used to before my marriage. However, I doubt it would be wise at present."

He heaved a deep sigh of relief. "Thank

heaven."

"May I ask one of the grooms to drive me into Ludlow?"

"Ludlow! That's ten miles!"

"Myfanwy tells me there is a good, cheap draper there. I must buy material and make up some gowns before I split all my seams."

"I shall have samples brought here for you to choose from."

"Thank you, but no tradesman would come so far for so little as I can afford to spend."

Gareth turned to her, letting the reins slacken. The placid horse continued up the hill at its own pace as he said seriously, "Cousin, while you are under my roof, I shall pay for your clothes. You will choose the best materials for your purpose, without regard to cost, and the village seamstress shall make your gowns." He smiled. "Maria is satisfied with her work, so she must indeed be excellent."

Disregarding this pleasantry, Laura demurred. "I am perfectly capable of making my own dresses. I enjoy sewing."

"I am aware of that. Please, content yourself with embroidery and such. Though I'm vague about the details, I'm sure dressmaking involves considerably more exertion."

"I cannot afford a seamstress and I will not hang upon your sleeve."

"Have you no regard for my reputation?" he demanded, half in earnest, half quizzing her.

"What do you mean?"

"What will the neighbours think when they call and find a relative of mine dressed in the dowdiest fashion? I shall become notorious as a pinch-penny, a veritable nip-farthing."

"But —"

"Or else they will suppose that I am all to pieces, one step ahead of the bailiffs."

"Surely —"

"No, I shall more likely be condemned as a clutchfist, since Maria is constant complaining that I will not set her up in her own household in Town."

"Is she really?" Laura asked, shocked. When he nodded, she went on unwillingly, "Oh, very well, I shall let you frank me — oh dear, that sounds shockingly ungracious. Thank you, Cousin Gareth. I appreciate your generosity and I shall like to have some pretty gowns." Even though they would all be black and big enough for an elephant, she thought with a mental grimace. On the whole, she was quite glad he had won his point this time. Gentlemen hated to lose, and she had no desire to vex him beyond bearing.

"Good, then that's settled." He drove around the stables and pulled up at the front door, where a groom was waiting to take the gig back to the carriage house.

"But I should still like to go to Ludlow," Laura said as Gareth handed her down, "to see the shops and the castle."

"So you shall, in full state in the carriage with coachman and footman and your maid, as soon as you have something to wear that will not disgrace me!"

Laughing, they went into the house.

Lloyd met them in the Great Hall. "If your ladyship is not otherwise occupied," he said, bowing, "Miss Burleigh would like to see you in her sitting room as soon as is convenient."

Laura threw a glance of panic-stricken appeal at Gareth. He pressed her hand.

"Are you too tired to speak to Aunt Antonia now?" he asked solicitously.

She shook her head, with the greatest reluctance. If she claimed fatigue he would never let her forget it, and she had to face Miss Burleigh sooner or later.

He continued in a low voice, "My aunt is straitlaced but charitable. You need not fear her."

It was easy for him to talk, she reflected forlornly as she trudged after Lloyd. Gareth, Baron Wyckham, had doubtless never given his aunt a moment's cause for uneasiness, never transgressed against the rules of propriety.

Would that she could say the same of herself.

CHAPTER 6

"What a pleasant room," Laura exclaimed. She had unconsciously expected Miss Burleigh's private apartment to be furnished in greys and duns. The reality of flowered chintz curtains and upholstery gave the room a cheerful, airy feeling.

Miss Burleigh, seated at an inlaid dropfront desk, bowed her head in response to the compliment. "Pray be seated, Lady Laura." She rose as Laura sat down on a low cabriole chair, and took a similar chair facing her, her thin face composed, her hands folded sedately in her lap. "I am willing to hear what you have to say."

Laura perched on the edge of the seat, her back stiff, trying to marshal thoughts that slithered and slipped from her grasp. Only the fact that she had begged for a chance to present her story enabled her to begin.

"It all started when my grandmother died just before my first Season," she said slowly, unfocused gaze fixed on her memories. "I was not expected to 'take,' being too thin and insufficiently docile, but I might have had a chance, that year, on my own. The next year I was brought out with my sister Cecilia, beautiful, compliant Cecilia. I might as well have been a doorpost for all the attention anyone paid me."

"The situation is not unfamiliar to me," said Miss Burleigh, and there was pain in her voice.

Her attention momentarily distracted from her story, Laura wondered if she, too, had been the despised, neglected sister of a Beauty. She had never married, devoting her life to that sister's children, but once she had been a young girl, with all the hopes and fears Laura remembered only too clearly.

And gradually the hopes had died. "Ceci caught a duke's heir. Once they were betrothed, Mama made no more pretence of trying to find me a husband. My so-called friends commiserated with me on having a younger sister wed first. Freddie Chamberlain was the only gentleman who still bothered to stand up with me at balls."

"Had you no fortune to attract suitors?"

"Nothing of significance. I had five sisters and four brothers to be provided for. Freddie was no fortune-hunter, though his pockets were generally to let. He was always kind, you know, when it cost him no effort and did not interfere with his pleasures. He was handsome, and amusing, and he danced with me. I thought myself in love."

"Inevitably," muttered Miss Burleigh.

"I persuaded him to marry me. Papa would never have considered his suit, for he already had a reputation as a gamester and a wastrel, so we arranged to elope. I sold my pearls to pay for the journey to Gretna Green. I was so sure I could reform him once I was his wife."

"Whoever first said that rakes reformed make the best husbands is responsible for a great deal of unhappiness. I suppose he changed his mind about marriage once you were on the road, my dear?"

"No, you must not think so very ill of him," Laura cried. She pressed the heels of her hands to her forehead, as if to blot out what came next. "We stopped at an inn for the night. He met some friends there, and the temptation to increase my small store of money was too much for him. He won a little at cards, lost a little, won again." She had to force her voice through her tight throat. "For near a fortnight we stayed there while he played and drank, drank and played. He never touched me. The cards and the brandy were more attractive."

"Oh, my dear, how very dreadful! How utterly mortifying. Do not cry, pray do not cry." Miss Burleigh jumped up and thrust a handkerchief into her hand, patted her shoulder. "It was then that Lord Medway found you?"

"Papa would not listen to a word I said." Bitterness combatted misery. "He had brought a special license and we were married that day. Though Papa did not believe it, Freddie was perfectly willing. He was sorry for me, and after all, he had no intention of allowing the acquisition of a wife to make the least difference to his life."

"Of course your elopement could not be hushed up, but only the families heard that you had not been married within a very few days. They were given to understand that you had voluntarily lived with Frederick as man and wife for two weeks."

"You are not related, ma'am. Since you know, everyone must."

"Your mama-in-law happens to be a friend of mine, as well as being my late sister's husband's cousin. We correspond frequently. Naturally she was deeply distressed by what the earl told her husband and she poured out her troubled mind in a letter, knowing I should repeat nothing. I despise gossip. Your story is safe with me."

"Thank you, ma'am." Laura was beginning to feel relief at having disburdened herself to a surprisingly sympathetic ear. "Not that it really matters, as I have no aspirations to reenter Society."

"I fear your father's utterly casting you off aroused suspicions that it was not a simple elopement. Indeed," she went on with a return to her usual austere manner, "I received an unpleasant letter the other day from Lady Frobisher, my brother-in-law's sister. Sybil Frobisher is an inveterate scandalmonger. I shall write to her today."

"You will not tell her —"

"I shall endeavour to defend you without revealing the unhappy truth. Now, Lady Laura, if you are sufficiently composed, I shall ring for tea."

Laura had not shed a single tear during her recital, though she had horribly mangled Miss Burleigh's tiny, lace-edged handkerchief. Smoothing it on her knee as they awaited their tea, she decided to make another to replace it, a simple task Gareth must surely approve.

Her curiosity revived now that her own

ordeal was past. She wondered if Miss Burleigh knew the reason for her otherwise imperturbable nephew's excessive excitability on the subject of childbearing.

She wondered if she dared ask. Miss Burleigh had softened, revealed herself not the dragon Laura had feared, but she would have every right to condemn inquisitiveness on so personal a matter. Before Laura had decided whether to risk a carefully phrased question, a maid came in with the tea.

Miss Burleigh poured, and passed a plate of fresh-baked Shrewsbury biscuits. The crisp, lemony biscuits awoke Laura's appetite. She was crunching her third when the door opened and Uncle Julius ambled in.

His thin grey hair straggled wildly. His chin sported a whitish stubble. His smock bore scorch marks and streaks of soot and his green satin breeches were badly creased. In one hand, like a demented Saracen with a scimitar, he wielded a deformed toasting fork.

"This is my private sitting room," Miss Burleigh pointed out coldly.

"Is it?" He peered about vaguely through his thick, smudged spectacles. "But Lloyd said the young lady . . . Ah, there you are, my dear." A sudden doubt struck him. "You are the young lady whose toast my nevvie burnt?"

"I am, sir." She flinched as the augmented end of the fork narrowly missed her nose.

"Careful, uncle!" Gareth strode into the room and gently removed the contrivance from the old gentleman's hand.

Uncle Julius made no objection, having spotted the plate of biscuits. He picked it up and consumed half a dozen with a thoughtful air. "I'm quite hungry," he said, sounding surprised. "I believe I left my dinner in my workshop." He headed for the door, carrying the emptied plate.

Gareth caught his sleeve. "Whoa, there. Why don't you explain your machine to us while a fresh meal is prepared." He nodded to Miss Burleigh, who rang the bell, looking martyred.

"Machine? Oh, that thing. I'd scarcely go so far as to call it a machine, nevvie." Nonetheless, he took back the fork and sat down. Miss Burleigh winced as the grimy smock met her flowered chintz sofa. "It's just a small improvement I thought up when one of you careless boys burnt the young lady's toast." He squinted at Gareth. "It wasn't you, by any chance, was it?"

"Yes, I was that careless boy," he confessed, grinning.

Uncle Julius turned to Laura. "I can't tell 'em apart," he confided. "That's why I call 'em all nevvie. Look here." To the prongs of the fork, he had welded a double grid of wire, about six inches square. On one side the two pieces were attached to each other by three small hoops of wire, forming a hinge. Opposite, a hook latched them together. This he now opened. "You put the bread in and close it again. These spikes stick through it. It can't possibly fall in the fire."

"How clever," Laura said admiringly. "Cousin Gareth, may we try it out this afternoon?"

"Certainly."

"If you do not mind, Miss Burleigh?"

"Should you dislike such carryings-on in the drawing room, Aunt Antonia, we can move our feast elsewhere."

"Not at all. I shall order a fire in the drawing room."

They turned back to Uncle Julius, to find him fast asleep, swaying slightly as he sat on the sofa, his latest invention clutched in his grimy hand.

The footman who came in answer to the bell was directed — instead of feeding Mr. Wyckham — to put him to bed.

"You must think I run a Bedlam," said

Gareth ruefully as they left Miss Burleigh in peace. "What with Maria's hysterics and Uncle Julius's little peculiarities . . ."

"I like him. Eccentricity and absentmindedness are pardonable in so clever a gentleman. Besides, it is the first time anyone has invented something just for me, even if he still has no notion who I am."

"Maria, his own brother's daughter, had lived at Llys six months before he began to recognize her, and he is still perplexed by the children. You must not be affronted when he fails to recall your name."

"How could I be, when he cannot tell you apart from your brothers?"

"Shocking, is it not? From Uncle Julius I never receive the deference due to the head of the family. Even Aunt Antonia occasionally recalls that I am Baron Wyckham of Llys, no longer a scrubby schoolboy." He sobered. "She was not unkind to you, was she?"

"Oh no, amazingly sympathetic and understanding." For a horrid moment Laura was afraid he would ask the subject of their conversation, but he went on speaking of his aunt.

"She has an acerbic tongue at times, but I am eternally grateful to her for the care she has taken of my brothers these many years.

I hope that in you she will find female companionship of a kind Maria is incapable of providing."

"I hope so, indeed." She would be glad to make some return for his hospitality. As they reached the Great Hall, she realized she was tired after the morning's exercise and emotions. Now, how to retire to rest without alarming him? "I must write to Lady Denham, my neighbour. There is a little writing desk in my sitting room, I noticed."

"I have letters to write, too. Will you not join me in the library? No stairs, if I may venture to offer that as an inducement."

"It is not offers I take exception to, but orders. Thank you, Cousin, I shall be happy to join you in the library."

The library was in the newest part of the house. Bookshelves ran up to a high ceiling ornamented with plasterwork. Opposite an elegant Adam fireplace on one wall, crimson velvet-curtained sash windows set in alcoves looked out on the avenue of oaks leading up to the house. Each alcove was provided with a small table and chairs. A huge mahogany desk dominated one end of the room, a long table the other, with a group of comfortable armchairs clustered about the fireplace. Newspapers, magazines, and books with places marked were scattered about, giving the room a pleasing air of being in regular use, not just for show.

"My father spent much of his time in here in his later years," said Gareth. "He became something of a recluse after . . . Well, no matter. I don't wish to bore you. Where will you sit?"

She chose a window table. He took writing materials from its drawer for her, mended a pen, checked the inkwell, reminded her to ask him for a frank, and settled to his own correspondence.

Laura found her letter difficult to write. Lady Denham, in her good-natured way, had made her promise to send news of her safe arrival, but she did not flatter herself she would be actively missed. Her neighbours in Swaffham Bulbeck had been friendly without ever becoming friends. A gentlewoman in reduced circumstances belonged among neither the gentry nor the villagers, nor yet the prosperous yeoman farmers.

In the end, she wrote a brief note stressing Lord Wyckham's kindness and Miss Burleigh's respectability. As she folded and sealed it, she saw Rupert striding towards the front door, a game bag and a shotgun over his shoulder, two panting terriers at his heels.

Gareth saw his brother at the same moment. Leaning out of an open window, he shouted, "Rupert, for pity's sake come in the back way. Aunt Antonia will have your ears for egg-cosies if she meets you in the hall."

The captain gave a cheery wave. "Rabbit pie for dinner," he called, and altered course for stables, kitchen, and gun-room.

"If Cousin Rupert is come home, it must be time for luncheon," said Laura hopefully.

After luncheon, she pleased Gareth by choosing to take a nap. She took a book to her chamber with her, but fell asleep. When she awoke, it was time for afternoon tea. Though the craving for hot-buttered toast had left her, she wanted to see the trial of Uncle Julius's toasting fork, and she was thirsty enough to drink a whole pot of tea. She made her way to the drawing room.

Miss Burleigh was just pouring the tea. Uncle Julius, neat and clean in an old-fashioned frock coat, his spectacles sparkling, was methodically devouring a plateful of ham sandwiches. Maria and her daughter wore matching blue-sprigged muslin today, and identical pouts. Two small boys in nankeen, their pink faces suggesting a recent scrubbing, had backed Rupert into a corner where he goodnaturedly regaled them with tales of derring-do.

Miss Burleigh smiled at Laura. Maria said, "Good afternoon, Lady Laura," with such half-hearted graciousness that Laura suspected she had just been ordered to do so by Miss Burleigh.

"Good afternoon, Mrs. Forbes," she responded noncommittally, taking a seat.

Without prompting, Arabella came to curtsy to her. "I'll bring your tea," she said eagerly.

"You'd best let George do that, Bella," said Rupert, coming forward. "Why don't you offer Lady Laura a biscuit? These two young rascals are George and Henry, Cousin. Make your bows, boys."

Maria looked on complacently as her sons bowed, then spoiled it by saying, "Henry, your wristband is torn. Lady Laura will think you a gypsy. Go and have Nurse mend it at once."

"But, Mama, I'll miss tea, and Cousin Rupert, and everything! You can't make me —"

"Henry, apologize to your mother." Gareth came in just in time to forestall a storm. "Maria, I daresay Lady Laura will overlook a torn wristband this once. Let the child stay."

"Please do, Mrs. Forbes," Laura requested and, deciding a change of subject was due, she turned to Gareth. "Do you mean to demonstrate Mr. Wyckham's new invention, Cousin?"

Uncle Julius tore his attention from his sandwiches for long enough to beam with pride. Gareth picked up the fork, propped by the fireside. He inserted a slice of bread and snapped the catch shut.

"Can I hold it?" begged the older boy. "Please, Great-uncle Julius. Please, Cousin Gareth."

"Oh no, George, you will burn yourself!" Maria at once objected.

"I'll see he doesn't," Rupert said firmly, "neither himself nor the toast."

Gareth came to sit by Laura, asking her a question about the book she had taken from the library. She was forced to admit to having slept the afternoon away. He was laughing at her when a loud "The devil!" from the fireplace turned all heads.

Rupert was sucking his fingers.

"I didn't do nothing," said Henry defensively.

Between objections to Rupert's language and Henry's grammar, Rupert managed to explain. The toast being browned on one side, he had tried to open the hook, which had not unnaturally burned his fingers.

"Back to the drawing board," said Uncle Julius, sighing.

Laura ventured a suggestion. "Perhaps you could fasten the sides together, half an inch apart or so, and leave off the hook and the spikes. Then one need only turn it upside down to remove the toast."

"My dear . . . er . . . young lady, an excellent notion. I shall try it at once." He took the fork from Rupert, half toasted bread and all, and trotted out.

As he departed, Laura felt a most peculiar sensation inside her. "Oh!" she cried, clutching her middle.

Gareth sprang to his feet. "What is it? You are ill! Rupert, ride for the doctor! Why did I not send for him when we arrived, fool that I am? Aunt, have you smelling salts? Laura, put your feet up. Lie down. Keep still. Oh God!" He swept her up in his arms and deposited her on a sofa. "Burnt feathers! Hot bricks! Brandy!"

CHAPTER 7

As Rupert pounded out of the drawing room, Laura obediently lay back against the sofa cushions. Kneeling beside her, Gareth took her hand and chafed it. He felt he had been plunged into a nightmare. Guilt and fear chased each other through his mind: Doctor McAllister should have seen her yesterday.

He glanced round distractedly to see if Aunt Antonia had rung for the servants and found her vinaigrette.

"I hardly think Lady Laura is in need of stimulants," said his aunt tartly.

"But she . . ." As he spoke he realized that the little hand nestled within his was warm and alive, not cold and limp. He looked at her face. Nothing could have appeared healthier. No sign even of the pallor of fatigue he had come to recognize on the journey.

Her cheeks bloomed with wild roses. Her lips curved in a tender, joyful smile. It was not aimed at him. Her grey-green eyes were focused inward, contemplating some private delight. She was radiant.

How could he have judged her no beauty?

He frowned. She had cried out and clutched her belly, yet she did not seem to be ill. Perhaps it was just one of the whims and crotchets pregnant women were known to be subject to.

Maria disabused him of that notion. "No doubt the baby is quickening," she advised him in a superior tone. She approached the sofa, forcing him to move. "Lady Laura, is it a sort of fluttering feeling?"

"Yes." Laura returned to the world. "Like butterflies, or birds' wings, or leaves in a breeze, only it's not. I cannot describe it. It took me by surprise, but it has stopped now."

"It will come again. Just wait till the little dear starts kicking you at two o'clock in the morning." She sat down on the edge of the sofa and the two began comparing experiences.

Gareth felt himself excluded. He glanced at Aunt Antonia, who had shepherded the children away from the pseudo-drama. He caught a wistful expression on her thin face. She, too, was an outsider.

But she had avoided making a cake of herself. His gnawing anxiety had made him jump to conclusions and overreact like the veriest featherbrain. Good Lord, he had sent Rupert for the doctor! That dour Scot would either guess what had happened and think Baron Wyckham a fool, or else he'd come, and rake said baron over the coals for dragging him from his dinner for nothing.

Now that the need for brandy and burnt feathers was past, a footman appeared at the door.

"Run after Captain Rupert to the stables," Gareth ordered. "Tell him he need not go after all."

Doubtless Rupert would also consider his eldest brother a knock-in-the-cradle. Gareth decided he did not care. Better to cry wolf than to risk Laura's life. Unlike the shepherd boy in the fable, he was in a position to make everyone do his bidding however often he proclaimed a false emergency.

He would have Rupert stop in Ludlow when he left for Town tomorrow, to ask Dr. McAllister to call at his convenience. There were London physicians who specialized in childbirth, he thought.

Aunt Sybil would know. He would call them in, and then there were midwives, nurses, wet-nurses for the child to be arranged. He had read reports of drunken midwives. No one without impeccable references was going to come near Llys Manor.

He turned back to the ladies on the sofa. "How many months?" he asked awkwardly.

"Five," Laura said, smiling at him. Her face was still aglow.

"Four to go," Maria clarified, obviously pleased to be instructing an ignorant male, though he was not quite that ignorant.

Laura laid her hand on his arm, a small, slightly work-roughened hand. That was going to end.

"Please, Cousin Gareth, may I have some toast?"

"Of course. I am remiss in my duties. We still have the unimproved fork." He suspected she was humouring him, trying to take his mind off the fright she had given him. As he went to the fireplace to make toast — or rather, to supervise an insistent George — he wondered whether he owed her an explanation of his fears.

"Not even the least hint of morning sickness?" asked Maria enviously.

"Nothing," Laura assured her.

"I had it with all three, and I was perfectly miserable the whole time I was carrying Arabella. But then, I always had a delicate constitution. I daresay you will simply sail through the whole horrid business. What do you want, Henry? Oh, don't bow when you are holding a plate. You will spill everything on my gown, you stupid boy."

"No I won't, Mama. See?" The sturdy little boy gave her a glance of disgust. "Lady Laura, here's your toast. George made it but I spread the butter."

"Thank you, Henry. You have both done very well."

"Do you want some more? Are you sure

not? Mama, Cousin Gareth says do you want some toast?"

"Gracious, no. If I ate such stuff I should have to go on a diet of biscuits and soda-water, like Lord Byron. Not that it would matter if I were round as a balloon," she added bitterly, "for there is no one here to see. Do you not wish you were in London, Lady Laura?"

"Not at all." Laura could think of few worse fates.

"I suppose not. In your condition you could hardly go about. But when I think that I shall miss all the entertainments in honour of the Tsar! Of course, I have received invitations to stay with friends, but one cannot take horrid, noisy children to a friend's house."

"Could you not leave them here? They have a nurse and a governess, do they not?"

"Abandon my little darlings to *his* tender mercies? Never! And he is too mean to take a house for me in Town. I shall positively waste away here in the wilds, I vow. Why I even bother to take pains with my dress when none see it but yokels, I cannot imagine."

"Even yokels must admire your taste," said Laura tactfully, doing her best to conceal her indignation at the unwarranted insults to Gareth. "Those of your gowns that I have seen are charming."

"I shall be happy to advise you." Maria was all graciousness now. "I am sure you are sadly in need of new clothes and even black can be made elegant."

"Cousin Gareth has offered me the carriage to go to Ludlow to the draper's."

"I shall go with you." She raised her voice. "Gareth, Lady Laura and I require the carriage tomorrow to go to Ludlow."

"If it is quite convenient," Laura hastened to add.

"Perfectly." He was apparently willing to waive his requirement that Laura have a new dress before going into town, no doubt because of Maria's unexpected and possibly short-lived amiability.

Laura thanked him, though Maria obviously considered it an unnecessary courtesy.

He smiled at Laura, and turned back to his nephew. "No, George, you may not make more toast. Everyone has had sufficient. Henry, pray ask Lady Laura and your mama if they would care for more tea. If so, bring their cups to Aunt Antonia and ask her politely if she would be so kind as to fill them. George, you may carry them back when they are filled. Arabella, were you not in charge of offering biscuits?"

The children scurried to do his bidding as he came over to the sofa and pulled up a chair. Laura decided that to be abandoned to his "tender mercies" would be quite the best thing for the three. She had not realized that Arabella had been squeezed in at her mother's side throughout the discussion of the symptoms of pregnancy. Maria had done nothing to shield the child from such untimely knowledge. With luck, she would not have understood more than one word in ten.

Rupert came in just then. "I collect you are not about to expire after all, Cousin Laura," he said cheerfully. "I'm deuced glad to hear it."

She guessed from the gleam in his eye that he was about to roast his brother about the false alarm. "I suffered a sudden twinge," she said quickly, "but I recovered in a moment. Thank you for dashing off so gallantly on my behalf."

"Ever at your service, Cousin." He winked and preened his mustache. "You have been eating toast, I see. I haven't had my share. George, to work!"

"Just a moment, Rupert," said Gareth. "The urgency has passed, but as Cousin Laura is going shopping in Ludlow tomorrow, I'd like you to stop on your way and warn Dr. McAllister to expect her."

Rupert assented, and made a hurried escape as Laura objected, "I don't need to see a doctor."

"Go to the doctor?" Maria exclaimed. "That will be a shocking waste of our time in Ludlow. Besides, it is most unsuitable for Lady Laura to call on him. Only the lower classes go to his house. He must come here."

"When we are going to be in Ludlow anyway?" Laura shook her head. "That would be a shocking waste of his time, which he could better use caring for his patients. I shall see him there."

Maria pouted. Gareth grinned, and Laura realized he had won his point without even trying: she had agreed to see the doctor.

"Rupert shall tell the landlord at the Feathers to reserve a chamber," he said. "We'll make the inn our headquarters and meeting place, and Dr. McAllister may call upon you there."

"Are you coming with us?" she asked, surprised, and added with a smile, "You mean to keep me under surveillance, I daresay, to make sure I see the doctor and buy materials appropriate to your consequence."

"Ludlow is our nearest market town. I always have business there," he answered, but his eyes laughed at her.

Rupert was long gone when they set out for Ludlow the next morning. Miss Burleigh had decided to go too, and her abigail, as the most senior, went with them to wait upon the ladies, much to Myfanwy's disappointment. Gareth rode alongside the carriage. Laura thought him a fine figure on his splendid dapple grey gelding, straight and tall yet relaxed in the saddle.

She enjoyed the drive, along the pretty little River Llys, sparkling in the sun, then across hills patchworked with crops, meadows, and woods. Living on the East Anglian plain, she had almost forgotten the beauty of a rolling countryside.

From a distance she saw Ludlow Castle, a vast stronghold looming over the Rivers Teme and Corve. Today, she would have no time to explore it, what with Maria determined upon shopping and Gareth insisting on the doctor, but she resolved to return.

Crossing a bridge they drove up through busy streets, past a huge church which also looked worth a visit. The carriage stopped before the Feathers Inn. A footman swung down from his perch behind and helped the ladies to alight as Gareth dismounted nearby.

Laura exclaimed in delight. The crooked façade of the Feathers was black-and-white half-timbering in elaborate patterns of crosses, circles, and diamonds. Each story leaned farther out over the street, beneath three gables. The carriage departed through an archway to one side and Laura stepped back to admire the building.

"I thought you would like it," said Gareth, pleased with her reaction. "It is three hundred years old, first licensed in 1521."

"The ceilings are horridly low," Maria said disparagingly, "and the floors are quite uneven."

"It is comfortable, however," Miss Burleigh pointed out, "and the food is excellent. What more can one ask of an inn?"

"Let us go in." Gareth shepherded his flock towards the entrance. "Rupert should have reserved a private parlour and a chamber for us."

Rupert having done his duty, the innkeeper showed them to an oak-panelled parlour. They sat down for a few minutes while the footman went to find out what time Dr. McAllister was free. He returned to announce that the physician would call on Lady Laura at two o'clock at the Feathers.

"I shall, of course, chaperon you," said Miss Burleigh. "Now I am going to perform a few errands and then to call on the Misses Rutledge. If I am offered refreshment, I may not join you for luncheon but I shall return by two." She and her abigail rustled out.

"And I shall be off about my business," Gareth said. "Maria is known to all the shopkeepers, so just tell them to send me the bills for your purchases, Cousin Laura. Unless you wish for my company, ladies?"

Maria strongly denied any desire to have him looking over her shoulder, so he departed. Laura and Maria, followed by the footman, set out for the shops.

Unexpectedly, Maria concentrated on Laura's needs as they made their way from draper to haberdasher to milliner. She enjoyed giving advice, and Laura had considerable difficulty refusing to purchase various extravagant fal-lals that Maria insisted she needed.

"Are you buying nothing for yourself?" she asked at last, to distract her companion from a glorious cottage bonnet of chipstraw with three black plumes and a white silk rose.

"I shall return to the shops when you are seeing the doctor. Fortunately, I am not entirely dependent upon Gareth, or doubtless I should be forced to go about in rags."

"He has been most generous to me," Laura said, unable to avoid a certain asperity in her tone.

"Well, perhaps not quite rags," Maria conceded reluctantly, "if only for his own credit. My dear, do look at that reticule. Black velvet and seed pearls, you simply must have it."

Despite Laura's efforts at economy, when they returned to the Feathers the footman's arms were loaded with packages. Several larger items had already been delivered by apprentices and porters. Laura gazed with dismay at the heap in the private parlour.

"Oh dear, I did not think I had bought half so much! How shockingly extravagant."

Entering at that moment, Gareth heard her lament. "Have you bankrupted me?" he enquired, amused.

"Nothing of the sort," Maria exclaimed with vicarious indignation. "She would not buy half what she needs."

Grinning, he said to Laura, "I knew if Maria went with you, you would be unable to indulge to the full your taste for frugality."

Maria gave an unladylike snort, but whatever retort she planned was forestalled by the appearance of a pair of waiters with loaded trays.

Though the soup was well-seasoned, the spring lamb sweet and succulent, Gareth seemed to have lost his appetite. By the time they reached the Welsh-cakes, he was showing signs of nervousness.

"Dr. McAllister is new to the area," he told Laura. "He took over the practice a few months ago when Dr. Powys retired. Of course, he does have an excellent reputation. He studied in Edinburgh and abroad, I understand, but he is rather young and untried."

She tried to joke his worry away. "Since I do not need a physician at all, I'm sure I shall be satisfied."

As usual, Maria had something negative to add. "If you are so uncertain of his abilities, Gareth, I wonder you should have called him to attend Henry and Arabella."

"He cured their earaches, did he not? Also, Mrs. Lloyd had him to one of the maids, and she was pleased with him. No, I am sure he is competent, Cousin Laura." There was a world of doubt in his voice.

Miss Burleigh returned and bore Laura upstairs to a bedchamber. She was quite glad to kick off her shoes and recline on the bed, leaning back against a pile of pillows, after tramping around the shops all morning. Her self-appointed chaperon seated herself by the diamond-paned window. Laura was asking her about the history of the town when the doctor joined them.

A tall, thin, untidy man with melancholy eyes, his head of flaming red hair brushed the low ceiling. He ducked under a beam as he approached Laura. Noting with pity and dismay that he carried an ear trumpet, she hoped he would understand what she said. Gareth's apprehensions were beginning to make her a little nervous herself, to make her wonder whether perhaps she did need a doctor. She told herself firmly that she had always been healthy, that she had never felt better, and that childbirth was a natural and irresistible process.

"Guid day tae ye, ma leddy." Without further ado, Dr. McAllister questioned her about the course of her pregnancy. He made no use of his ear-trumpet and seemed to hear perfectly well. She answered readily, the answers at the tip of her tongue after discussing everything with Maria the day before.

Several of the questions were so personal, intimate even, as to draw a gasp of protest from Miss Burleigh. However, the Scot's sober, matter-of-fact manner altered not a whit and Laura replied with a minimum of embarrassment. At the end of the interrogation, he favoured her with a restrained but approving smile.

"Moderrn medicine preferrs information to guesswork," he informed her. "I'll listen tae your heart the noo." He brandished his ear-trumpet, reminding Laura of Uncle Julius and his toasting fork.

Miss Burleigh jumped up in alarm. "What is this? I never heard of such a thing. You will do nothing of the sort, young man. Is something wrong with Lady Laura's heart?"

"Noo, how am I tae tell, madam, if I canna listen tae it?" he asked reasonably.

"Is this more of your modern medicine?" Laura asked with interest.

"It is, ma leddy. 'Tis the notion o' a young pheesician I met while studying in France, Laënnec by name. Much can be inferred aboot the condeetion o' heart and lungs by the sound they make. Monsieur Laënnec working to develop a special contrrrivance for the purpose, a stethoscope he ca's it."

"We must tell Uncle Julius," said Laura with an irrepressible giggle. "Perhaps he can invent this stethoscope before Monsieur Laënnec. I beg your pardon, sir. Lord Wyckham's uncle is an inventor."

"I hae treated Mr. Wyckham for a chemical burrn," said the doctor drily, but with a twinkle in his eye. "Be that as it may, in the meantime I find an ear-trumpet more ef-feeecient and less disconsairting than pressing my ear tae a patient's chest."

"Oh yes, doctor," said Miss Burleigh with a shudder, "pray continue."

So Laura variously held her breath and breathed deeply while Dr. McAllister pressed his ear trumpet to various portions of her chest and back.

"Well?" she said as he straightened at last.

"Weel, noo, ma leddy, I never heard better. Eat weel, but not ower heartily, gentle exercise daily, rest when ye feel tired, and I'll recommend the midwife at Llysbury. Mistress Owen is a clean, willing body, and expeerrrienced. She has even read William Smellie's *Midwifery*."

"I do not need to consult you again?"

"Not unless ye hae untoward symptoms: bleeding, airly contractions, any severe discomfort, and I dinna mean a backache. 'Tis nae likely."

Laura hesitated. She liked him, despite his somewhat severe demeanour. He had taken the trouble to explain about the ear-trumpet; he was definitely amused by Uncle Julius, and not unkindly.

"If you don't mind, sir, I think I had best see you again, regularly. Lord Wyckham is . . . unused to having a pregnant female about the place, and inclined to be over . . . careful. If it is more convenient for you, I can come here."

"That willna be necessary, ma leddy. I can verra weel call at Llys Manor, for my work takes me that way often."

Miss Burleigh looked upon both of them with benign approbation. "You will always be very welcome to take pot-luck with us, Dr. McAllister," she said.

He bowed and took his leave.

Laura lay back. "I believe I shall rest for a while," she said. "If you have no more errands, ma'am, I should like to hear more of the history of Ludlow."

Miss Burleigh had scarcely embarked upon a recital of the royal and otherwise celebrated historical personages associated with the castle, when the door burst open.

"What is wrong?" cried Gareth. "Damn his eyes, the man will not tell me because we are not blood-relations."

"There is nothing to tell," said Laura soothingly. She held out her hand to him. He came to sit on the chair by the bed, taking her hand in a convulsive clasp. "What did he say to you?" she asked.

"That all is as well as can be expected."

"I do believe he was teasing you, though he spoke nothing more nor less than the truth. I am exceedingly well, sound as a bell, and my heart is in the right place."

He grinned at her sheepishly. "Teasing me? The devil! Oh, pardon my language, Aunt. What do you mean, your heart is in the right place?"

So she told him about the ear-trumpet. Somehow she forgot to retrieve her hand, but after all, he needed the comfort. Not until much later did she realize she had let both Dr. McAllister and Miss Burleigh assume she meant to stay at Llys until her baby was born.

CHAPTER 8

Laura retired early after the expedition to Ludlow, and woke early the next morning. The sun was shining again, but Myfanwy swore the puffs of cloud sailing in from the west meant rain before noon. The dressmaker, Mrs. Davis, was expected at ten — they had stopped in the village on the way home to request her visit — so Laura decided to take a walk before breakfast.

She left by the front door and headed across parkland towards a knoll with a pavilion on top, sheltered by a crescent of trees. Red Hereford cows raised their white faces to inspect her as she passed, then returned to cropping the short grass.

Approaching the little hill, she realized it was steeper than it had looked from a distance, but the view from the top must be worth the climb. The path, cutting diagonally across the slope, was not too steep, and if it tired her, the way back was downhill. She made for the beginning of the path.

"Laura!" Gareth's voice, sharp with reproach.

With a sigh, she swung round as hooves thundered behind her and stood with hands on hips watching him dismount from his dapple grey.

"Good morning, Cousin," she said peaceably, stroking the horse's nose. "Another beautiful day, is it not?"

"You promised to have breakfast in bed."

"As I recall, I said I was considering making a habit of it."

"Well, perhaps," he conceded.

"The morning is too fine to waste, and my maid swears it will rain later."

He turned to gaze into the west, where white mare's tails streaked the sky over the Welsh mountains. "Well, perhaps," he conceded.

"Dr. McAllister recommended gentle exercise, and it is much pleasanter to walk outdoors than up and down the Long Gallery."

"Well, perhaps," he conceded, then grinned. "No, of course it is, but the ascent of Ash Hill cannot be described as gentle exercise."

"Well, perhaps not," she conceded, "but I should so like to see the view from the top. I don't suppose you would lend me your arm?"

"Well, perhaps, if you will make me a promise."

"Well, perhaps, depending on what it is."

He looked down at her seriously. "Don't walk in the park without company. In the gardens, someone is always around, but if you came to grief out here there would be no one to help."

"I shall not come to grief. Dr. McAllister says I am excessively healthy. Do you not believe him?"

"Doctors are not omniscient. Besides, you might twist your ankle in a rabbit hole — Rupert has not been home enough to wipe out the population — or —"

"Or fall out of a tree and break my neck, or drown in four inches of water in a fountain," she said tartly.

"Oh Lord, do I sound like a hysterical mother?"

"A little. I really must see what I can do about Maria's children now that she and I are friends. But no, I daresay you are right. I will not walk alone except in the gardens."

"Is that a promise, or merely a habit under consideration?"

"A promise. Now will you help me up the hill?"

"Your wish is my command. Just let me hitch Fickle to that bush."

"Fickle?"

"By Wanderer, out of Flirt."

The gelding rolled his eye at her and she laughed. "Most of the horses Freddie wagered on were fickle, at least where he was concerned."

"Do you miss him?" Gareth asked, busy tying the bridle to a shrubby elder heavy with strong-scented flowerheads.

"Now? No. Is that very shocking?" She tried to explain. "When I stopped travelling with him and settled at Swaffham Bulbeck, at first I used to miss him when he went off without me. But soon it was more a . . . a sort of wondering where he was and when he would come home, not really missing him. I grew accustomed to his absence." After all, Freddie had paid her little enough attention when he was at home.

"One can grow accustomed to anything."

He offered his arm. As they started up the path, he spoke from some deep inner emotion, "Time does not necessarily lessen the pain."

"Not necessarily. For me it did. I was always pleased to see him when he arrived, but to tell the truth, I was always pleased to bid him good-bye, too. He could be dreadfully tiresome."

"That I can imagine," he said wryly, doubtless recalling the times his cousin had sponged on him.

"So now, you see, when I am not constantly wondering what he is up to, I seldom think of him." She remembered the relief she had felt after relating to Miss Burleigh the mortifying story of her elopement. Now, another sort of confession had liberated her from another burden. Now she recognized clearly that if she had been an undesirable wife, Freddie had been a most unsatisfactory husband. Almost gaily, she begged, "Pray do not tell anyone what an unnatural creature I am."

"My lips are sealed. As you are not a grieving widow, should you object to a small dinner party? I generally invite the local gentry to dine at the Manor when I am in residence. If I do not, they will be affronted.

If I do, and you fail to attend, rumours will fly."

Gaiety fled. Her hand tightened on his arm. "Rumours that I am not respectable enough to meet your neighbours."

Gently teasing, he reassured her: "I was thinking of rumours that you are too high and mighty to associate with country nobodies. They are unpretentious folk, with short memories for London scandals if they even bother to read about them in the newspapers."

"I shall be happy to meet them," she muttered, abashed at her overestimation of the interest her affairs had aroused, "if Miss Burleigh agrees that attending a dinner party is not improper in a supposedly grieving widow."

"We shall ask her. And then we shall ask Mrs. Davis when she can have an evening gown ready for you. The party shall be in honour of your new finery."

"You will not tell your guests!"

"No? Will you deprive me of the triumph of announcing publicly that I have cleverly induced you to accept a few dresses?"

"Odious wretch." Reaching the top of the hill, she stopped.

The pavilion was a simple circular structure, unenclosed, with a paved floor and white-painted pillars. Laura was glad to see the wooden bench around the sides and back. She had scarce noticed the climb, supported by Gareth's arm as they talked, but now she was ready for a rest.

"Come and sit down," he said. "You must be ready for a rest."

Though he echoed her thought, words of denial sprang to her lips. She swallowed them unuttered. For once he was right. Crossing to the far side, she sat down. He joined her and named the points of interest in the panoramic view that spread before them: Llys village with the river and the castle ruins on their mound; Radnor Forest in the distance, and Beacon Hill; ancient Celtic earth forts; the sinuous line of Offa's Dyke, built in the tenth century by a Mercian king in a vain attempt to keep out the Welsh; and lastly, the sprawling south façade of Llys Manor, with the central Tudor block and the idiosyncratic wings.

Laura listened with interest, but a part of her mind was elsewhere. Dr. McAllister's opinion had clearly not set Gareth's mind at rest. She could not help wondering if the painful memories he had hinted at were connected with his fears for her.

She had found relief in voicing her unhappy memories. Might he do the same?

Did she dare ask him?

"Bang, bang, you're dead!"

Two small heads popped up above the bench-back, one on each side. Two sticks took unwavering aim.

"I shot you, Cousin Gareth," cried Henry.

"You're Frenchies," George explained. "We are Wellington's Guards and you're our prisoners."

"We can't be your prisoners if we are dead," Gareth pointed out, his mouth twitching.

"All right, you can be alive. We're going to take you to our castle and put you in a dungeon." He pointed at the Manor. "We won't tie you up if you give your word you won't run away."

"If there is breakfast waiting at the castle," said Laura, "I shall willingly give my word. I am ravenous."

"What's ravingous?" the younger Guardsman enquired.

"Hungry, gudgeon," his brother informed him condescendingly.

"I'm not a gudgeon!"

They trained the guns on each other in a chorus of bangs.

"This would be a good moment to make our escape," said Gareth, "but I think we had best take our captors with us. Maria is doubtless still asleep, but Miss Coltart may be frantic."

"Coley's not frankik," Henry said, abandoning the battle.

"Frantic," George corrected. "She told us to go and play, Cousin Gareth, and she hung her watch round Henry's neck so's we can tell what time to go home."

"See?" Henry hauled on a chain about his neck and George consulted the steel-case watch that emerged.

"Five to nine! We'll have to run. Come on, Henny-Penny."

"Don't call me that," bawled Henry, pursuing George down the path. They rolled down the last part of the hill and set off towards the house like a pair of foxhounds on the scent.

Laura and Gareth followed at a more decorous pace.

"I suppose I must speak to Miss Coltart," Gareth said with a sigh. "I hate to spoil their fun but she ought to know what is going on."

"Since she lent her watch, I suspect she knows very well."

"Possibly. That makes it the more imperative that I see her. For one thing, George ought to have his own watch. I cannot think hers safe in their care."

How typical of his generosity, Laura thought. "You do not mean to ring a peal over her then," she said. "I am glad."

"No, I gave her a certain latitude with the boys, to keep her when she threatened to leave. They seem to like her. I just want to be sure she is aware of their roaming. Maria need know nothing of it."

"She shall not hear it from me. You know my opinion of her crotchets. I ought to meet Miss Coltart if I am to help the boys. May I go with you?"

"I shall be glad of your support."

"After breakfast?"

"After breakfast," he agreed, grinning. He unhitched Fickle and, leading him, walked with Laura back to the Manor.

Gareth sent for the governess to come to the library, partly because he did not want the boys present when he spoke to her. His other reason was to spare Laura the climb up three pair of stairs to the schoolroom, though he did not venture to tell her that. She had had enough "gentle exercise" for one morning, he reckoned.

When Miss Coltart joined them, he invited her to sit down. She shook her head and stood there before them, square and pugnacious in her drab gown.

"If it is about this morning, my lord, the boys have told me that they met you and her ladyship on Ash Hill."

"Did they tell you they had taken us prisoner?"

She ignored this irrelevant interruption, continuing in her dogged way, "I take leave to remind you, sir, that you said I might follow my own method of education, provided Mrs. Forbes is not vexed. George and Henry were outside with my permission. They study better after exercise, and I find the time useful to concentrate on teaching Miss Arabella her letters. The boys have promised not to play in the gardens and not to climb trees, as forbidden by their mama, and to stay within sight of the house. They always return on time, well before there is any chance of Mrs. Forbes seeing them from her window."

"Admirable," said Gareth cordially, taking the wind out of her sails. "The time is what I wished to discuss with you. I take it your watch has no sentimental associations or you would hardly have lent it to them?"

"No, my lord." Puzzled, she sat down at last, frowning.

"Then may I suggest that you give it to them, and I shall provide you with a replacement, in token of my appreciation. Something pretty in gold, with a gold chain, would be appropriate, do you not agree, Lady Laura?"

"Most appropriate," she murmured, with a look of such warm approval that he flushed and hurriedly turned his attention back to the governess.

She appeared flabbergasted. "Th-thank you, my lord," she stammered, then pulled herself together and said, belligerent again, "As you approve my methods, sir, may I be so bold as to say that Master George must have a tutor. I have taught him all the Latin I know, and I have no Greek."

"I am amazed you have taught him anything," Laura said, "since you are not permitted to discipline the boys, I collect."

Miss Coltart turned to her eagerly, with no trace of pugnacity. "I try to make their lessons interesting, my lady. Besides, George is a natural scholar, and Henry struggles to keep up to prove himself as good as his elder brother. However, George's love of learning will go for nothing if he cannot study the classics."

Laura turned to Gareth. "Is there some difficulty about hiring a tutor, Cousin?"

He grimaced. "The worst. Maria is convinced that a male teacher will beat her little darlings."

"Ah," she said in a thoughtful voice.

"Also, my lady, it is past time the boys learned to ride."

"I take it there is no difficulty about providing ponies, Cousin Gareth?"

"Only that they might fall off —"

"— and break their dear little necks. Do not despair, Miss Coltart, I believe I see a way to your ends." She cast a glance sparkling with mischief at Gareth.

What the devil was she up to?

Miss Coltart appeared to have perfect faith in her. "Thank you, my lady," she said, standing up. "That is a load off my mind. Now, if you will excuse me, I had best get back to my pupils."

As she left, Lloyd came in to announce that the dressmaker had arrived. Laura went off to the sewing room.

Gareth decided he, too, must have faith in her. Having made himself responsible for the boys, he owed them a decent education, but dealing with Maria was beyond him. He could only be grateful for Laura's intervention, whatever the result.

In the sewing room, Laura found Mrs. Davis just taking off her tall Welsh hat. A short, rolypoly woman, she took Laura's measurements with painstaking care. That done, they opened the packages from the

Ludlow shops. Laura was horrified anew at how much she had purchased.

There were black cambric and jaconet muslin for walking dresses and morning gowns, black crape for family evenings, and a beautiful black figured silk for special occasions. For trimmings she had black, grey, and white ribbons of velvet and satin; lace, narrow and wide; bugle beads; and a few white silk flowers.

"A pity it is your ladyship cannot wear colours, pretty as you are," observed Mrs. Davis, echoing Myfanwy's flattery. She stroked the silk with its pattern of tiny grey ivy leaves. "Still, there's elegant you'll be, look you. How will I make up the silk?"

They were discussing necklines and sleeves when Maria invaded the sewing room armed with Ackermann's plates and *La Belle Assemblée.* Since the fashionable styles she favoured would be unwearable after a few more weeks of pregnancy, Laura refused, as tactfully as possible, to follow her advice.

"These must last me the next four months and be easily alterable thereafter," she pointed out. "I cannot be sure when I shall be able to buy new gowns again."

"True." Maria gave a martyred sigh. "You cannot count on Gareth's continued generosity, as I have good cause to know."

Though agreement would have aided her plan, Laura's tact wore thin. "How can you say such a thing, when he provides a home for you and your children?"

"It is his duty as head of the family," Maria snapped. "I am his first cousin, after all, not merely the widow of a second cousin." She flounced out.

Greek and riding lessons would have to wait until she recovered from her pique.

Mrs. Davis emerged from the corner where she had discreetly busied herself during the altercation. A commonsensical woman, she and Laura soon came to an agreement. With Myfanwy's aid, she said, she could run up a decent dress for church on Sunday, and the first evening gown would be ready by Monday.

On hearing this news, Gareth invited his neighbours to dinner, as promised.

Laura could not help a frisson of excitement as Myfanwy fastened the buttons of the figured silk, her first pretty new gown in years. Narrow rouleaux of grey and white satin, twisted together, trimmed the hem of the full skirt; the high waist was bound with white satin ribbon laid on so as to be easy to let out; white lace edged the short sleeves and modest décolleté. She had bought a frilly cap adorned with a white rosebud, and Miss Burleigh had lent her a necklace of jet beads. She felt elegant, but even better, she felt comfortable. She had not realized just how much her old, too-tight clothes had cramped her as her body changed.

Shyness made her hesitate on the threshold of the Long Gallery, but Gareth came to meet her. "That is worth celebrating," he murmured with an appreciative look.

"I'm glad you approve. I should hate to have bankrupted you for nothing."

She took his arm and he introduced her to those of his neighbours she had not met after church the previous day. As he had predicted, the country gentry greeted her placidly. Laura enjoyed their unpretentious cordiality, their chatter of crops and hunting, of recipes and children.

Miss Burleigh was a coolly gracious hostess, Gareth a genial host. Uncle Julius peered into the faces of the guests, recognizing some and failing to recognize others, all of which they accepted with good-humoured patience. The Reverend Cornelius seemed to be attempting to combine the benevolence he felt proper in a clergyman with the condescension permissible in the younger son of a noble family.

Maria, in a gown of white net over a blue satin petticoat, outshone every other woman. Pleased with herself, she relented towards Laura and deigned to say, "Your gown has come out tolerable fine, I see, considering."

Laura decided to tackle the subjects of tutor and ponies tomorrow, before Maria found another cause for contention.

After dinner, when Gareth managed to tear the gentlemen from their port to join the ladies in the drawing room, the squire's wife beckoned him to her side. A stout, hearty female, known throughout two counties for the volume of her "Tally-ho!" on the hunting field, she announced, "We have been talking of the present celebrations in London, Lord Wyckham. I daresay you will be going up to Town and meeting all those kings and emperors and whatnot in person, will you not?"

"Some of them, I expect. Since half the Ton has gone to Paris, I feel obliged to do my part to make the Allied Monarchs welcome."

The squire's lady remarked in ringing tones on the famous bonnets and the notorious rudeness of the Tsar's sister, the Grand Duchess of Oldenburg. Maria complained bitterly about missing the splendid entertainments. The Reverend Cornelius told Laura he thought he might, hm, dash up to Town for a few days to see what was going on. She was not attending to him.

Gareth was going away? Her heart sank.

She scolded herself. She should be glad to be relieved of his surveillance for a while. As yet the reason for it was still a mystery to her. Since their talk on Ash Hill, no suitable opening for asking him had presented itself.

But he would be back. If not before, he would surely want to be at Llys when his younger brothers came home from university and school.

That time was several weeks hence. She had to admit she was going to miss him.

CHAPTER 9

At last the last guests departed. Laura heard Gareth bid them good night at the top of the stairs, and then he returned to the drawing room. He came to sit beside her on the sofa.

"Tired?"

"A little. That was the first dinner party I have attended in many years." Lady Denham's friendship had never extended to a dinner invitation. "I enjoyed it. Your neighbours are agreeable people."

Cornelius, who was to spend the night at the Manor, nodded complacently. "I am fortunate in my parishioners," he said. "Gareth, I've a mind to see the celebrations. I suppose you and Rupert can squeeze me into your, hm, lodgings for a few days?"

"Of course, old chap. Rupert can always sleep at the barracks so you shall have his chamber."

"But you will not make room for me," said Maria sulkily.

"A lady cannot possibly stay at a gentleman's lodging," said Miss Burleigh, shocked.

"Oh, there is always some excuse to stop me having any fun!" Maria stalked out.

"When do you leave, Gareth?" his aunt asked. "I had not realized you meant to return to Town."

"I'm sorry, Aunt Antonia. To tell the truth, I had half forgotten about the wretched Monarchs. I've no great desire to go but I know I ought. I feel sure poor Prinny will need all the support he can get, for not only has the Grand Duchess taken him in dislike, the Princess of Wales is in London at present. Cornelius, can you leave tomorrow?"

"So soon?" Laura exclaimed involuntarily.

"Shockingly inconsiderate in me, is it not, to give my aunt so little notice? But today is the sixth already and Prinny's royal guests may reach London any day. Cornelius?"

"Tomorrow? Yes, if you will give me until, hm, noon to make arrangements for next Sunday's service."

"I shall pick you up at the vicarage at noon. Aunt Antonia, the Tsar and the King of Prussia will not stay above three weeks, I believe."

"Then we shall look for you at the end of the month," said Miss Burleigh, rising. She smiled at Laura. "You may be only a little tired, my dear, but I am not so young as I was. I shall retire now."

"So shall I," said Laura quickly, feeling Gareth's anxious gaze upon her. On his last evening at home, she wanted to reassure him that she did not intend to run wild the moment he was out of sight.

Cornelius declared himself ready to turn in, and they all left the drawing room. The vicar and Miss Burleigh went off in opposite directions. Laura started towards the minstrels' gallery, on the way to her chamber.

"Wait, Cousin Laura. If you please." Gareth laid his hand on her arm. "You will take care of yourself while I am gone?" he said urgently.

"Of course."

"And you will call in Dr. McAllister if . . ." He paused as Lloyd and a pair of footmen went past them into the drawing room.

"If there is the slightest need," she promised.

"I am glad you are on such good terms with Aunt Antonia. She will look after you. I wish I did not feel obliged to go."

"Believe me, I admire your devotion to duty, a concept unknown to Freddie. I daresay you will enjoy the festivities once you are there."

"Possibly. In leaving so soon after your arrival, I am treating you as a member of the family, not as a guest. I mean no discourtesy."

"I do not regard it."

"No, I daresay you will be glad to see the back of me and my nagging for a while," he said ruefully.

"You have been amazingly restrained these last few days." Smiling, she was about to confess that she was going to miss his nagging when Lloyd and the footmen came from the drawing room, laden with heavy trays of cups and saucers and all the tea-making apparatus.

Following them came Uncle Julius. He squinted after them, deep in thought.

"Wheels!" he said, the light of inspiration in his face, and trotted off towards his workshop.

Laura laughed. "There will be a new invention awaiting your return, Cousin. An urn on wheels, perhaps? I'd forgot I saw him earlier snoozing in a corner."

"Day and night mean nothing to Uncle Julius. Still, he will not trouble you. I cannot say the same of Maria, I fear, though I doubt she is capable of intimidating you."

"Far from it. I believe I have her measure. I shall tackle her tomorrow on behalf of George and Henry."

He smiled down at her. "I have such faith in you, Cousin, that before I leave I shall instruct my head groom to keep an eye out for a pair of Welsh ponies, and while I'm in Town I shall make enquiries for a tutor."

"Sluggish ponies and a mild-natured tutor."

"Of course." He kissed her hand and bade her goodnight.

As always when she passed that way, Laura dawdled in the minstrels' gallery to study the painted frieze. Age-faded musicians played lutes, pipes, drums, tambourines, and other ancient instruments she could not name. Ladies in tall, pointed hats tipped with veils danced unknown dances

143

with gentlemen in doublet and hose. Every time she looked at it she saw something new.

Not till she reached her bedchamber did she realize she was holding to her cheek the back of her hand that Gareth had kissed. The old-fashioned courtesy had deranged her wits, she decided, and she quickly rang for Myfanwy.

She slept late the next morning. When she went down, Gareth was closeted with his steward. She saw him only to say good-bye.

Miss Burleigh stood with her on the front steps, sheltered from a misty rain by the porch, waving as the carriage departed down the drive. Maria was absent, either sulking because she was not going with him, or simply not yet ready to show her face to the world. After all, it still lacked ten minutes of noon.

Laura and Miss Burleigh returned into the house. The absence of its master somehow made it feel empty — or was it Laura who felt empty?

The best thing to fill the void, she decided, was to do her utmost to repay a part of her obligation to him. Before tackling Maria, she must visit the children and talk to their governess. The stairs up to the schoolroom would serve in place of the morning walk she had missed today.

Miss Burleigh gave her directions, and she found her way to the wing that housed the Forbes family. Of Jacobean vintage, the staircase was much grander than the arched Tudor stone stair in the Great Hall. She slowly ascended one side of the superb double sweep of polished oak, imagining bewigged cavaliers and ladies in stiff brocades and stomachers.

Maria's rooms, off the first landing, had once been the state apartment. No crowned head had ever rested there, Gareth had told her, but Prince Rupert had spent one night while seeking allies for his unfortunate uncle, Charles I. Maria revelled in the magnificence — without any feeling of gratitude — whereas Gareth prefered more modest quarters in the newest wing.

Laura hurried past the door. She did not want to have to explain that she was going to see Miss Coltart. If Maria had any suspicion of her plan, the careful approach she had worked out would fail.

The entire top floor of the wing, beneath the garrets, was given over to the Forbes children. Laura had no difficulty finding the schoolroom. The cheerful sound of a French nursery song in several different keys led her to a scarred door. She waited to the end of the last verse, knocked, and went in.

Arabella, dressed in plain blue cambric, ran to take her hand. "Did you hear me singing, Cousin Laura? I was singing a French song. Can we sing it again, Miss Coltart, for Cousin Laura?"

"Please, ma'am," George and Henry seconded her.

"May we." The governess, rather pink in the face, stood up and curtsied. "I hope you do not think we are wasting time, my lady. I find singing vastly improves their pronunciation."

"That sounds quite likely. Pray do not stand for me, Miss Coltart." To set the woman at ease, she drew out a chair and sat at the battered, ink-stained table. "If it will not interrupt your schedule, I should like to hear the children sing."

They lined up, the boys with hands clasped behind their backs, and a ragged chorus of *Frère Jacques* rang out, enthusiastic if unmusical. Laura clapped.

A maid stuck her head around the door. "Please, miss, it's time for Miss Arabella to change her dress and go down to her mama. Oh, beg pardon, my lady. I din't see your ladyship."

"I won't go!" Arabella screeched. "I want to stay wiv Cousin Laura."

Miss Coltart threw a helpless glance at

Laura. She recalled that the unfortunate governess was forbidden to punish her charges. The maid, who would doubtless suffer if Arabella did not go to Maria, came in and took the little girl by the arm.

"I'll hold my breaff till I die!"

"You will do nothing of the sort," Laura snapped. "Do you really suppose that I wish to stay with a child who behaves so horridly?"

Arabella stared at her, mouth drooping, blue eyes so like her mother's filling with tears. "I'm not horrid."

"No, your behaviour is horrid. However, if you continue to act so, in the end you will be a horrid girl."

"Arabella's horrid," chanted George, and Henry chimed in for the repeat. "Arabella's horrid. Arabella's . . ."

Their voices died away as Laura gave them a withering look. "A fine example you set your little sister," she said scornfully. "Such gentlemanly manners. I am sure I shall never wish to visit the schoolroom again."

"Oh, please come again!" Arabella sped to her and hung on her arm. "I won't be horrid, promise. See, I'm going now." She pulled the maid after her out of the room.

George, crimson-faced, stuttered, "I b-beg your pardon, ma'am. Please, you won't tell

Cousin Gareth when he comes home, will you?"

He nudged Henry, who burst into tears. "I'm sorry," he wailed. "I want to be a fine genkleman like Cousin Gareth."

They were only little boys, after all. Laura opened her arms and they ran to her for a hug.

"Cousin Gareth is a true gentleman," she said, "never unkind nor unmannerly. You cannot do better than to follow his example." They both nodded solemnly. Over their heads, Laura saw that the governess's expression was grim. "I must not keep you any longer from your lessons. Miss Coltart, may I have a word with you?"

The boys were set to copying *Frère Jacques,* Henry on his slate, George struggling with quill pen and ink. Miss Coltart joined Laura by one of the windows that made the room so light and airy.

"I must beg your pardon," Laura said ruefully, in a low voice. "I did not mean to cause such a disruption."

"You dealt with it very neatly, my lady." The governess was unappeased. Laura guessed it was not the disruption that had set her on her high ropes.

"I have the great advantages of being a novelty to them, being someone they wish

148

to conciliate, and being able to leave when I wish. Your task is much more difficult."

"It is not easy," the woman acknowledged, relaxing. "I sometimes feel I am balanced on a tightrope, with Mrs. Forbes's reproaches waiting on either side, whether I allow the children to run wild or attempt to discipline them. Not that they are bad children. I am fond of them. Only that, and Lord Wyckham's appreciation of my labours, keep me here. He is, as you said, ma'am, a true gentleman."

Laura glanced at the boys. George was absorbed in the task, Henry fiddling with his slate pencil and peeking at his brother's paper. She turned back to Miss Coltart and lowered her voice still more. "I came up to tell you that Lord Wyckham is seeking a tutor, and his head groom has orders to find two ponies. Now it is up to me to persuade Mrs. Forbes to accept them."

The governess impulsively stuck out her hand. "Good luck to you, my lady, and my thanks." They shook hands.

As she returned down the stairs, Laura felt the weight of expectations on her shoulders. Never before had anyone relied upon her. She must not fail, for Miss Coltart's sake, for the children's, and for Gareth's. He obviously cared deeply for his nephews and considered himself responsible for their welfare, yet she could not blame him for dreading Maria's furies and sulks. To help him in this would be to repay a small part of what she owed him for his generosity.

Running over her plan in her mind, polishing it, she smiled to herself. She hoped that if Gareth knew her intended method, he would laugh, not seethe with indignation.

When she reached Maria's chamber, she knocked on the door, but as she expected, the abigail said Mrs. Forbes had gone down to luncheon. Laura found her in the breakfast room, elegant in pink India muslin with white ribbons, picking delicately at a slice of cold chicken. Miss Burleigh glanced up as Laura entered.

"We do not usually have a collation set out when none of the boys are home," she said dryly, "but I have been charged most particularly to see that you are well nourished. A mere snack on a tray will not do, according to my nephew."

Laura smiled at her. "I daresay I might order a tray laden with sufficient nourishment even for my appetite, ma'am, if this is inconvenient."

"Not in the least. Carrying trays all over the house gives the servants much more trouble."

"Just what I thought," came Uncle Julius's voice behind Laura.

She turned as, with a gleeful face, he pushed in his latest contraption. A framework set on two small wheels and two wheelless legs held two large trays, one above the other. Raising the legs off the floor by means of a pair of shafts sticking out at that end, he rolled the curious handcart up to the table.

"I call it a tray-barrow," he said proudly. "With it, one servant can manage two trays without any risk of dropping them." He seized Miss Burleigh's plate and a couple of empty glasses, and set them on the top tray. As he lifted the shafts, tilting the tray-barrow, the plate and glasses slid down the slope. Crown Derby china, Waterford glass, and Miss Burleigh's luncheon landed on the Turkey carpet.

"Back to the drawing board," said Uncle Julius, sighing.

"I was about to remark," said Miss Burleigh, "that your tray-barrow is scarcely practical in a house with so many stairs. I see it has other drawbacks."

"Stairs? Hmm. Good point." Lost in a brown study, he stood there between the shafts of his invention.

Lloyd appeared with a footman to clean up the mess, so promptly that Laura suspected he had been keeping an eye on the inventor. He gently moved the old gentleman and his barrow, without disturbing thought processes. The shards were swept into a dustpan, and the footman was on his knees scrubbing the carpet with a damp cloth when Uncle Julius announced, "I have it," and trotted out.

Miss Burleigh uttered a quiet moan.

Laura fetched her a new plate of food, served herself, and sat down. She could not make her approach to Maria yet, for Miss Burleigh would be justifiably shocked by the way she went about it. Instead, she asked Maria's advice about a gown Mrs. Davis was about to make for her.

As a result, Maria was in a thoroughly good humour when Arabella scampered in, in pink India muslin with white ribbons matching her mama's dress. She curtsied to her mother and Miss Burleigh and bade them good-day. Then she went to Laura.

"Please, Cousin Laura, will you help me get some food?"

Maria frowned. "I am sure I do not know why you will trouble Cousin Laura when your own mama is here."

"But when I ask you, Mama, you awways

sigh and say children are such a nuisance."
She imitated Maria's languid tone to perfection. Miss Burleigh raised her napkin to her lips and coughed, her eyes gleaming with a hint of malice.

"I do not mind helping," said Laura hastily. She took the child to the sideboard. "What would you like, Arabella?"

"Gooseby tart wiv lots of cream."

"You shall have gooseberry tart, as soon as you have eaten some meat and vegetables. Do you prefer chicken or ham?"

Arabella opened her mouth to screech, looked at Laura, and closed it again, tight. "Ham, please," she said in a small voice.

Maria turned to regard them with astonishment and suspicion. Seeing that Laura was not actually torturing her daughter, she said pettishly, "I daresay she minds you because . . ." and then she could not think of a reason.

A bad omen, Laura feared, but she smiled at Arabella, served her with ham, tiny new carrots, and bread and butter, and helped her up on the chair at her side.

That afternoon, several neighbours came to call at the Manor. An elderly lady restored Maria's temper by remarking on how delightfully picturesque she and Arabella appeared together. However, Laura despaired of ever finding an opportunity to speak to Maria alone. At last the visitors departed and Arabella was sent off for her nap. Miss Burleigh went off to her sitting room to interview a girl who had applied for Myfanwy's old position as housemaid.

"Mrs. Lloyd has approved her," she explained to Laura, "but I always judge for myself before any indoor servant is hired. I take it Myfanwy is proving satisfactory as your abigail?"

"Most satisfactory." She was already fond of the cheerful young Welsh maid.

"Interfering old busybody," said Maria as the drawing room door closed behind Miss Burleigh. "I daresay Mrs. Lloyd is perfectly capable of choosing servants. When I first came to Llys, Aunt Antonia tried to tell me how to bring up my children, as if a dried up old maid could possibly know better than their own mother."

Laura refrained from pointing out that Miss Burleigh had brought up her late sister's sons with a fair degree of success. Instead she used the spiteful comment as an opening.

"If Miss Burleigh must approve every indoor servant, I suppose it is she who has decided against hiring a tutor for George and Henry? I had thought it must be Gareth's refusal to pay the extra wages that was depriving your sons of a proper education." She hated to malign him so, but Maria seemed to be taking the bait. "Tutors earn more than governesses, I believe, and you would still need a governess for Arabella. Perhaps he cannot afford to hire both."

"Of course he can afford it," Maria said with scorn. "He can afford to go gallivanting up to Town, can he not? He is a niggardly nip-cheese, who does not care how my boys suffer from his penny-pinching."

"They will grow up ignorant, alas. And what a pity that his, er, thriftiness prevents his providing them with mounts, unless there is not room in the Manor's stables?" Having defended Gareth in the past, she felt she was less likely to arouse Maria's suspicions if she provided him with excuses now. "If they do not learn to ride soon, I expect they will present but poor figures on horseback when they are men."

Maria appeared more struck by this shocking notion than by the prospect of George and Henry living in ignorance of the classics. Her voice quivered with indignation. "There is plenty of room in the stables. Gareth is forever buying hacks and hunters and carriage horses for himself and his brothers.

It is most unjust the way he neglects my boys."

"Have you ever pointed out to him that their ignorance and poor horsemanship must inevitably reflect upon him, once they are old enough to go about?"

"I shall speak to him at once. Oh, botheration! He has left already. I might have known he would not be here when he is wanted."

"If I were you, I should write to him." Laura was afraid that time would change Maria's capricious mind. "While he is in Town, he can surely spare time from his gallivanting to deal with a matter of such importance."

"Oh, writing letters is what I do not care for." Maria pouted, already losing interest.

"I shall be happy to write for you."

"Will you? Pray do. I am quite glad you came to Llys after all, Laura. Only, what if Gareth agrees, and finds a tutor who will beat my poor little orphans?"

"He cannot beat them, if you forbid it, without risking his position."

"True. But what if George and Henry fall off their ponies and hurt themselves?"

"They will come to no serious harm if you give orders that they are to learn to ride in a paddock with long grass to cushion their falls. I shall go and write to Gareth immediately. He shall no longer escape his obligations." On that note, Laura made a hasty exit, choosing to assume she still had Maria's assent. With any luck, she had left Maria dwelling on her grievances, not on her qualms.

The letter she wrote would not have pleased Maria. She had not intended to reveal her method of persuasion to Gareth, but in the end she told him everything, picturing the way his eyes crinkled at the corners when he was amused.

She told him everything except that she missed him. He had been gone a few hours, and already she missed him.

CHAPTER 10

The Reverend Cornelius returned ten days later, bringing with him a young man who was to serve as both his curate and the boys' tutor. Peter Renfrew had just taken holy orders. Slight but wiry, he was inclined to be bashful and over-eager to please. He thanked Miss Burleigh profusely for the bedchamber prepared for him and listened attentively to Maria's exhortations, agreeing with every word.

Laura hoped the boys and Miss Coltart

would take to him.

Cornelius stayed to dine. He entertained them with ponderous descriptions of the splendid celebrations and the crowds that everywhere greeted the visiting allies. After dinner, he drew Laura aside.

"Gareth decided to, hm, let Renfrew settle in to his duties in his absence."

"The lily-livered poltroon!"

Cornelius gave her an engaging grin that made him look much less pompous. "That's more or less what I told him. He said you are much more capable of dealing with Maria's, hm, high flights than he will ever be."

"That is not true," she said, though she flushed a little at the compliment. "He is perfectly capable of dealing with her, only he prefers not to. I daresay he expects me to teach George and Henry to ride, also?"

"No, no. He specifically said that you are to have nothing to do with the riding lessons."

"Oh, did he!"

Alarmed at her vehemence, he laid a soothing hand on her arm. "I believe he fears that you might try to lift the children into the saddle, or pick them up when they fall. My brother is very much concerned for your welfare, Cousin, as are we all, of course. I beg you will not, hm, feel obliged to act

158

contrary to his wishes. He would be, hm, devastated should you come to any harm."

His earnestness and his care for Gareth impressed Laura. She guessed that he knew the reason for his brother's undue alarm and she nearly asked him. However, she doubted she would be able to bear to listen to him pontificating about a matter that touched Gareth so deeply.

"Very well, I shall stay away from the riding lessons," she promised. "In any case, there are no ponies as yet."

"True. Oh, I nearly forgot. Gareth asked me to give you this."

Taking the folded sheet of paper, she pried open the seal. No polite greeting; no "humble and obedient servant." In a large, neat, masculine hand was written simply: "You wretch. I daresay you consider that the end justifies the means? Thank you. W."

She laughed. Though she had hoped he would be amused by her stratagem, a niggling doubt had remained. She folded the sheet small and tucked it into her reticule.

When she retired to bed that evening, she took out the note, smoothed it, and put it in the drawer of the little writing desk in her sitting room. Then she retrieved it. It was not the sort of thing one wanted to risk someone reading.

It would be safer in her dressing table drawer, under her chemises, a traditional place to hide love-letters — though no one could possibly mistake Gareth's brief message for a love-letter.

Lord Wyckham returned to his ancestral home just two days later, walking unexpectedly into the breakfast room when the family was at luncheon. Laura glanced up as the door opened. Her heart gave a peculiar lurch as she saw him standing there in mud-splashed riding boots and breeches. His blond hair clung in damp tendrils to his forehead where his hat had failed to keep off the wind-blown mizzle.

His gaze went straight to Laura and his weary face relaxed into contentment. She reminded herself fiercely that it was her obvious health, not her mere presence, that pleased him.

"Forgive my dirt, ladies," he said. "If you insist I shall change at once, but I left the inn very early this morning and I am ravenous."

"You may join us, Gareth," said his aunt magisterially. "What brings you home so soon?"

"London was unbearable." Filling a plate with veal-and-ham pie and cold beef, he came to sit opposite Laura. "The Tsar and his wretched sister have been so rude to poor Prinny, even the opposition leaders are beginning to balk."

"Why, what have they done?" asked Maria.

"Right from the first, they seem to have gone out of their way to humiliate him. The Tsar avoided the ceremonial route from Dover and went to the Pulteney Hotel, which the Grand Duchess has rented in its entirety. The Prince Regent waited for him with a royal welcome at St. James's Palace, and waited and waited. Tsar Alexander decided to stay with his sister instead of at the palace."

Laura watched him as he continued the sorry tale of snubs and insolence, eating as he talked. Prinny was no angel, but he did not deserve such treatment, he said. His indignation on his sovereign's behalf animated his handsome face and lit a fire in the dark blue eyes.

"The Tsar was all politeness to the great Whig lords," he went on, "attending their entertainments, which Prinny could not possibly go to in the present political climate. Prinny took his visitors to Oxford, to receive honorary degrees, on the day Lady Jersey had planned a ball. The Tsar left in the middle of dinner to drive back to Town just to dance from three till six in the morning."

"How splendid it must have been. I wish I had been there," Maria mourned, the point of the story lost on her.

Gareth exchanged a glance of amusement with Laura. How good it was to have him back!

And how dangerous her joy at his return! Like the veriest featherhead, she was succumbing once again to the charm of a handsome man. Gareth was utterly different from Freddie in every other respect, yet to let herself believe she was in love with him was to court pain. He was a wealthy baron of upright principles and unstained character. She was the disgraced widow of a ne'er-do-well, cast off by her family, pregnant, and without even beauty to recommend her.

To him, she could never be more than an object of charity, his duty as head of the family, and the cause of some unexpressed disturbance.

"You are not eating, Laura."

"I was too engrossed in your tale," she lied, and took a forkful of the pie. The crisp brown crust turned to dust and ashes in her mouth.

She had to leave, as she had originally

intended, no matter what she had implied in agreeing to see Dr. McAllister regularly. If she had almost decided to stay until after her confinement, that decision was prompted by sheer cowardice. The journey back to Cambridgeshire would be difficult and uncomfortable. Gareth could not be expected to provide his luxurious carriage when he was bound to disapprove of her departure.

He would be hurt by her departure, and she could never tell him she was leaving to protect herself from him.

"And then the Princess of Wales entered her box," Gareth continued. "Alexander bowed to her and the theatre erupted in cheers. Poor Prinny pretended . . . Laura, don't look so stricken, pray. I shall not tell you any more if you are going to take Prinny's woes so much to heart."

She forced a smile. "I do think it most unfair, when he went to so much trouble to entertain them in magnificent style."

Did she dare allow herself a week of his company? To rush off when he had just come home would be the height of discourtesy.

When they left the room after the meal, she felt him watching her. She was wearing a new gown, black muslin she had embroidered with pale grey silk thread, but she rather doubted he was admiring her handiwork.

In the fortnight he had been away, her belly had grown so much her condition must be obvious to even the most unobservant gentleman. If he had arrived in Swaffham Bulbeck now, instead of a month ago, he would have had the greatest difficulty deciding whether to make a pregnant woman travel or to leave her in her cottage.

The thought of his consternation amused her, and she turned to him with a smile when he said, "May I have a word with you, Cousin?"

"Of course. I was going to walk in the Long Gallery, in view of the weather."

"You are laughing at me, I see," he said with resignation as they made their way thither. "I suppose you have guessed what I wish to talk about."

"Your arrant cowardice?"

"I plead guilty. However, I assume all is well, since Maria has not yet rung a peal over me?"

"She is persuaded that she won a great victory over your parsimony."

"Is persuaded? Say rather that you persuaded her, you odious creature. I am surprised that she is not gloating at my defeat."

"I also persuaded her to gloat silently, lest you retaliate by cutting back your expenditure on her family in some other way."

"What a character you give me! How goes it with young Renfrew?"

"The boys have taken to him, Miss Coltart mothers him, and Arabella has decided to marry him."

His shout of laughter startled a footman crossing the Great Hall on some errand. "How fortunate that Arabella is five, and not fifteen," he observed. "I hope Maria will be equally unruffled by the riding lessons. I am going to look at a couple of ponies tomorrow."

They strolled up and down the gallery, chatting of his stay in London and her occupations during his absence. She had read and sewed, played with the children, visited tenants and villagers with Miss Burleigh, called on neighbours with Miss Burleigh and Maria.

"And of course I walked about the gardens, and in the park . . ." she paused, teasing, ". . . with Myfanwy. But I have not yet been back to Ludlow to see the castle. Miss Burleigh says you know more of the history of the town than she does. Will you go with me?" She could imagine no more delightful memory to take back with her to Swaffham Bulbeck.

His instant glance at her non-existent waist warned her of his reaction. "Do you think it wise? Will you not wait and see what Dr. Croft has to say?"

"Dr. Croft? Who is he?"

"A famous London accoucheur." He avoided her eyes. "I offered him the use of my carriage and a holiday in the country."

"And he is coming to Llys to examine me? Gracious heavens, I might see the point in calling in a London physician if Dr. McAllister had found aught amiss, but . . ." She bit her lip. Soon she must break it to him that she was going to leave, and she did not want to distress him any sooner than she must. "Oh, very well."

"Thank you."

"But in common courtesy, Dr. McAllister should be here, too. When will Dr. Croft arrive?"

"He was supposed to leave Town today, so he ought to arrive tomorrow. If he agrees, I shall take you to Ludlow the day after, weather permitting."

"If!"

Gareth pretended he had not heard. "I had best go and see how things go on in the schoolroom," he said, and made his escape.

Dr. Croft had a smooth, soothing, gentlemanly manner. Laura instantly disliked him. He was condescending to Dr. McAllister, lecturing him like an incompetent student. Though he did agree that Laura was healthy and might go to Ludlow, he also prescribed a regimen of weekly cupping and a lowering diet.

Catching Dr. McAllister's eye, Laura saw that though he had been grimly patient until now, he was about to protest. She had no intention of submitting to either starvation or the letting of her blood, but there was no sense in setting up Dr. Croft's back. He would soon be off to Town again. She shook her head slightly at the flame-haired Scot.

Dr. Croft instructed his country colleague in the amount of blood to be let and the proper diet to be followed, then left the room.

"Cupping? I never heard such nonsense," said Miss Burleigh roundly.

"Ower ma dead body. Whit's yon bairn tae use for bluid if we tak' its mither's?"

"I shall not allow it," Laura assured them both, "but Cousin Gareth will expect me to obey his fine London doctor."

"I wad nae tell his lairdship ma conclu-

167

sions, and Dr. Crroft has nae the right tae do so, Laird Wyckham being but a distant rrelation by marriage."

"I hope Dr. Croft realizes that."

"I shall make sure he does." Miss Burleigh swept towards the door of Laura's chamber. "Come, doctor."

Laura heard her calling after Dr. Croft in a way she would surely have stigmatized as thoroughly unladylike in other circumstances.

Gareth drove Laura in the gig to Ludlow. The sun shone and the air was full of the fragrance of dog-roses and the humming of bees. He had been forced to agree that the day was much too fine to be shut up in a stuffy travelling carriage.

He was still a trifle suspicious of her capitulation over seeing Dr. Croft. Nor did a certain air of conspiracy between her and his aunt escape him. Every now and then, he caught Laura's wistful gaze upon him and wondered what was afoot. He was not going to let her out of his sight today, except of course for necessary feminine occasions, during which, he was sure, he would bite his nails to the quick.

Glancing at her happy face, he dismissed his misgivings. Soon — surely! — she must agree to stop gadding about the countryside. Today she should have a day to remember.

Leaving the gig in the Feathers' yard, they went into the inn. The landlord welcomed them with promise of a private parlour and a fine luncheon, and a chamber if her ladyship wished to rest later. Gareth said they would eat in the coffee room as they had brought no chaperon for Lady Laura. He trusted mine host for the menu, except that there must be plenty of cherries and strawberries for dessert.

"You have noticed my weakness," Laura said laughing as they walked up to the castle, her little hand on his arm. "I cannot resist summer fruits."

"Raspberries and currants still to come, and even peaches, nectarines, and apricots. They do well at the Manor in a good summer, espaliered on a south-facing wall."

A fleeting sadness crossed her face. "I have not tasted a peach this age. Gracious, I believe the church tower is even taller than the castle. I should like to go inside."

"We can see it this afternoon, when you have rested," he said, and at once wished he had not. He did not want to quarrel with her on this day of pleasure.

"If I need to rest," she murmured, but he refused to be provoked.

Laura was fascinated by the huge castle, with its massive keep, towered walls, circular chapel, and roofless Great Hall, where Milton's masque Comus was first performed. Gareth had read up the history in preparation and entertained her with stories of Norman barons and marauding Welsh, Edward IV, Catherine of Aragon and her first husband, Prince Arthur.

"He died here at sixteen, a year after their marriage, leaving both widow and throne to his younger brother, Henry VIII."

"Knowing Henry's subsequent history, one wonders what Arthur died of," Laura observed drily. "Look, there are steps up the wall. Let us walk around the top. The view must be superb."

"No!" His heart leaped into his throat and tried to strangle him. Though he knew all too well her reaction to a direct order, his tongue had a life of its own. "You must not go up there."

She stopped, her hand tightening on his arm, and turned to face him. Beneath the black brim of her bonnet, garlanded with funereal black roses, serious grey-green eyes searched his. "Explain," she said.

"The stone is crumbling; the parapet is too low for safety, broken in places; the wind is strong so high above the ground."

"No." She shook her head, impatient. "That is not what I mean. You owe me an explanation. I have seen Dr. McAllister and Dr. Croft. I take Myfanwy when I walk in the park. I eat breakfast in bed and rest in the afternoons. Still you are not satisfied." Her tone softened. "Still you are terrified by my pregnancy. Tell me why."

He groaned, a flood of dreadful memories engulfing him. When she drew him over to a fallen stone and made him sit, he scarcely noticed. He was scarcely aware of the words pouring from him, setting loose the horror within.

He was fourteen again, his voice beginning to break, home from school for the holidays. Christmas and Twelfth Night had passed without the usual festivities, for Mama was breeding again and far from well. He gave it little thought. Mama had been in fragile health as long as he could remember, always gentle, loving, sweet-tempered, always ready with a comforting embrace, but not to be troubled with her sons' rough-and-tumble ways.

The short, dark January days were heavy with foreboding. Gareth and Cornie whispered about it and decided another little grave was expected to join the row in the churchyard. In their schoolboy lives, a stillbirth was nothing new, a matter of small moment. Their three younger brothers were nuisance enough; who needed more!

They accepted Papa's preoccupation and made do with a groom or the gamekeeper when they went riding or shooting. Nothing prepared them for the day they came home and found the servants standing about the Great Hall in solemn, low-voiced groups, some of the maids weeping.

Lloyd stepped forward to say, "God send you are come in time, Master Gareth. You are to go to her ladyship's chamber at once."

He ran. The stairs had never seemed so steep; the endless hushed passageways echoed to the thud of his boots. His heart pounded with fear and his breath roared in his ears. Reaching his mother's chamber, he did not dare knock, but someone had heard him and opened the door.

The room was in semi-darkness, lit by a single branch of candles, the curtains closed against the gloom of a winter afternoon. Mama lay in the bed, still and white as the pillows, an ivory carving, her eyes closed. Papa knelt at the bedside, clasping her hand, his head bowed on his hands. Dr. Powys and the vicar stood nearby, talking quietly. In a corner, Mama's abigail sobbed, her apron over her head.

Aunt Antonia took Gareth's arm to lead him towards the bed. He saw she had been crying. His own eyes were dry, burning dry, and when he attempted to swallow the lump in his throat, he discovered his mouth was dry, too.

As he approached, Mama opened her eyes and smiled at him. She was not dead! She was going to be all right! He rushed forward, grasped her icy hand, tried to pour his own strength and vigour into that frail, beloved figure.

Her lips moved. He bent low to hear her.

"Gareth . . . dearest . . . take care of . . . your brothers . . . and poor Papa."

Papa? But Papa was there to take care of him and the others. Even as he stared in astonishment at his father's bowed head, the faded blond hair thinning, it lifted. From Papa's lips came a cry of anguish that tore at Gareth's soul.

"Emily, don't leave me!"

Aunt Antonia's arms had closed about Gareth, had drawn him away, half uncomprehending. And then, in the nursery, he had found the scrap of life his mother had died bringing into the world.

Gareth was suddenly conscious of Laura's presence beside him, of her compassionate eyes, of the new life growing within her. He

173

must not tell her about the baby sister who . . .

"I didn't understand even then," he said tiredly. "I suppose I blamed some unknown disease. It was not till the funeral that I realized bearing a child had killed my mother. I can quote you the words that opened my eyes, from a local gossip to a stranger: 'Died in childbed she did, like many another. A dangerous time it is for any woman, look you, and her ladyship no different from the rest of us. Ah, but it's missed she'll be.' "

"Even the villagers missed her. It was much worse for you."

"It was worst for my father. He became a recluse. I never exactly had to look after him, but I did my best for my brothers." He gave her a crooked smile. "So now you know why the very fact of your pregnancy terrifies me. There is nothing logical about it, I admit. All over the world, millions of women give birth without trouble, otherwise I daresay the human race would have died out long since."

"But you are not responsible for those millions. I do understand, Gareth. I shall try to make allowances for your quirks."

He stood up, pulled her to her feet, and just for a moment held her very tight.

CHAPTER 11

Gareth's brief embrace shook Laura to the core. His hard body pressed against hers, his strong arms about her, reawakened the aching longing she had learned to suppress because Freddie never satisfied it.

As they walked back to the inn in an awkward silence, she struggled for control. He had hugged her in gratitude for her understanding, in a need for comfort, even with some affection. Nothing more. She was six months pregnant with another man's child.

He was even more dangerous to her peace of mind than she had supposed, yet now she could not leave Llys. The glimpse he had given her of his pain made that impossible. Within the confident, powerful head of a noble family dwelt a sensitive boy still suffering from that long-ago hurt. How could she add to his torment, refuse him the solace of taking care of her?

She glanced up at him. He was pensive, a trifle embarrassed, but behind the embarrassment she thought she saw relief, a scarcely perceptible relaxation of taut muscles about his mouth and eyes. She was glad she had pressed him for an explanation.

They turned into the Bull Ring, the oddly named street where the Feathers was situated. Stopping to allow a slow farm cart to pass, Gareth said in a low voice, without looking at her, "I beg your pardon. For . . . er . . . taking liberties."

Her cheeks grew warm and she fixed her gaze on the cart's squeaking wheel. "Pray do not regard it. A . . . a cousinly salute."

"And for burdening you with my troubles."

"That was my doing. I asked. You need not fear that I will tell anyone, though your aunt guesses, I believe."

"Aunt Antonia is no slowtop. I have always been surprised that Cornelius was not . . . similarly affected."

"He is a year younger, is he not? At that age, a year can make a vast difference."

He nodded. The cart had passed and they crossed to the inn. The landlord ushered them into the panelled coffee room, to a corner table near a window. While waiters scurried to serve them, Gareth drew Laura's attention to the ceiling. Ornately plastered, it was decorated with James I's coat of arms surrounded by thistles, acorns, and grapes.

"The thistle of Scotland," she said, "but why acorns?"

"The English oak?" he hazarded, "though

it is not a common symbol of the nation. And why the grapes I cannot imagine."

"For the good wines served at the Feathers, my lord," suggested the innkeeper.

They laughed, and the stiffness between them eased. It vanished entirely a few minutes later when Laura dropped her knife, clutched her middle, and exclaimed, "Oh!"

"You'll not catch me again that way," said Gareth. "The baby is moving again, I take it?"

"Moving?" she said indignantly. "The brute is kicking me!"

"How very disconcerting," he observed, grinning. "Perhaps the trout is not to his taste, or hers, as the case may be."

"Well, it is very much to mine." She picked up her knife to return to her meal, but her attention was on the vigorous performance inside her.

His or hers? For the first time, the baby was real to her, not just as a new life but as a person-to-be, real enough to wonder whether she was carrying a girl or a boy. She wanted a girl — not a boy to try to bring up without a father, a boy to remind her of Freddie.

As if she had any choice! I shall love you anyway, she thought, patting her stomach apologetically.

Gareth was watching her with an odd, almost wistful expression, the look of a male faced with a mystery beyond his understanding. She smiled at him and picked up her knife again.

"The trout really is delicious."

"Watch out for bones," he said severely.

After their outing to Ludlow Castle, Laura clashed less often with Gareth. She understood his feelings, and so made allowances for his qualms, as she had promised. He in turn, aware of her sympathy, did his best not to attempt to impose restrictions upon her.

At first, her physical attraction to Gareth caused many a secret pang, but as time passed the increasing discomforts of pregnancy distracted her.

Myfanwy was a great help. With a dozen little brothers and sisters at home, she knew what to expect and how to relieve some of the awkward symptoms. Dr. McAllister assured Laura that everything was proceeding normally. He encouraged her to continue her walks in the gardens, but more and more she was content to sit on the terrace or under a tree, with a book or embroidery in her hands.

Gareth was delighted. He often came to sit with her and chat, as did the rest of the family, including the children and even, occasionally, Uncle Julius. The inventor was working on a complicated project he refused to discuss until it was perfected.

"It's dashed mortifying when things go wrong just as you are showing them off," he confided to Laura. He recognized her on sight, now, and even recalled her name correctly now and then.

She had long been on first name terms with Maria — at least when Maria was in charity with her. After Dr. Croft's visit and the conspiracy to keep his odious directions from Gareth, Miss Burleigh had invited Laura to call her Aunt Antonia. Cornelius no longer felt compelled to put on his most sober clerical face in her presence. When Rupert came home again, after seeing off the Allied Monarchs, he treated her with easy cameraderie, as if she were his elder sister.

In short, Laura became so much a part of the family that when Lancelot and Perry came home for the summer holidays, everyone was shocked to realize she had never met them.

Rupert drove Gareth's curricle into Ludlow to meet his younger brothers off the

179

Mail. When they returned, Laura was strolling in the rose garden, holding Arabella's hand. They were singing a nursery song the child had just learned. Arabella's ability to hold a tune had much improved since Miss Coltart had more time to spend with her, and she loved to sing.

Reaching the top of the steps to the English garden — Laura was not at all tempted to try the descent now — they turned, just as Rupert hallooed from the terrace. He and the two youths with him started towards them.

"Perry!" squealed Arabella and took off, little feet twinkling over the gravel, ringlets and ribbons fluttering. She flung herself at her youngest cousin, who caught her up, held her high, then set her on his shoulders.

Smiling at the enthusiastic welcome, Laura walked slowly to meet them, already predisposed in Perry's favour. He was a sturdy fifteen-year-old, freckled, obviously a Wyckham despite curly hair of a darker blond than his brothers. Lancelot was also very much in the family mould. At twenty, his slender build set off by the sober nicety of a dandy's dress, he bore himself with a somewhat stiff dignity.

Rupert introduced them. Both had some difficulty bowing, Lancelot because of his high, starched cravat and shirt points, Perry because Arabella refused to get down. Her hands buried in his curls she resisted Rupert's efforts to dislodge her.

"Ouch!" yelped Perry. "Come on, Bella, enough is enough."

"I don't want to get down. If you make me, I'll scream and scream till —"

Rupert promptly desisted, but Arabella caught Laura's eye and closed her mouth.

"You will scream and scream until your cousin never wants to give you a ride again?" Laura asked.

"Perry likes me," she said uncertainly.

"Not when you are pulling my hair!"

"Perhaps, if you get down now, your cousins will listen to your new song."

Lancelot, who had held aloof from the fracas with an air of disdain, grimaced. So did Rupert, as Arabella held out her arms to him to be lifted down. Perry grinned at Laura.

"You're a great gun, Cousin," he said. "Let's hear it, Bella."

" 'Mary, Mary, quite contrary,' " carolled Arabella.

The three young men glanced at each other and their lips twitched. Under Laura's stern gaze, all three managed to hold back their laughter until Arabella finished the verse.

Arabella took Laura's hand. "Why are they laughing?" she asked, disconsolate.

"Because silver bells and cockle shells and pretty maids do not really grow in gardens," Laura invented hastily.

"Pretty maids do," said Perry. "At least, one pretty maid who sings very nicely. Do you want a ride up to the house, Bella? I'm sure it must be time for tea. Promise you'll get down without a fuss when we get there, though."

She promised and he galloped her back towards the house. Rupert offered Laura his arm, saying gallantly, "One pretty maid and one pretty lady grow in this garden."

"One quick-witted lady," Lancelot said, falling in beside them, his manner, though not his neckcloth, having lost some of its starch. "I thought I'd die when she started singing about Contrary Mary."

Laura frowned at him. "Don't you dare say anything to Maria — nor to anyone else, come to that — that even hints at a connection. She has not heard it yet."

"We'll have to warn Gareth," Rupert pointed out. "If Bella sings that in the drawing room, he'll split his sides."

"Your brother has more self-control than

you suppose," she said tartly. "However, you may warn him."

"Yes, ma'am," said Rupert, saluting with a grin. Laura blushed. She had no possible right to issue orders to the Wyckhams and could only be glad they took her presumption in good part. Somehow she had fallen into the rôle of older sister instead of that of poor relation which belonged to her.

Gareth apparently had no quarrel with her on that account. He took her aside in the Long Gallery before dinner and said, "Lance told me about 'Mary, Mary.' Thank you for directing the boys to hold their tongues."

"It seemed wise, though Maria cannot take offence at the words without admitting herself contrary."

"She is quite capable of that. I cannot help wondering whether Miss Coltart taught Arabella the song deliberately. She has had a good deal to suffer from Maria's megrims."

"Even if she did, you must see that to take her to task can only make matters worse, in acknowledging that the words apply to your cousin. Better to pretend nothing is amiss. It is a common nursery song, after all."

"Yes, you are right."

"All the same, I am glad I succeeded in

persuading Arabella to sing 'Hickory, dickory dock' instead at tea time."

"So am I." His voice was warm. "Once again, you have saved me from a dust-up."

"If that means what I think it means," she said, taking refuge from confusion in primness, "then I saved myself as much as anyone. I like your brothers — Lancelot and Perry, I mean."

"I am glad you have made friends with them so quickly, not that it is difficult with Perry. He is like an eager puppy who only wants a bit of attention to be your friend for life. Lance is more of a challenge. Your skill at deflecting Arabella's tantrums impressed him enormously." He looked at his exquisitely dressed brother and sighed. "I could wish he had not chosen to ape the dandy set."

"At least he is no fop. I daresay he may grow out of it." Thinking of her own misjudgements at nineteen, Laura echoed his sigh. "You are lucky in your family. I like them all."

"Even Maria?"

"Even Maria, when she is not in the boughs," she said firmly.

When they were all seated at the dinner table, Gareth and Aunt Antonia at either end, she recalled her words. Cornelius had come up from the vicarage and Uncle Julius had torn himself from his workshop. Maria was in an excellent mood as Lancelot, whose taste was clearly not to be despised, had praised her gown. To Laura, the lively discussion of the events of their lives since they all had last been together exemplified the happy family.

Yet she was wrong to say that Gareth was "lucky" in his family, she realized. Luck had little to do with it.

Since Lady Wyckham's death and the late baron's withdrawal, Aunt Antonia had provided physical comfort and discipline, even a distant, unspoken fondness. It was Gareth's love for his brothers that had accomplished the rest. Somehow the suffering boy had found the strength to create a family where differences of temperament and diverging interests were overcome by the bonds of affection.

How could she help but . . . admire him?

By the next day, talk of the past had given way to plans for the future. Everyone had friends they wanted to invite for a week or two, and picnics, cricket matches, and outings to be arranged for their entertainment. However, the high spot of the summer at Llys was always the thirteenth of August, feast day of St. Wigbert, the patron saint of the parish church.

"A rather dull English monk, I fear," Cornelius apologized when Laura enquired. "He is, hm, deservedly obscure."

On St. Wigbert's Day, since time immemorial, the Wyckhams held open house, for their neighbours, tenants, farm workers, villagers, tradesmen, and house guests. The day was taken up with archery and bowling tournaments; three-legged, sack, and egg-and-spoon races; a greased pig-catching contest; a puppet show and morris dancers; and a concert by the choir of the Welsh Methodist Chapel who, in the name of tradition, abandoned their feud with the Anglican Church for the day. In the evening, a supper for the commoners and dinner for the gentry, would be followed by dancing for anyone still capable of the exertion.

At her own insistence, Laura was set to work by Aunt Antonia. She helped sort out dates and accommodations for visitors, discussed menus with the cook, wrote lists and invitations. For the first time she was able to put to use what she had learned as a girl about running a great household. She found the reality fascinating. Spending a good deal of time in consultation with Mrs. Lloyd, she came to like the housekeeper and admire her efficiency.

Inevitably, Gareth asked, "Are you sure all this business is not too tiring?"

"Not at all. All I do is sit here in the morning room, like a queen granting audience, and everyone comes to me."

"I had not realized the fête involved so much labour." He sat down on the chair beside the drop-front desk where she was writing one of the endless lists, with the aid of last year's.

"Aunt Antonia has managed it for years without assistance," Laura said, "but she is not as young as she was."

"And Maria is not the least help."

"Nor is she any hindrance. She is in her element, with the house full of visitors and gaiety. Not a sign of a megrim for a week."

"No doubt that makes your task easier. Nonetheless, we are lucky to have you. I would not have you think I am idle, however! Besides the normal work of the estate, the outside events take some organizing."

"I know. Perry and Lance were in here only this morning squabbling about what to give as prizes for the races. I hope I convinced them that the winner of the ladies' egg-and-spoon race will appreciate neither a snuff box nor a new cricket bat."

"Gudgeons," he said affectionately, then

hesitated before continuing, "I have been thinking that I ought to warn you about Aunt Sybil."

"The name sounds familiar."

"Lady Frobisher. She always comes home for St. Wigbert's Day."

"Oh yes, I addressed an invitation to Lord and Lady Frobisher, purely as a matter of form, Aunt Antonia said. But that is not it. I know, she painted those watercolours of local scenes, did she not?" Something else nagged at the back of her mind, an unpleasant memory that refused to come forward.

"Yes, the landscapes are hers, schoolroom efforts."

"You want to warn me to make some complimentary reference to her paintings?"

"I wish that were all." He grimaced. "Aunt Sybil, alas, prides herself on her knowledge of the *Haut Monde,* and she never forgets any item of gossip."

"She is your father's sister? I remember now." Laura's cheeks burned. She looked down at her hands, clenched in her lap. "Aunt Antonia told me that Lady Frobisher is an inveterate scandalmonger, and that she wrote . . . she wrote an unpleasant letter . . . about me."

"The devil she did!" He leaned forward and put his hand on hers, his face dark with anger. "Laura, I cannot forbid my aunt her childhood home, but I can and will ensure that she spreads no tales while she is here."

"How?" she asked doubtfully.

"Aunt Sybil indulged in one or two youthful indiscretions herself, that I discovered when my father died and I went through his papers. I shall make it plain that if she tells tales, she will receive a dose of her own medicine. Her 'bosom friend,' Mrs. Payne, will be only too happy to provide a wide circulation."

"It is very kind in you, but I cannot like to be the cause of discord between you and your aunt. Perhaps it will be best if I just go home before she arrives."

Gareth sprang to his feet. "Home! This is your home. Your home, no longer hers. Let me hear no more of such talk. And enough of Aunt Sybil. Come, you have been cooped up in here too long. If you would care to walk down to the English garden with me, I shall have the gig brought to drive you back up the hill."

"That will be delightful," she said, composure restored. With such a champion, she had nothing to fear from Lady Frobisher. Enough of Aunt Sybil, indeed.

Yet it was Gareth who raised the subject

again, as they reentered the house after their stroll.

"One more thing you ought to know about Aunt Sybil, Laura. She is determined to see me wed and may well bring with her some eligible young lady. She is wasting her time. I shall never marry."

"Then you will not mind if Aunt Antonia writes to inform her that every chamber in the Manor is already bespoken for the week of St. Wigbert's Day, as is the case." Laura spoke lightly but she wondered at his determined tone. Though it made no difference to her, of course, whether he married or not, she thought it a pity when he would be so splendid a husband and father. On the other hand, she could not wish him wed to any female chosen by Lady Frobisher.

A little voice in her head whispered that she could not wish him wed to any female except . . . but that was ridiculous.

CHAPTER 12

Lady Frobisher paid not the least heed to Aunt Antonia's letter. She arrived at Llys with a pretty, meek girl in tow, the Honourable Miss Daphne Overstreet, the well-dowered daughter of a viscount. Daphne was by far too timid to make the slightest push to attract Gareth. Instead, she took refuge with Laura, to Lady Frobisher's fury.

Her ladyship bristled with disapproval but, after a brief interview with her nephew, it was silent disapproval. Laura scarcely noticed her black looks since the Manor was abustle with upward of two dozen other guests. Though she held herself a little apart, feeling slow and heavy at eight months pregnant, everyone except Lady Frobisher accepted her without fuss as one of the household.

Daphne was not the only unexpected guest to be squeezed in somehow by the imperturbable Mrs. Lloyd. Three days before the fête, Sir John Pointer turned up.

Lloyd ushered him out to the terrace, where Laura, most of the ladies, and a few gentlemen were taking afternoon tea. Those about her politely turned their attention elsewhere when they realized the plump dandy had come to call on her.

"Thought I ought to see how you was doing," he explained. "Good friend of mine, Freddie. Popped into the cottage on the way to Newmarket, found you gone, remembered Wyckham asking after you, so here I am."

"You are very welcome," Laura assured him, touched, though the reminder of her past life disturbed her.

He looked about appreciatively. "Glad to see you're in clover. Freddie'd be pleased. Good fellow, Freddie. Things ain't the same without him. All's bowman with . . . er . . . hm . . ." His round face turned scarlet above his high collar. "With . . . er . . . is it?"

Laura rescued him. "Everything is going very well. Will you take a cup of tea, Sir John?"

"Or perhaps something stronger, Pointer?" Gareth had come out of the house on returning from a ride with some of his guests. To Laura he sounded inexplicably belligerent.

"No, no, tea will suit me down to the ground," said the baronet with a hint of alarm.

"Sir John has come all this way, Cousin, just to make sure that all is well with me."

"Indeed. Could you suppose otherwise, Sir John, when Lady Laura is in my care?"

"No, no, assure you, Wyckham, . . . didn't know . . . wasn't sure . . ."

"It is excessively amiable in him, is it not, Cousin? Since you have arrived at this opportune moment, Sir John, may we hope you will be able to stay for the fête on Saturday?" Laura had no desire whatsoever for his company, but she was obliged to him

192

for his concern, however delayed, and she could not let Gareth treat him so rudely.

Her unspoken rebuke must have registered, for Gareth relented. "Certainly you must stay, Pointer." In a display of effortless social mastery, with a single glance at the assembled company, a slight gesture of the head, he brought several people over to join them. Sir John was absorbed into the group.

"And after treating him so horridly, you never even gave him a chance to refuse the invitation," Laura whispered.

"Shockingly discourteous, was I not?" Gareth said ruefully. "My first thought was that his presence must distress you, but then you appeared to want him to stay."

"I was a little upset to see him," she admitted, then scolded him, "but your churlishness upset me more, which is the only reason I asked him to stay."

"Then you don't really want him here? I shall send him to the rightabout at —"

"Gareth, don't you dare! Leave the poor fellow be. He misses Freddie far more than I do, I fear."

"Which only goes to show that you have more sense in your little finger than he in his head," said Gareth roundly.

He greeted with pleasure the next uninvited

arrivals. Sir Henry and Lady Wyckham, Maria's parents, returned unexpectedly to England from a diplomatic post with the Portuguese court in exile in Brazil.

Sir Henry was a distinguished figure, who combined Rupert's height, Lancelot's slenderness, Gareth's quiet elegance of dress, and Cornelius's pompous manner. Lady Wyckham was exactly as Laura would have imagined Maria's mother and the wife of a diplomat. Her dress, though unostentatious, was fashionable and extremely becoming, and she was able to converse with anyone. Laura suspected she had no deep interest in people, yet she set them at their ease, even her eccentric brother-in-law, Julius, and bashful Daphne Overstreet.

After a dutiful visit to the schoolroom, Lady Wyckham showed little interest in her grandchildren. With her parents arrival, Maria abandoned any pretence of devoted motherhood. Reverting to the rôle of an unmarried young lady — with the licence of widowhood — she flirted with every unattached gentleman within reach.

Naturally, this rôle had no room for children. Even Arabella seldom saw her. At first, Laura was concerned, but Miss Coltart and Peter Renfrew kept them busy and happy. On their occasional appearances among the guests, Maria studiously ignored them but everyone else spoiled them so they hardly noticed.

St. Wigbert's Day arrived. In front of the Manor blossomed a huge red and yellow marquee in case of rain, but the sky was a deep and cloudless blue. The parkland sprouted archery butts, bowling alleys, racecourses, refreshment tables, a puppet booth, a stand for the choir. In a large enclosure a young sow rooted contentedly, unaware that she was to be slathered with lard and chased by hordes of youths.

Chairs and small tables for the gentry had been set out in the shade of scattered trees. Laura found a vantage point beneath a chestnut on a slight rise and settled there with the inseparable Daphne to watch the festivities.

Swarms of people flocked to watch the contests and entertainments. Children ran about squealing and ladies and gentlemen strolled through the crowd, their progress marked by parasols of a dozen different hues. Laura easily picked out Rupert and his friends by the glory of the full dress scarlet and gold uniforms they wore in honour of the occasion. Now and then she caught sight of the other Wyckham brothers.

As host, Gareth was never still for more than a moment. He seemed to know everyone, to have a word or two for everyone. Laura saw him laugh with a farmer, pick up a fallen child, bow over a lady's hand, take a shot at the skittles, present prizes, quaff a tankard of ale, all without ever looking hurried or harassed. She wished she dared go and join the throng. Though she knew it was foolish, she felt excluded from the warmth of his hospitality.

The feeling vanished when a footman arrived with his lordship's compliments and a tray of lemonade, Welsh cakes, and Shrewsbury biscuits. In the midst of all the bustle and confusion, he had thought of her comfort.

The afternoon grew hot. More and more ladies and gentlemen retreated to the shade of the chestnuts and oaks. Laura saw that some were heading for the house, and then she noticed that Uncle Julius was often to be seen in the midst of these groups. Curiosity coincided with discomfort from the heat, from sitting too long, and from two glasses of lemonade.

"I believe I shall go and lie down for a while," she said to Daphne. "There is no need for you to tear yourself away from the spectacle. Lady Frobisher is just over there —"

"Oh please, let me go with you." The girl's eyes filled with alarm. "You can lean on my arm."

So together they slowly walked towards the house. Before they had covered a third of the distance, Gareth caught up with them.

"Laura, are you unwell?"

"I am dying" — a dramatic pause — "of curiosity."

He shook his head at her, at once exasperated and amused. "Is she not a wretched tease, Miss Overstreet?"

Daphne turned scarlet, fixed her gaze on a patch of bird's foot trefoil at her feet, and mumbled something incoherent. How Lady Frobisher had supposed she might possibly fix Gareth's interest, Laura could not imagine.

"Do you know what Uncle Julius is up to?" she asked.

"Yes, did you not hear? He is demonstrating his latest invention. So far, I gather, it is working perfectly. Shall we go to see it?"

Laura was about to accept when the lemonade made its presence urgently felt. "I must not keep you from your guests," she said regretfully.

"They can spare me for a few minutes."

Flattered, but beginning to be not a little desperate, she glanced back for inspiration. "No, they cannot. The choir is assembling. How shocking if you were not there to hear them sing. I wish I could stay."

"So that's it. I beg your pardon for delaying you." With an ill-concealed grin he turned away.

Scarlet-faced as Daphne, Laura continued towards the house at a fast walk. Someone — Dr. McAllister? — had described the difficulties of pregnancy to Gareth. How dared the odious man laugh at her, she fumed.

Another problem was breathlessness. When she had to slow her walk, she was very glad Gareth had not come with her. Far from laughing, he would have worried, though Dr. McAllister had told her it was perfectly normal, the result of the baby's pressure on her diaphragm. Lying down flat made it worse, so having relieved her bladder, she reclined on the pretty Sheraton chaise longue in her sitting room with several pillows behind her.

"Shall I ring for your abigail?" Daphne asked anxiously.

"Myfanwy is at the fête. Let her enjoy it.

Why don't you go back out and see the fun?"

"Oh no, dear Lady Laura, pray don't make me! I shall just sit here, quiet as a mouse. I shan't disturb you, I promise."

Loath as she was to further antagonize Lady Frobisher, Laura had not the heart to drive the poor child away. "Perhaps you would like to read to me?" she suggested. "Lord Wyckham bought a new novel in London which I liked so much he ordered another by the same author, which I have not yet had time to start."

"A novel! I fear Mama does not allow me to read novels."

Laura had no great opinion of mothers, judging by the two she knew best: her own and Maria. "I am sure no mama could object to *Mansfield Park*," she said. "I daresay *Pride and Prejudice* will prove as innocently amusing. Do let us try it."

With an air of recklessness, Daphne acquiesced. " 'It is a truth universally acknowledged,' " she read, " 'that a single man in possession of a good fortune must be in want of a wife.' "

Not Gareth, Laura thought. He had not said he was not in the market for a wife, which left room to change his mind in the future. He had said in the most resolute

199

fashion that he would never marry. At the time she was too busy to ponder his words. Now she wondered whether his resolve stemmed from his father's heartbroken withdrawal from the world on the death of his wife. Perhaps Gareth simply did not choose to risk so great a loss.

Poor Gareth!

"Oh, how very like Mama!" cried Daphne.

"Is it? I'm sorry, I was not attending."

" 'The business of her life was to get her daughters married,' " Daphne read. "Speaking of Mrs. Bennet, you know. Was not your mama thus?"

"No." After the triumph of catching a duke-to-be for Ceci, Lady Medway had not cared a fig whether her plain elder daughter dwindled to an old maid. Seeing Daphne's surprise at her vehemence, Laura qualified her answer. "Not really. Do go on."

Though Daphne read well and the story was even more to Laura's taste than Mansfield Park, she drowsed off. She was distantly aware of Daphne creeping out, but she did not rouse fully until Myfanwy bustled in.

"There now, is it a good nap you've had, my lady? You said to come and dress you early, seeing it's needed to help the visiting ladies I am. You'll be sorry to have missed the fun, but there's always next year."

Chattering and giggling about the games and shows and contests, the maid helped Laura to put on the figured silk, now let out to its full extent.

Laura made her ponderous way down to the Long Gallery. Gareth and Cornelius were there, both staring at the ceiling.

"Well, I wouldn't let him," the vicar advised. "It may work now but you know very well there is always a, hm, snag, and by the time it becomes apparent, he has lost interest."

"True, but I hate to disappoint the old man." Gareth turned. "Oh, Laura, what do you think of Uncle Julius's raiser?"

"Razor? I have not seen it, and I don't know much about the subject, except that Freddie frequently nicked himself while shaving. Has Uncle Julius invented a way to avoid such hazards?"

"No, no, raiser — *r a i s e r.* A tray-raiser, he calls the contraption."

"Tray-raiser? Oh dear, a successor to his tray-barrow?" She giggled, remembering that minor disaster. "I cannot give an opinion without seeing it. Is it in the workshop?"

"Yes, and it can wait until tomorrow," Gareth said firmly. "It's miles away and I'm not having you . . . I mean, it's quite un-necessary for you to try to dash there and back before dinner."

"I'm not very good at dashing these days," Laura conceded.

"I shall be happy to show you in the morning."

"For pity's sake, Gareth," said Cornelius, "don't go and demonstrate the mechanism without Uncle Julius. You are liable to, hm, hang yourself. You must restrain him, Cousin Laura."

"I shall try, only whenever I go into the workshop, I find my fingers twitching to fiddle with all that curious equipment."

Gareth laughed. "It is tempting, is it not? When we were boys, Cornie and I —"

"Gareth, recall that I am now a, hm, man of the cloth. Have a care for my dignity."

"I'll tell you tomorrow, Laura," Gareth promised.

The next morning several house guests departed, including — to Laura's relief — the Frobishers and Daphne Overstreet, and Sir John Pointer. What with seeing them off and Gareth being closeted for near an hour with Maria and her parents, the visit to the workshop was postponed until after luncheon.

"Is it not time for your nap?" Gareth asked when Laura reminded him of their plan.

"No, I cannot lie down so soon after eating. Do let us go, unless you have other business?"

"Nothing that cannot wait, and I need your advice." He had the harassed look only Maria could bring to his face.

Laura had noticed at luncheon that Maria was unusually excited even for that excitable lady. "Anything I can do to help," she assured Gareth, "you know you have only to ask."

"I know," he said gratefully. As they strolled along the corridor to Uncle Julius's workshop at the far end of the longest wing, he explained. "Uncle Henry is on his way to Vienna — the Allies are going to hold a Congress there to decide how to carve up Europe after Napoleon. And my aunt has invited Maria to go with them."

"To a diplomatic congress?" Laura said in astonishment.

"I daresay there is bound to be a good deal of jollification, with most of the crowned heads of Europe present to make sure they get their piece of the pie. The thing is, Uncle Henry refuses to take the children."

"Maria does not appear precisely distraught at the prospect of leaving them."

"She says the poor little things will be much better off here," Gareth said dryly.

"Of course they will."

"You don't think they will suffer from being parted from their mama?"

"I think they will go on much better under your guidance without Maria's interference," Laura said frankly, "but it is a great deal to ask of you."

"Of me! Not at all. I am very fond of them, and thanks to you, Miss Coltart has them well in hand. My chief concern is for their welfare."

"Then let Maria go."

Gareth smiled down at her. "I knew I could count on you for a candid opinion without roundaboutation. That leaves me with but one concern."

"Which is?"

"I cannot allow Maria to desert them unless I have your promise not to regard her responsibility for them as transferred to you. Between Miss Coltart and Renfrew, Aunt Antonia, my brothers and me, and a horde of servants, the children are not likely to suffer from neglect." He glanced at her swollen belly. "Soon enough you will have responsibilities of your own."

"I trust you are not predicting twins?"

"Good gad, no!" he said in horror.

Laura laughed. "Teasing aside, I expect one will be enough to keep me fully occupied for a while. But I, too, have grown very fond of George and Henry and Arabella. I shall acknowledge that they are not my responsibility, but I don't wish to be shut out of their lives."

"As though I could! Unlike Maria, you will always be welcome to interfere in their upbringing if you see anything which needs righting. But after all, she will only be gone for a few months." He sighed heavily.

And I shall be gone in a few months, Laura thought. It was all too easy to forget, to let her resolve weaken, to persuade herself she could be satisfied with his friendship. Yet even now, heavy with child, she felt a tremor of desire as she laid her hand on his arm, accepting his help down three steps to a lower level. If he guessed, he would turn from her in disgust.

No, she must not stay at Llys.

They reached the workshop. Uncle Julius was there, seated at one of his workbenches. He was fast asleep, his head pillowed on his arms. Close to the back of his head, brass scales in perfect balance had one pan occupied by a browning pear-core, the other by the remains of a stale sandwich with the edges curling. On his other side, inches from his nose and reflected glinting in his spectacles, a set of shiny cogwheels clicked as they turned.

A finger to his lips, Gareth beckoned. On tiptoe, with exaggerated caution, he threaded his way between benches littered with tools and bits of metal and India rubber, and half-finished, incomprehensible machines. Larger machines stood on the floor. Unable to raise herself on tiptoes, Laura followed as quietly as she could. Despite her care she brushed against a switch. With a squeal and a rattle, something moved.

"Well, bless my soul!" Uncle Julius blinked at the mechanism before his nose. "Of course, clockwork, why didn't I think of it? Much simpler to construct than hydraulics." He caught sight of his visitors. "Clockwork requires far less precision," he explained kindly, "at least when it's not for telling time."

"Good afternoon, Uncle," said Gareth. "I've brought Cousin Laura to see your raiser. Will you demonstrate?"

Uncle Julius vaguely felt his grey-stubbled chin. "Yes, yes, I could do with a shave. No time, you see. But as for bringing a lady to watch, what odd manners you young modern people have, nevvie!"

Laura kept all but the merest tremor of laughter from her voice. "Cousin Gareth means your tray-raiser, sir. Perhaps you should call it a lifter, to avoid confusion?"

"An excellent notion, my dear young lady." He beamed. "However, it's no use showing you that now."

"Has the lifter broken down already, Uncle?"

"Good gracious, no. Broken? No, no. But at present it works by manpower, and as I am about to construct a clockwork mechanism, there is little point in demonstrating the primitive version." And he went into one of his creative trances.

In a whisper, Gareth observed, "At least I shan't have to decide for a few more weeks whether to let him cut through from the Long Gallery up into the drawing room." With a grimace, he pointed out a hole in the ceiling in one corner of the workshop, with ropes dangling from it.

"You must not ruin those beautiful rooms," Laura whispered back. "If it seems really useful, put it in a hallway, or next to the back stairs."

"An excellent notion," Gareth exclaimed aloud.

Uncle Julius remained lost in his brown study, so they left him to it. As they returned along the long passage, Laura said, "I don't know what tricks you and Cousin Cornelius got up to in your youth, but if you install a mechanized tray-lifter, Henry and George are bound to try using it as a small-boy-lifter."

"True. Or, worse, a small-girl-lifter."

"I expect Uncle Julius can fit some kind of lock to . . . Oh!" She stopped and pressed her hand to her bulging abdomen.

"Kicking again?"

"Yes, one never quite grows used to it. I could swear I feel a foot under my hand."

He reached out, then quickly drew back, flushing. "I'm sorry, I —"

"No, Gareth, it is all right." Laura took his hand and laid it on the spot where the tiny foot was thumping at her from the inside.

A stunned expression spread across his face. When they started walking again, after a few moments, he was silent, still looking dazed. Laura was afraid he was shocked by her impulsive action — bold, not to say improper! — yet she dared hope his silence had a quality more akin to wonder than disgust.

As they came to the Great Hall, he turned

to her and said softly, "Thank you."

If only he were her baby's father!

CHAPTER 13

The guests were all gone. Maria departed with her parents, euphoric but for a brief, tearful appeal to Laura to make sure Gareth did not allow Mr. Renfrew to beat her poor little boys. Lance and Perry and Rupert went off to visit friends. After all the hustle and bustle, Llys Manor seemed excessively quiet, especially as Gareth was often out and about supervising the harvest.

Laura grew sluggish. Increasingly clumsy and awkward, she began to feel as if she had been pregnant forever. The children were so used to her condition that when they came down to tea they no longer asked how long they had to wait before their new cousin's arrival.

They scarcely missed their mama. In fact, Laura missed Maria more. Aunt Antonia was all sympathy with her discomfort but she could not really understand.

As for Gareth, he enquired with maddening frequency whether she was sure of her dates. When Dr. McAllister, called in unnecessarily for the second time, told him nine months was merely an inaccurate average length for pregnancy, he was horrified.

"You mean the baby could arrive any day now?"

"Aye, m'laird, but dinna fash yersel'. Wi' a first birth, there's ay plenty o' warning."

"Always?"

"Near enow, though there's the odd wumman draps e'en her first quick and easy as a ewe draps a lamb."

"You mean a first birth is generally difficult?"

"Nay, mon, I mean nowt o' the sort, and I'll thank ye not to be putting such notions into her leddyship's head."

"I don't care how difficult it is," Laura said wearily, "so long as it comes soon."

"As to that, ma leddy, it could be a week or it could be a month," said McAllister with a cheerfulness as maddening as Gareth's oversolicitude. "Now, as to the back cramps, that wee abigail o' yourn ha' the right o' it. A good rub wi' any kind o' liniment'll do more to help than aught I can prescribe. Good day to ye, ma'am," he said to Aunt Antonia, and departed.

"A month!" Laura groaned.

"A week!" Gareth groaned. "Or any day now! I must send for Dr. Croft, and the midwife, and the lying-in nurse, and the wet-nurse —"

"Not Dr. Croft!" Laura and Aunt Antonia exclaimed at once.

"He is the most eminent physician-accoucheur in London. I want the best."

"Laura did not care for him," said Aunt Antonia astringently. "At this of all times, you cannot wish to surround her with those she dislikes."

"But he is vastly popular with the ladies of the Ton," Gareth protested. "They flock to him."

"There is no accounting for tastes," his aunt observed. "I myself did not take to the man."

With a grateful glance at the old lady, Laura soothingly pointed out, "If Dr. Croft is so busy, Gareth, he is unlikely to be willing to travel so far for an indefinite period for a single patient. Indeed, I have every confidence in Dr. McAllister and the midwife he recommended."

"And you really disliked Croft? Not just because I called him in without consulting you?"

"He somehow succeeded in being obsequious and condescending at the same time. What is more, I believe he has only one prescription for all his patients, regardless of the individual constitution. If I had followed his regimen of regular cupping and a lowering diet, I should not be half so healthy as I am, besides being thoroughly miserable."

Gareth stared at her in dismay. "He recommended regular bleeding? When you've a baby growing inside you?"

"Really, Gareth," snapped Aunt Antonia, "you are becoming positively indelicate in your speech. Dr. Croft is unacceptable. Leave it at that."

"Yes, Aunt. I'm sorry, Cousin. I meant it for the best."

"I know," said Laura, touching his hand. "If it makes you feel better, perhaps Dr. McAllister would agree to stay at the manor and go on his rounds from here."

"I'll catch him and ask him." Gareth jumped up and ran from the room with a lack of dignity most indecorous in Lord Wyckham of Llys.

Offered a sum which would enable him to treat several dozen poor patients for free, Dr. McAllister took up residence at the manor. Likewise Mistress Owen, the midwife from Llysbury, agreed to move in, with the use of his lordship's gig to convey her to any confinements she was called to.

Gareth also summoned a surgeon from Worcester, recommended by a neighbour; two monthly nurses, one for day and one for night duty; the wet-nurse, a village woman who had given birth a few weeks ago; and a nurse and nursery-maid for the baby.

"Really, Gareth, these hordes of people are quite unnecessary," Laura told him crossly the day the surgeon arrived.

He sat down beside her on the bench on the terrace. He had taken to dashing home at midday from even the farthest fields and orchards. "Don't be vexed," he pleaded. "I have to do everything I can. I could not bear the burden of guilt my father carried the last years of his life."

"Guilt? I thought it was grief made him a recluse."

"Grief and guilt. Laura, I've never told anyone, not even Cornelius, but afterwards, after the funeral, I heard Papa talking to the vicar in the library. I recall every word as if it was yesterday. 'It was my fault,' he said. 'I killed her.'"

Oh God, he had cried, *why could I not leave her alone?* But that Gareth could not bring himself to repeat to Laura. He was not — thank God — responsible for her pregnancy.

Yet if anything went wrong because he had failed to take every possible precaution, he knew he would blame himself forever.

"Poor man," said Laura soberly. "I suppose he felt he had failed to take proper care of her. I'm sure he must have, though, loving her as he did."

"You see why I must leave no stone un-turned."

She smiled at him. "Yes, I do, though I hope your use of that particular phrase does not indicate that you mean to administer earwigs and centipedes and leeches."

"No leeches, I promise. Dr. Croft was a mistake. No reducing diet, either. Come on in, it's time for luncheon and I am sharp-set."

Laura said no more on the subject. Silently blessing her for her understanding, Gareth told the hordes to stay out of her way. Still, he felt more and more foolish as the days passed and no baby appeared.

Rupert, Lance, and Perry came home. In deference to Laura's condition, none of them brought friends with them, a decision arrived at between the three of them before they left. Gareth was proud of them for their thoughtfulness. He would also have been proud of the way they made a point of sitting with her, entertaining her with tales of their doings, had they not all so obviously enjoyed her company.

"You see," Perry explained seriously, "Cousin Laura isn't a bit like Cousin Maria. She's actually interested in us. And you can tell her anything. She doesn't disapprove of half the fun, like Aunt Antonia."

The good-natured Perry spent much of his time playing with George and Henry and Arabella, taking them fishing for minnows and building tree houses. None of them either drowned or broke a leg. Rupert was well occupied with riding and shooting. Lance, with little scope for his dandyism in the country, unexpectedly took to Dr. McAllister, the least dandified of men. He even accompanied him on his rounds. Nonetheless, Gareth was startled when Lance announced that he wanted to leave Oxford and train as a physician.

"I've decided to tell him he may," Gareth said to Laura, again joining her on the terrace, this time to watch the sunset, "if he's still of the same mind when he finishes at Oxford. He only has one year to go. It's an unusual choice of profession for the son of a noble house, but at present I'm hardly in a position to disparage it."

"The more doctors, the merrier?" she teased.

"If we had one in the family, you could not object to his presence," he retorted.

A shadow crossed her face, and he silently cursed himself. She was never likely to find herself pregnant again and in need of a doctor.

Unless she remarried, in which case her welfare would be her new husband's concern, not Gareth's. The notion gave him a peculiarly unpleasant sensation somewhere beneath his waistcoat. Of course, it would mean her leaving Llys, and she had become so much a part of the family her departure would leave a gaping hole.

He gave himself a mental shake. For the present, she was well and truly fixed at the manor. Even going to Church on Sunday was such an effort that Cornelius had persuaded Aunt Antonia to excuse Laura from attendance the past few Sundays.

Somehow her great, unwieldy belly in no way detracted from her prettiness. Without being aware of the change, he had come to find her looks much more attractive than Maria's undeniable beauty. Perhaps it was because her dark hair was a pleasant contrast amidst his blond family. Or perhaps because Maria's delicate features were so often marred by petulant discontent.

Except that even when she frowned Laura was . . .

"Laura? What is it?"

She was frowning, not crossly but with an air of extreme concentration, her hands pressed to her back on either side.

"I think . . ." She hesitated. "Yes, I do believe I am going into labour."

"Here?" Gareth said idiotically, starting up.

"Here." She smiled up at him. "I've been having pains for several days —"

"Pain? Why the devil did you not tell me?" he howled.

"Because it is what Dr. McAllister calls false labour. He and Mistress Owen and Myfanwy all say it is quite commonplace. But now the pains seem to be coming regularly and getting stronger, so — Oh!" She turned bright scarlet and clutched at her knees. "Gareth, I . . . I'm afraid the waters have broken."

"I knew everything would go wrong! I'll carry you up to your chamber."

"No! It's perfectly normal, only rather . . . rather embarrassing. Please, just send Myfanwy to me."

"But —"

"Go away, Gareth!"

He raced into the house, across the Long Gallery, into the Great Hall, bellowing for Myfanwy, for McAllister, for Aunt Antonia, for midwife and surgeon and nurses. Footmen ran. Lloyd appeared, with a decanter and a glass on a tray.

"The doctor is out, my lord. I have sent to the stables to dispatch a groom after him. He left instructions to have brandy ready to hand in case —"

"Then take it to her, hurry!" Gareth recalled her peremptory command to him to go away. "No, wait, her maid —"

"For you, my lord," said the butler, setting down the tray and filling the glass.

Hardly aware of what he was doing, Gareth tossed back the brandy, just as his aunt hurried into the hall.

"Really, Gareth, drinking at such a time!"

"Doctor's orders, madam," Lloyd murmured.

"At least," Aunt Antonia continued, "I assume all this commotion means Laura's time has come?"

"The waters have broken," Gareth blurted out.

She looked dismayed. "Oh dear, you were with her?"

"Is it serious? She assured me it's quite normal. Was she just trying to set my mind at rest? What can I do?"

"Nothing, dear boy, except keep away. It is perfectly normal but, oh dear, not something one would wish a gentleman to witness."

"She's on the terrace. Go to her, Aunt,"

he pleaded.

Aunt Antonia ambled towards the Long Gallery with an appalling lack of urgency. Everyone was conspiring to try to persuade him nothing was wrong, his own fault for making a fuss when there was nothing to fuss about, he acknowledged wryly. But now something was happening. Laura was in pain and McAllister was absent. How could he trust Mistress Owen and the surgeon to know what to do?

Drawn by an invisible but inexorable force, he followed his aunt.

Through the windows, he saw Myfanwy and one of the nurses already with Laura. At that moment, Aunt Antonia realized he was just behind her.

Turning, she said severely, "You are quite in the way, Gareth."

"I'll wait here."

She studied his face, and softened. "Very well. But not a step closer, and turn your back."

Swinging round, he glared at the First Baron Wyckham, hanging on the wall opposite the windows in all the glory of a full-bottomed wig. "What are they doing to her?"

"Making her comfortable and decent so that she can go up to her chamber." Aunt

Antonia's tart voice faded as she moved away, out onto the terrace.

"I shall carry her!" he shouted, to no response.

His ears strained to catch the murmur from outside, he stood there for several minutes unmindful of his illustrious ancestor. Then he heard footsteps behind him and Myfanwy said, "Mind the step, my lady."

Not waiting to find out if the prohibition was still in force, Gareth turned, rushed to Laura's side and scooped her up in his arms.

"I'm carrying you," he said firmly.

"So I see. It is not at all necessary, but I shall not object."

Laura smiled at him as he strode out to the Great Hall. He saw she appeared just as healthy as before whatever mysterious emergency had just occurred. The only change he noticed was that she now wore a loose robe over her gown.

He wished he had pressed McAllister for details of the normal course of labour, so that he would understand what was happening.

"Put your arms around my neck," he ordered, reaching the bottom of the stairs.

She obeyed, and laid her head on his shoulder, relaxed in his arms, trusting in him to take care of her. But half way up the stairs she stiffened, her clasp tightening. He did not dare look down at her for fear of stumbling.

"What is it?" he demanded, feeling the blood drain from his face.

"Just another pain," she gasped.

"Dammit, where is that doctor?"

"Gareth, pray mind your tongue," snapped Aunt Antonia, hard on his heels. "Vulgar language is of no more assistance than drinking."

"Laura's in pain," he protested.

"It's more of a sort of twinging spasm," Laura assured him, "not real pain, not yet."

"Not yet? My God!"

"Gareth, please!" his aunt remonstrated. "If you wish to discuss Heavenly shortcomings in the arrangements He has made for childbirth, then take the matter up with Cornelius."

"My lord." Omniscient as every good butler, Lloyd stood at the top of the stairs, tray of brandy in hand. "I took the liberty of sending word to Mr. Cornelius." He moved ahead to open the door to Laura's chamber.

Gareth carried her in and laid her gently on the bed. He stood looking down at her helplessly until Aunt Antonia took his arm

221

in a firm grip, turned him around, and pushed him towards the door.

"Out," she said. "It is out of your hands now."

The door clicked shut behind him.

Waving away the glass of brandy Lloyd offered, Gareth went down to the library, intending to read to distract his thoughts from Laura's sufferings.

He sat at one of the crimson-curtained windows so he would see when Dr. McAllister arrived. After staring for an age at the same page of one of his favourite books without absorbing a word, he gave up and simply stared out of the window instead.

Inactivity growing unbearable, he paced up and down the room, until Perry rushed in, liberally bedaubed with mud, his young face anxious. "Gareth, they told me —"

"Where are the children?"

"I sent them up to the nursery. They are even filthier than me. But Cousin Laura, she's going to be all right, isn't she?"

Gareth was torn between the need not to alarm the boy and a wish to warn him so that if anything did go wrong it would not be too great a shock. He compromised. "I've done everything possible to ensure that she will be all right."

Perry looked at him dubiously. "But you

can't be sure. It would be dreadful if she died, like Mama."

"Cousin Laura is much younger and healthier than Mama was." Trying to reassure himself as much as Perry, he appeared to succeed with his brother, at least. Cheered, Perry went off to take a bath.

Gareth resumed his pacing. Had he really done everything? He should not have let McAllister leave the house. What if his groom had missed the doctor? he thought suddenly. He must send out another man — two men, three! — to scour the countryside.

As he strode towards the door, it opened and Lance came in. "So Cousin Laura is in labour at last," he said blithely.

"You were with McAllister?" Gareth scowled at his insensible brother, neat and trim as ever despite his outing in the doctor's gig. "He's back? I didn't see you come up the avenue."

"We drove up the back lane. He's already gone up to Cousin Laura."

"Devil take it, I wanted to see him."

"What, and keep him from her side?"

Gareth groaned and clutched his head. "No, of course he should be with her."

"I was roasting you. She doesn't really need him, you know," said Lance, laying a comforting hand on Gareth's arm. "He says he wishes half his patients were as healthy and he has no doubt the midwife is quite capable of doing all that's necessary."

"I'm paying him to attend her!"

"That's why he's there. Gad, if every patient's relatives were as difficult as you, I'd pretty quickly change my mind about becoming a physician. You will let me, won't you?"

"We'll discuss it later. I can't think about that now."

Lance looked at him and sighed. "I told you, she's going to be all right. Well, I might as well go and change for dinner already as I must get rid of my dirt."

"My dear Lance, you're as impeccable as ever."

"There's dust on my boots, and my wristbands are definitely dingy, and I shouldn't wonder if my hair is all blown about."

"Doctoring can be a bloody business," Gareth pointed out.

"That's different," said Lance dismissively, departing.

Gareth wished he had not reminded himself of the bloody side of the medical profession, not when Laura was up there surrounded by medical attendants. He must go and find out what was happening.

On the stairs he met Myfanwy. "My lady sent me to tell you all's going well, my lord."

"What does Dr. McAllister say?"

"Just the same, my lord."

"How much longer?"

"There's hours yet it'll be. First babies come slow, look you."

"Take care of her, Myfanwy."

"As though I wouldn't, my lord!"

He went back down, meeting Cornelius and Rupert in the hall, just come in from the stables. Rupert's bloody game-bag made Gareth shudder; so did Cornie's homily on the consolations of religion, which seemed to Gareth to assume the worst possible outcome. To escape, he went to change for dinner.

He was not surprised to find his appetite had deserted him, though Aunt Antonia, joining them, assured him Laura's labour was proceeding perfectly normally. "Else I should not have left her, of course."

The evening seemed endless. At last his brothers retired to bed, leaving Gareth pacing the Long Gallery. Though Myfanwy turned up with periodic bulletins, the gallery seemed too far away, in case anything happened. He moved out to the Great Hall, then up to the landing, then to the passage outside Laura's apartments.

Lloyd, brandy and a sandwich on his tray, found him there.

"I don't want anything," he told the butler impatiently.

"It's past two o'clock, Master Gareth."

"Go to bed, go to bed. I shan't. Listen, what's that?" From behind her chamber door, a groan came faintly to his ears.

Reaching for the door-handle, he hesitated. A lifetime of training told him a gentleman simply does not burst into a lady's chamber. So he burst into her sitting room instead. No one was there, and through the connecting door came more groans, growing fainter, stopping. A lifetime of training deserted him.

CHAPTER 14

"Gareth!" Aunt Antonia was the first to spot him as he rushed into Laura's chamber. "What on earth has come over you? Go away at once."

"I had to come! What's wrong?"

"Nothing, Gareth." Laura sounded weary, but not in agony. Between two of those surrounding her, he saw her face, red and shiny with sweat, not deathly pale as he had feared. She smiled at him. "Dr. McAllister says I'm doing . . . Aaah!"

"Dinna bear down yet, ma leddy," said McAllister sharply. "Ye'll only exhaust yoursel'. Try to relax."

"Gareth, hold my hand," she whimpered. "Please! I cannot . . . Oh, oh, oh . . ."

Myfanwy stepped back out of his way and Laura took his hand in a convulsive grasp. He kept his gaze on her face, taut with strain, her eyes screwed shut.

"Relax," he said, his voice coming out in a strangled squawk.

Her eyes opened and he caught a flash of amusement in the grey-green depths before they closed again. "I'm . . . trying," she panted.

"Doing verra nicely," McAllister grunted.

At last the pangs ended and she loosed her grip. Myfanwy thrust a handkerchief wet with lavender water at Gareth. Gently he wiped Laura's face, marvelling at the peace he saw there after the pain, knowing the pain would come again. Myfanwy handed him a glass of water. His arm around her shoulders, he raised Laura a little to drink.

"That is enough," said Aunt Antonia firmly. "Out you go, now."

"Let him stay, Aunt," Laura said with a chuckle, "else he will only fret himself to flinders."

"Most improper!"

"I shan't look round, Aunt Antonia, I swear it. God knows, I don't wish to look round. I can help her. Can I not help you, Laura?"

"Yes," she said soothingly, "for I am afraid I might hold Myfanwy's hand too tight and hurt her."

Ye gods, she was soothing him! "No fear of hurting me," Gareth vowed. "Hold as hard as you can."

So she did, and he kept reminding her to relax until the moment came when McAllister, after consulting his colleagues, said as yet another pain began, "Noo, ma leddy, 'tis time to bear down. Push!"

The pushing phase seemed to Gareth to go on for ever. In between the scarlet-faced, concentrated efforts, Laura grew paler and quieter.

"Push!" ordered Dr. McAllister for the hundredth time.

"I cannot," she moaned. "I'm tired."

"Do something!" Gareth commanded, just catching himself in time as he started to turn to glare at the doctor. "Help her!"

"You help her, ma laird. Encourage her. The harder she pushes, the sooner 'twill be done, and we're nearly there noo. I'll no use the forceps wi'out the need."

Gareth leaned down and said in her ear, softly but urgently, "Push, Laura. You can do it. Not long now. Keep it up. You can do it, I know you can. Good girl, that's it. Don't flag now, we're nearly there."

"We?" she gasped as her fingernails bit into his hand.

Once, twice, thrice more she bore down, then McAllister barked, "Ye can stop. The babby's head is oot; the rest will follow."

Then Mistress Owen announced, "A girl it is, my lady." The sound of a sharp slap was followed by a thin wail.

"Let me see. Let me hold her." Laura was bright-eyed now, fatigue forgotten.

"Ye'll wait a wee bitty, ma leddy, while I cut the cord."

A moment later, the midwife came around the bed, the scrap of humanity squalling in her hands. "There's lusty," she said admiringly, pausing by Gareth.

He looked down. The child was hideous, with blotchy skin, a wizened body, its bald, oversized head misshapen, the nose squashed, the toothless mouth open to bawl its outrage at being reft from its safe haven. Not knowing what to say, Gareth touched one tiny, waving hand.

The babe clutched his finger with an extraordinary strength. He saw its minuscule fingernails, unbelievably perfect. It stopped crying, opened big blue eyes, and gazed at him.

"She's beautiful," he said, and he meant it.

Laura reached out both arms. "Let me have her."

With utmost care, Gareth disengaged his finger. The infant opened her mouth, took a deep breath, spluttered and coughed and started to wail again, turning bright pink.

"Just learning to breathe she is, look you," said Mistress Owen, and placed the child in Laura's arms.

At once the wails stopped as the baby turned her head to nuzzle her mother's breast. The wonder and love in Laura's face brought a lump to Gareth's throat. She too was beautiful, despite the dark shadows under her eyes, the lank, sweat-soaked hair.

"She is trying to suck," Laura said urgently. "I must feed her."

"A few minutes she can wait," the midwife advised. " 'Tis washed and wrapped up warm she needs to be."

"And there's the afterbirrth yet, ma leddy," Dr. McAllister advised her. "Ye've a wee bit more work tae do, but it willna take long."

"What is it now?" Gareth demanded as

the midwife whisked the baby away.

"Ye've no seen calves born, ma laird, nor foals?"

"Oh yes, of course." He felt downright bacon-brained.

"Just think of me as a cow or a mare," said Laura, laughing.

"Laura, my dear." Aunt Antonia came up, moving stiffly, her lined face sagging. She took Laura's hand. "I'm so sorry, I fell asleep and missed all the excitement. You have a fine, healthy daughter. Let me offer my congratulations." She bent down, steadying herself with one hand on the bed, and kissed Laura's forehead, then straightened with difficulty.

"Thank you, dear Aunt. You should not have waited up. Gareth will lend you his arm to your chamber now, will you not, Gareth?"

"Certainly. Come, Aunt Antonia. I shall be right back, Laura."

"I sent your maid to sleep, Laura," his aunt said, "so that she would be fresh when you need her. I believe I shall retire now. I am not as young as I used to be."

She leaned heavily on Gareth's arm, her pace painfully slow. She was usually so self-contained and competent, it was easy to forget she was an elderly lady, not up to a long night's watch. At her chamber door, he impulsively kissed her thin cheek, as he had not done since childhood.

"Thank you, dear Aunt, for your care of her. Goodnight, or rather, good morning."

Pink-faced, she bade him goodnight and hurried into her room.

He sped back to Laura's chamber. About to open the door, he hesitated, then knocked. Her abigail opened it, bare-footed, clad in a cotton wrap and nightcap, her hair in a long braid down her back. Gareth grinned as she curtsied.

"I woke up, my lord," she said with dignity, drawing her small frame up, "so to see how my lady does I came. You cannot come in now, it's nursing the babe she is."

If she was his wife, he could watch, he thought with a touch of wistfulness. But the child was not his, and he would never marry, never have the right to see that charming sight. Not that she was supposed to be suckling the babe herself, he recalled suddenly. He had hired a wet-nurse for that. Well, time enough to remind her in the morning.

"Tell Dr. McAllister I'd like a word," he said. "I'll wait in Lady Laura's sitting room."

The doctor came through a few minutes later, drying his hands on a towel. He looked tired, his fox-red hair standing on end. "The babbies ay arrive in the wee, sma' hours," he said, "or so it seems. 'Tis not many confinements I attend, mind, just the difficult ones. Lady Laura's was smooth sailing a' the way."

"She is well?"

"Aye, weary but happy. Nae mair bleeding than's usual, and there's little fear o' puerperal fever wi' the preecautions Mistress Owen and I tak as a matter o' course."

Puerperal fever? An alarmed question on the tip of his tongue, Gareth decided that too could wait until the morning — or more accurately later in the day. "What of the child?" he asked.

"A bonny wee lassie." McAllister's eyes twinkled. "Though I'll wager ye thought otherwise."

"At first," Gareth conceded.

"There's nae birth is easy for the babby, squeezed and pushed and thrust into the cauld, cauld worrld. Weel, if your lairdship will excuse me, I'll be off tae bed, for I've calls tae make in a few hours."

The porcelain clock on the mantelpiece showed five o'clock was past. Gareth went to the window and pulled aside the rose-patterned curtains. The sky was pale, and a pale mist wreathed across the park, curling

between the trees. He was not at all sleepy
— rather the reverse, bursting with energy
and in a mood to celebrate.

He went to wake his oblivious brothers.

Laura swam up from the depths of sleep.
She felt strange. Her hand went to her
stomach — flat as a flounder! She had had
the baby. She had a daughter, and her
daughter was crying.

Wide awake, she started to sit up.

The sound cut off as the door to her
sitting-room closed.

"No need to disturb yourself, my lady."
The lying-in nurse appeared at the bedside.
A sallow woman dressed in black, with her
grey hair pulled back so tightly beneath her
cap the sight of it was enough to make one's
head ache, she went on, "Mrs. Barley, the
nurse, is changing the child's napkin and
I've sent for the wet-nurse. She'll be here in
a moment to take it to the nursery and feed
it."

"Fiddlesticks, I shall feed her. And she is
not to be removed to the nursery."

The woman's mouth primmed in disapproval. "His lordship hired the wet-nurse
for you, my lady."

"Then his lordship will just have to unhire
her." She should have spoken sooner, she

knew, but she had put off the inevitable battle until it became unavoidable. It was inevitable. She had stayed at Llys because of Gareth's fears. Pride would not allow her to hang on his sleeve forever, as he seemed to assume. Soon she must leave, and she could not take the wet-nurse with her.

Besides, as soon as she held her baby in her arms, she knew she had no intention whatsoever of letting a stranger suckle her.

"Tell Mrs. Barley to bring her to me," Laura ordered. She would have to learn to take care of her daughter herself, but at the moment, she realized, she was tired and sore and feeling rather frail.

Time enough when she was up and about to sort matters out — and Gareth need not suppose she was going to lie abed for a month just because lying-in nurses were also known as monthly nurses. To have that disapproving witch frowning on her for four weeks was out of the question.

Her stiff back a reproof, the witch stalked through to the sitting room. Laura heard a murmur of voices, then the baby began to cry again.

Laura flung back the bedclothes, but as she swung her feet over the edge of the bed, a woman in blue bustled in with the child in her arms. Comfortably padded, Mrs.

Barley had round, rosy cheeks, and her greying hair was not scraped back but pinned up in a loose knot.

"You'll excuse me not wearing a cap, my lady," she said, her soft voice countrified but not Welsh. "Somehow babies always end up grabbing the ribbons and untying them. Hark at her bawling, the sweet little mite." She beamed down at her charge.

"She must be hungry. I am."

"Not that hungry, my lady, she just wants to suck a bit. Your milk won't come in proper for a day or two, so babies aren't made to need it for a while. You let her suck, though, she'll get what she needs from you, not from any wet-nurse."

Laura smiled at her, relieved to have an ally. Mrs. Barley helped her arrange herself so that both she and her daughter were comfortable, then plumped herself down on a chair.

"I were nurserymaid to his lordship and the Reverend," she said, "and nurse to Master Rupert and Master Lance and Master Perry. A proper handful they was, I can tell you. Her late ladyship put each one to her breast, delicate as she was, poor dear, and couldn't manage it more than a month or two. Still, it gave them a good start in life. Mrs. Forbes, now, she sent hers out to a wet-nurse all three, or so I heard. She weren't here at Llys then. And when she came, she brought her own nurse. A good enough body, but without the gumption to stand up to madam's crotchets."

Laura let the flow of words wash over her, her entire being concentrated on the tug at her nipple, the warm weight of her child in her arms. All the humiliations of those few nights of Freddie's fumbling embraces were vindicated by the tiny head at her breast.

Poor Freddie! His daughter had his fair hair, so fine her pink scalp showed through. She was not by any means so handsome as her father — despite Gareth's kind remark — but Myfanwy had warned Laura that the process of birth distorted a baby's features. In any case, Laura was by no means so certain as she had once been that she wanted her child to be beautiful.

She herself had suffered through not being beautiful, but Maria was beautiful and yet far from contented, still less happy.

For the first time, Laura wondered whether Ceci was happy with her heir to a dukedom. Their father had made it quite plain Laura was not to attempt to communicate with her sister, but Ceci was a married woman now, able to decide for herself. Though her husband might prevent a meeting, he could hardly control her correspondence. Perhaps Laura would write to notify her of the birth of her niece.

"She's asleep, bless her heart," Mrs. Barley's voice interrupted Laura's musing. "You'd best wake her, my lady, and let her have a go the other side to keep things even. She won't like it but she'll soon settle down again. Sleep's what she wants most now. Slept right through, good as gold, when his lordship brought his brothers to see her. Have you decided yet what she'll be christened?"

"Priscilla," Laura said at once, though she had not considered the question. She had once had a dearly loved rag doll called Priscilla, which had been taken away when it grew shabby. The wax and porcelain replacements were too fragile to be hugged or slept with.

Whatever else she lacked, her Priscilla should never lack for love and hugs and kisses.

On the third day, when Gareth went up to see Priscilla after luncheon (his third visit of the day), he was startled to find Laura in her sitting room, on the chaise longue by the window. She wore a dressing-gown, lavishly trimmed with lace, in Maria's favourite shade of blue — doubtless a cast-off. She must have new gowns for her new figure, he realised; in half-mourning colours, he thought with distaste, but at least not black.

The September sunlight gleamed on her dark head, bent over the babe in her arms, cooing. As he stopped on the threshold, she looked round and smiled.

He spoke softly. "I'm sorry, I ought to have have knocked — I didn't want to wake her and I didn't know you were here. You should be in bed."

"Balderdash! Do come in, Gareth. I have finished feeding her and she is wide awake for once."

"The wet-nurse is supposed to feed her." He crossed the room and looked down at Laura, frowning.

She shook her head, and the child, gazing intently into her face, blinked. "Don't stand towering and glowering over me," she said tartly. "Sit down, pray. I have been hoping for a chance to talk to you."

With a hollow feeling in his middle, Gareth pulled up a chair. Was she going to tell him she wanted to leave Llys? He suspected she had only stayed for his sake. Her cursed independent streak made it so difficult for her to accept what she saw as charity, though to him it was simply his duty.

It had started out as simply his duty, he corrected himself. Unlike his duty to Maria, it had become a pleasure. He could no longer imagine Llys without Laura.

"Now you are brooding." There was a question in her voice.

With a start, he realized he was still standing, his hand on the back of the chair. "I was just wondering," he said hesitantly, "do you think I might hold her? Just for a minute? Barleysugar wouldn't let me."

"Barleysugar?" Laura chuckled. "Is that what you called her when you were children?"

He grinned. "Barleycorn when she scolded. She doesn't believe in men handling infants, especially as I'm not Priscilla's papa, but may I?"

"You will be careful?"

"Of course!" Not through him would any harm come to the babe.

"You have to support her head. That's it. Barleysugar says she is not half so fragile as she appears, and so does Myfanwy, but I own to being a trifle apprehensive."

So did Gareth. His hands felt huge and clumsy, but as he felt with the back of his knees for the chair and cautiously sat down, Priscilla did not burst into tears. Her great

240

blue eyes stared up at him with a serious expression. She blew a bubble.

He fell in love.

Which was precisely what he ought to have made every effort to avoid. What a fool he was! She was not his daughter. He had no possible claim upon her. And he must never forget the row of tiny graves in the churchyard. To grow too attached to a newborn child was to court heartbreak.

CHAPTER 15

Laura knew the exact moment when Gareth lost his heart to Priscilla. The look on his face changed from solicitude to wonder to enchantment. His mouth curved in a slow smile, a beam of delight, and he said, apparently quite unconsciously, "Goo-goo, who's a pretty poppet, then?"

She had not foreseen his abject surrender to her daughter's charms. Her father had never visited the nursery. Even when his children reached years of discretion, Lord Medway had shown no interest in the girls. Cecilia's betrothal pleased him because it brought a connexion to an ancient, wealthy, and influential family. Laura's elopement displeased him because it brought only scandal. For their feelings he cared naught.

As for goo-gooing to a newborn baby, the very notion would have left the earl dumfounded.

Gareth's response to Priscilla made Laura esteem him the more, but left her as much dismayed as gratified. When the time came to leave Llys, his affection for her daughter would make her feel a brute to part them. She noticed he looked disconsolate now, as though foreseeing that moment. She must not let him grow too close.

"I shall take her now," she said quickly.

"Too late. She has my shirtfrill in an unbreakable grip and I believe she has dropped off to sleep. I should hate to disturb her." Gazing down at Priscilla, nestled in the crook of his arm, he sounded part smug, part rueful.

"She seems to like to hold onto something when she sleeps."

"Laura," Gareth said in sudden alarm, "her skin looks awfully yellow to me. Is she ill? Tell me my eyes deceive me!"

"She is a bit yellowish, but not ill. Dr. McAllister and Mrs. Barley and Myfanwy, who has dozens of brothers and sisters, all assure me it is a normal change soon after birth. It should clear up in a few days."

"Should?" he said with deep misgiving.

"Will. Dr. McAllister also says I shall

regain my strength far quicker if I don't lie abed. Mistress Owen agrees. Their poorer patients have no choice but to resume caring for their families, and they do none the worse for that. So the monthly nurses can go. Myfanwy is all the help I need."

"No." His sharp tone made Priscilla jerk, losing her grip on his frill. Apologetically he touched her hand and she grasped his finger instead, calming. He lowered his voice. "No, Laura, the nurses must stay. McAllister swears they know what to do in case of puerperal fever, or I'd not have let him return home."

"He comes in every day," Laura pointed out.

"But the fever can grow worse very fast and it can be . . . very serious."

The word "fatal" hovered between them, and Laura knew she was going to give in. "I loathe having those women always about me," she grumbled. "The witch is lurking in my chamber right now, listening at the door, no doubt."

"Oh, if that is all! They need not lurk about you, I daresay, as long as they are in the house, and you promise to call them the moment you feel the least bit unwell."

"Tyrant. Very well, I promise."

"And the wet-nurse — will you not let her

take over that chore for you?"

"Chore? It's a joy, not a chore, and better for Priscilla besides. But so that you do not think me horridly ungrateful, I will confess I am excessively glad to have Mrs. Barley to change her napkin and deal with her fussing in the middle of the night. All I have to do is feed her. I am truly grateful, Gareth, for all your care and . . ." Laura hesitated, her cheeks growing hot. Aunt Antonia had not failed to reiterate the shocking impropriety of allowing him into her chamber, especially at such a time. ". . . And for being with me when she was born."

"I still have the marks of your fingernails on my hand," he said with a grin, "but I'd not have missed it for the world. Er, speaking of napkins, I believe my sleeve is growing damp. I'd better ring for Mrs. Barley."

"Heavens no." She swung her feet off the chaise. "She is sleeping to make up for her disturbed nights. I shall change Pris."

"That's what I hired a nurse for."

Laura looked him in the eye and said determinedly, "I have to learn to take care of her myself."

His stricken expression told her he guessed her reason, and already dreaded being parted from the child. How could she convince him her self-respect gave her no choice but to return to Swaffham Bulbeck? For his sake, the sooner she left the better, but all her advisers — even Dr. McAllister who had no stake in the matter — agreed on the imprudence of a long journey with a small baby.

"Definitely damp," Gareth announced, apparently as willing as Laura to defer argument on that subject.

Or perhaps she had completely misread his feelings, she thought as he handed over Priscilla, waking and beginning to whimper. Perhaps he had no desire to prevent their departure once she had regained her strength and her daughter was sturdy enough to travel. No longer pregnant, she was no longer a focus for his fears, nor could he wish for the responsibility of another child not his own.

Yet he had fetched her to Llys in ignorance of her pregnancy. His sense of duty to his family was powerful, and though Laura was not a blood relation, Priscilla was his own cousin's child. Of all the family, he had never utterly cast off poor Freddie. Gareth and Rupert, tolerant as they were generous, had lent Freddie money without any real expectation of being paid back.

Even if Gareth had not succumbed to Priscilla, he would never let Freddie's widow leave Llys without protest. He was nobly postponing his arguments because of her weakness. How she loved him!

Priscilla, her little bottom clean and dry and well powdered, fell asleep again before Laura finished tying the tapes. As Laura tucked her up in the beautifully carved cradle brought down from the nursery, someone knocked on the door. Gareth went to answer it.

"It's my turn, Gareth." Perry's hushed voice was indignant. "It's not fair, you'll be able to see Pris any time when I have to go back to school."

"She's asleep, and Cousin Laura is here."

"Come in, Perry," said Laura. "You will not disturb her if you are quiet."

"May I rock the cradle, Cousin Laura?" Perry asked eagerly. "Barleysugar let me. Oh, I'm glad you're well enough to be up," he added at a minatory glance from his eldest brother.

She smiled at him. "Thank you. Yes, you may rock her."

"I'd better go," said Gareth. "We have been taking turns to come and admire your daughter so as not to overwhelm her."

"Not to mention that you wish to change your coat," Laura teased.

"That too. Will you take exception if I suggest you return to the chaise?"

"I should strongly object — but that I'm quite ready to sit down."

At the door, Gareth looked back. Perry was on his knees beside the cradle, his freckled face a mirror of awe and adoration. Gareth blenched as he recognized himself in the half-grown lad bending over the cradle which had sheltered Wyckham babes for centuries.

Stepping blindly out into the passage, he pulled the door to behind him and leaned against it, his eyes closed. When Mama died, he had found some comfort in his desolation in the infant she left behind. He had hovered over the cradle, begged to hold his baby sister, given his heart into her tiny hands, then watched as she sickened and grew pale and wan — and followed her mother to the graveyard.

He could not let Perry suffer as he had suffered then. He had to warn him.

Perry came to him in the library later. "Lance said you wanted to see me. Is it about Arabella tearing her new frock? Her nurse was mad as a wet hen, but Miss Coltart says it's good for her to run about with the boys. She'll have all the time in the world to worry about ladylike decorum when she grows up. I'll pay to replace the frock out of my allowance if it's really too badly ripped to mend."

"Lord, no, I hadn't even heard about the frock, though you might make sure she's not wearing a new one when you take her out with the boys."

"I will," his brother promised with an ingenuous grin. "What is it, then?"

"Sit down, Perry," Gareth said soberly.

Perry sat, obviously running through in his mind all his recent peccadilloes and wondering which had come to Gareth's ears, and which were worthy of a serious raking over the coals. Meanwhile Gareth ran through all the possible openings he had thought of, but there was no easy way to approach the subject.

"You have been spending a lot of time with Priscilla," he began.

"I don't disturb her, truly. If she's asleep, I just rock her. When she's awake she . . . she seems to quite like me," he said modestly.

"And you like her."

"Oh yes, of course. That is, I like George and Henry and Arabella, but Pris is special. Maybe it's because she's so tiny and new, one can't help wanting to take care of her."

"Tiny and new and fragile."

"I know, you don't have to tell me. I'm

always as gentle as can be with her. Why, I don't even scuffle with Arabella as I do with the boys."

"My dear chap, you are very good with the children and I have no doubt of your gentleness. What I mean is — and don't repeat this to Cousin Laura — small babies don't yet have a very firm grasp on life. The slightest indisposition can carry them off."

Perry's freckles stood out on his suddenly white face. "You mean Priscilla is going to die?"

"Good Lord no! I wouldn't even go so far as to say she is likely to die. Certainly she will lack for nothing I can provide to prevent it," Gareth declared, hating himself for bringing that stricken look to the boy's eyes. "Yet it's best to recognize that babies are fragile creatures, and not to let oneself grow too fond lest . . . lest they should be taken."

"I see." Perry stared down at his hands, clenched in his lap, then raised his head and said simply, "But one cannot choose whom to love. Thank you for warning me, Gareth, only it doesn't make any difference, you see."

As Perry went off, subdued and still pale, Gareth hoped he had at least spared the lad a shock if not the pain should anything happen to Priscilla.

If anything, Perry spent more time than ever with the child during the next ten days. Gareth sympathized, since he himself found it difficult to tear himself away from Priscilla, who appeared to flourish on all the attention. She went through her christening without a murmur.

Nonetheless Gareth was glad when, the next day, his youngest brother returned to school where friends, lessons, and sports would turn his thoughts elsewhere. At the same time, Lance returned to Oxford and Rupert to his regiment. Tranquillity descended upon the manor — or dullness, depending on one's point of view of the moment.

Actually, Gareth missed his brothers less than usual. With Maria beyond reach, unable to interfere, he took much more interest in his niece and nephews than had seemed wise before.

The boys scarcely seemed to miss their mother. Arabella had at first, but she was fascinated by the baby. She sang songs to her, and drew dozens of pictures in coloured chalks for her, of which Laura pinned up the best on the walls of her sitting room, now transformed into a nursery. Gareth thought the little girl regarded Priscilla rather as a particularly marvellous doll. She was too young, he hoped, to be badly upset if the worst came to the worst.

But Priscilla continued to thrive, as did Laura, and Gareth's fears began to calm.

A period of heavy rains ended in what the Shropshire folk called St. Luke's little summer. Gareth rode out on Fickle every day to oversee the apple harvest and ploughing and planting of winter wheat. Coming home at midday he often found Laura strolling in the gardens with the babe in her arms, sometimes alone, sometimes with Aunt Antonia or Cornelius or the children. At first Gareth protested at her taking Priscilla outside — it was October, after all, however fine. However, she would no more allow him to wrap her daughter in cotton-wool than herself.

One day Uncle Julius was with her in the rose garden, where a few late blooms lingered. Ever since St. Wigbert's Day the old man had been working on the mechanization of his tray-lifter, a slow business as each cogwheel had to be forged. Now, as he stood contemplating Laura with Priscilla in her arms, his eyes were bright behind the blurred spectacles. Not the charm of the scene, Gareth guessed, but a new inspiration.

"What is it, Uncle?" he asked. "Thought lies heavy on your brow."

"No, no, nevvie," said Uncle Julius, "it must be light, d'you see, or she'll have to have a footman along. Wicker? Wicker!" And he scampered off.

"Is he reinventing the basket?" Gareth enquired of Laura, beaming at Priscilla as she smiled and gurgled at him.

Laura's smile was effortful. "No, he is going to make a baby-barrow so that I can push Priscilla when she grows heavier. I hope it will work better than his tray-barrow."

"Lord, yes! We cannot risk her in whatever contrivance he comes up with. I shall dissuade him."

"Don't do that. He would be so disappointed not to be allowed to help, and we can always try it with one of Arabella's dolls or a sack of flour first."

"Then if not that, what is troubling you?"

"Nothing. I am just a little tired, I suppose, and I have the headache. Not a bad one, truly."

"Are you eating enough? Getting enough sleep? I knew I should not have let the monthly nurses go. I'll send for McAllister."

"I don't need a doctor," she snapped. "Do stop fussing, Gareth, and leave me alone."

"I'm sorry," he said stiffly. "I didn't mean to vex you. I shall see you at luncheon."

Laura turned away. "I'm not hungry."

Chagrined, he went into the house. By the time he had washed his hands and joined his aunt in the breakfast room, worry had replaced chagrin.

"Laura said she is not hungry, Aunt Antonia. She's not her usual cheerful self. She rapped my knuckles when I suggested sending for McAllister but perhaps I ought to anyway?"

"Quite unnecessary," his aunt assured him. "Many women go through a period of despondency soon after a child's birth, when they feel out of sorts and everything is wrong with the world. It rarely becomes a serious disturbance. What she needs is sympathy and comfort and reassurance."

"The devil!"

"Gareth!" Aunt Antonia drew herself up ramrod straight, pursing her lips with a frown of censure.

"I do beg your pardon, ma'am." Pushing his chair away from the table he stood up, a sick sensation rapidly destroying his appetite. "Instead of comforting Laura, I took offence when she spoke sharply and I fear I've made her more unhappy, not less. I must go to her. Excuse me, if you please."

Laura was no longer in the rose garden. Gareth went up to her apartments, only to be told she had just lain down on her bed for a nap.

Myfanwy gave him a shrewd look. "No cause to be all of a fidget, my lord. The megrims my lady has, that's all. There's better she'll feel after a rest."

"But she must eat to be able to feed Priscilla. I shall send up a tray. Tell her I beg her to eat, for the babe's sake."

With his own hands he prepared a tray, buttering a roll, peeling and slicing an apple, cutting slivers of ham so thin they would be no trouble at all to eat. Adding a dish of her favourite junket flavoured with bramble jelly, he sent a footman up with it.

He would have liked to stay at home until Laura emerged from her chamber, but he and his steward had an appointment with a drover to discuss the sale of fat lambs. The man was coming from Worcester to look over the flock and could not be put off. Gareth had to leave without even knowing whether Laura had eaten.

Worse, as he swung up into Fickle's saddle, he suddenly wondered whether she would consider the carefully chosen tray of food as a peace offering or as another attempt to coerce her.

■ ■ ■ ■

When Myfanwy set down the tray on the bedside table and told Laura his lordship begged her to eat for the babe's sake, she burst into tears. How dreadfully selfish Gareth must consider her to risk depriving her daughter of proper nourishment! No doubt he thought she did not love Priscilla half as well as he did. She was an utterly incompetent mother; she should have left the baby's care to Mrs. Barley and the wet-nurse.

Though she had no appetite whatsoever, she sat up in bed and let Myfanwy place the tray on her knees. She regarded the food with loathing.

"His lordship prepared it himself, look you," Myfanwy said encouragingly. "All cut up small, nice and easy to eat."

Laura cried the harder. He had forgiven her for snarling at him. He was the kindest man in the world and she was an ungrateful wretch for wanting not kindness but love. She simply could not bear to go on living at Llys. She had to go away, to leave Myfanwy and Aunt Antonia and dear, stuffy Cornelius and the children. She would never know how Uncle Julius's baby-barrow turned out. She would never see Rupert or

Lance or Perry again. Gareth might visit her in Swaffham Bulbeck, and she'd have to face his hurt at her having removed Priscilla from his house.

Or maybe he would not visit. Maybe he would be too hurt, too offended to want to see her, even for Priscilla's sake. She did not want to hurt him!

The only thing worse than a bleak future without him was an agonizing future with him always nearby but never close enough. All life held for her was a struggle to do her inadequate best for the beloved child of an unloved and unloving father. Poor little girl, growing up with no papa and a useless mama.

"Only one hankercher you have left, my lady, till I wash some. Do try to eat a morsel," Myfanwy coaxed. "There's better you'll feel for a bite and a bit of a sleep."

"I'll try," Laura sniffed, mopping her eyes.

She forced herself to nibble a piece of the roll and to swallow a morsel of ham and a slice or two of apple. The junket went down easily, though somehow it did not taste as good as usual. Before she finished it, from the sitting room came Priscilla's preliminary whimper, followed by a full-throated bawl. Wearily Laura pushed aside the tray and turned back the bedcovers.

"Stay there," ordered her maid.

"I told Mrs. Barley I'd take care of her all day."

"There's none the worse she'll be if I change her for once, my lady, so's you can stay in bed to nurse her afore you lie down to take your nap."

Laura listlessly agreed. Priscilla fussed over her feeding, confirming Laura's belief that she was an incompetent mother. She shed a few more tears, using up the last handkerchief, and then fell into an exhausted sleep.

She awoke feeling mopish but not quite so desperate. If she stayed in bed glooming, which was her first instinct, Gareth would be certain she was ill. The ensuing commotion would only make her feel worse, so she rang for Myfanwy and dragged herself out of bed.

The maid arrived with a pile of clean, pressed handkerchiefs. "Borrowed from Miss Burleigh," she said, "just in case."

Laura's nose and eyes were still red from her earlier bout of crying. Looking so haggish, she could not face anyone, but now she was too restless to sit about in her rooms.

"I shall walk in the shrubbery," she decided, donning an aged black-dyed stuff gown. Priscilla was so sound asleep she hesitated to wake her, but Myfanwy offered to watch her. "If I don't have her to carry," Laura said, "I believe I shall venture as far as Ash Hill."

"Likely exercise'll blow the cobwebs away, my lady, but wrap up warm. The sun's gone in, look you. Rain before morning there'll be."

As Laura tramped across the park, the gusty west wind did begin to blow away the cobwebs enveloping her mind. She took off her black bonnet to facilitate the process. She had always loved windy autumn days, with leaves swirling down from the trees.

No wonder she had been down in the dumps, confined for so long to the house and its near environs when she was used to long country walks. Now she was fit again, she must take advantage of Mrs. Barley's presence to exercise properly. All too soon she would have to manage without that help.

The thought cast her straight back into the dismals again. Trudging up Ash Hill, she tried to cheer herself by recalling and anticipating the glorious view from the top, but what came to mind was her confession to Gareth that she did not miss Freddie. Gareth had been as kind as ever, but he must have been disgusted by her unnatural lack of grieving.

How could he ever love such a freakish, ramshackle female? What a dreadful mess she had made of her life!

CHAPTER 16

"Ash Hill!" Gareth exploded.

"Yes, my lord." Lloyd did not turn a hair. "Myfanwy did not attempt to dissuade her, being of the opinion that a good walk'd do her ladyship good. Were her ladyship not to return after a reasonable period, I should of course send out a groom."

"No need, I shall go," said Gareth, calming down. After all, what did he know of female post-childbirth megrims? Less than the little abigail, certainly. And, though steep, Ash Hill was no precipice off which Laura might throw herself.

Nonetheless, striding out to the stables he yelled for a groom to resaddle Fickle and he galloped across the park.

He tied the bay gelding to the same elder bush — now leafless, its berries stripped by the birds — as last time he had found Laura here. No doubt his anxiety was equally futile today. At least he could carry Priscilla back for her, he thought. Perhaps Uncle Julius's baby-barrow idea was not so addlepated as he had assumed.

Gazing up the hill, he could not see her. She must be sitting down. Exhausted? Or just sensibly recruiting her strength before the walk back to the house. As he started up the slope, he vowed to himself not to fret her with his concern. She needed sympathy and comfort, not remonstrance.

She sat on the bench at the rear of the pavilion, shoulders slumped, staring with blank despondency at her hands in her lap. Her empty hands . . .

Gareth glanced around. "Where is Priscilla? Did you not bring her? She is not ill, is she?"

To his horror, Laura burst into tears. As he approached, cursing himself, she jumped up and moved away, to stand with her back to him. "I kn-now you think I'm an ut-utter failure as a mother," she sobbed, "but even I am not so s-selfish as to leave my baby if she was i-i-ill."

"I think you a bad mother?" he said in astonishment. His hands on her shoulders, he turned her to face him, then enveloped her in his arms so that she was crying on his chest.

"Y-you said —"

"I spoke without thinking," Gareth said ruefully, his cheek against her soft, fragrant hair. "Which I seem to do altogether too often to you, though I trust not to others. You are the most devoted, loving mother imaginable. Little Pris is thriving under your care. Why, Barleysugar says she has never known a happier baby — I and my brothers, I collect, were a fretful lot!"

Laura raised her head and gave him a tremulous smile. He was shocked to discover he desperately wanted to kiss those quivering lips, and the tearstained eyes. She fitted quite perfectly into his arms, her supple slenderness intoxicating.

He wanted her.

Dismayed, afraid she might perceive his arousal, for she was no naïve girl, he released her and stepped back. His hand on her arm he led her back to the bench, trying hard to concentrate on what she was saying with such adorable earnestness.

"But Priscilla has been fretful recently. She seems to know when I'm feeling crossgrained and out of spirits, and it makes her the same."

"Then the solution is obvious: we can cure her by curing you." He sat down leaving a careful two feet between them, and fought down the temptation to hold her hand. "Even the best of mothers must wish for a change of company. Should you like a din-

261

ner party?"

"Oh yes!"

"That will not only serve as notice to our neighbours that you are ready to receive callers, it will be an excuse for a new gown. Indeed, I have been meaning for weeks to point out that you need a new wardrobe since . . ." He hastily turned his eyes away from her delectably full bosom and slim waist. "Since your shape has altered."

"My old gowns from last winter still fit well enough."

"But they are all black and it is past time you went into half-mourning. Come now, we have had this argument before. You must do me credit or you will ruin my reputation."

"Maria is no longer here to slander you," she pointed out with a smile, a proper one. Why had he never noticed before what an enchanting smile she had, especially when she was teasing?

"New gowns, no argument," he said firmly. "I'm quite certain black is detrimental to babies. Since you cannot leave Priscilla for long enough to go into Ludlow, I shall send for the draper." He glanced with disfavour at the black bonnet on the seat beside her. "And the milliner."

"That is new," Laura objected. "I bought

it last time you coerced me into accepting new clothes."

"I don't like it. Whoever heard of black roses?"

She laughed. "Oh very well. But I should like to go to Ludlow, taking Priscilla along. It is not so far, after all, and your carriage is very comfortable. I daresay she would come to no harm on such a short journey. I shall ask Mrs. Barley."

Gareth managed to limit his protest to a mild, "As long as Barleysugar is quite sure it is safe, my carriage is at your disposal. You would take her with you, of course, to look after the child at the Feathers while you shop."

His real fear, he realized, was not for Laura's or Priscilla's safety. It was that she would find travelling with the baby unexpectedly easy. What would he do if she announced she wanted to leave Llys?

He needed to be alone to think. "Shall we start back?" he suggested. "It grows dark early at this season, especially with a cloudy sky."

"Rain before morning, Myfanwy prophesied, which I suppose means postponing Ludlow." Laura pouted, but her eyes twinkled. At least he had succeeded in raising her spirits.

On the way back across the park, leading Fickle, he entertained her with a description of the drover's visit. His head shepherd, fiercely proud of the excellence of his lambs, spouted a paean in their praise — in Welsh. His steward was more concerned with wringing the highest possible price out of the drover, who was naturally determined to pay the lowest possible price.

Laura was amused by the tale, but she also asked several very sensible questions. Gareth had never before talked to her about the estate, not seriously, no more than a casual mention of how he had spent his day. In his experience, ladies were not interested in farm work or the latest ideas in agriculture. Laura's intelligent curiosity and her close attention to his answers took him by surprise.

Somehow he had never before seen her as a person in her own right. First she had been Freddie's impoverished widow, then a mother-to-be, with all that implied to him, and most recently simply Priscilla's mother. He had a great deal to think about.

Leaving her at the front door, he took the patient gelding around to the stables, then went up to his dressing room. Instead of ringing for his valet to bring hot water and help him change out of his riding clothes, he sat down, stretched out his legs, and un-seeingly contemplated the muddy toes of his boots.

So he desired Laura. In itself that pre-sented no difficulty. Accustomed to celibacy while at Llys, he visited London often enough to satisfy his baser instincts with the fair Paphians who there abounded.

The trouble was, he was beginning to suspect he loved Laura.

He rolled the notion around in his mind, recalling the months since he brought her to Llys. His sense of responsibility as head of her dead husband's family had soon changed to liking and admiration, not to mention gratitude for her help with Maria. He had been vastly pleased when Laura made friends with all his brothers, and even with Aunt Antonia. Had his compulsive care of her during her pregnancy been driven less by fear of the burden of guilt if she died than by the simple fear of losing her?

Love had quietly grown in his heart until, enlightened by a flare of desire, he recog-nized it.

Love and desire: the obvious answer was marriage. But if she was his wife, he'd never be able to keep from her bed. All too soon the terror would begin again, ten times worse because this time he knew he loved her — and her pregnancy would be his fault.

His father's anguished face rose before him. No, he would never marry.

When Gareth left for London in spite of persistent foul weather, though he claimed he went on business, Laura knew it was her fault. The driving rain had forced postponement of the trip to Ludlow and the dinner party and sunk her once more in gloom. She was growing as spoilt as Maria, falling into the vapours at the least sign of her plans being crossed.

She knew it was absurd to be overset by such a petty matter. The truth was, she had looked forward to the outing and the party to distract her from her woes. The delay simply gave her time to brood, but she could not tell Gareth so, because he was the object of her brooding.

When he took her in his arms in the pavilion atop Ash Hill, for a glorious moment she had hoped that he loved her. But his sole concern had been to cheer her for Priscilla's sake. He had succeeded in reassuring her that she was a good mother, while confirming that to him she was no more than a good mother to the baby he adored. Why had she ever dared hope he might see her as a desirable woman, when

Freddie had made it perfectly obvious she was not?

The leaden clouds swept in over the Welsh mountains in an endless procession, and it went on raining.

Aunt Antonia suffered a painful attack of rheumatism and unwillingly took to her bed. When her favoured James's Powders did not help, Laura insisted on sending a groom through mud and flood for Dr. McAllister. Through mud and flood the good doctor came. He prescribed hot fomentations applied to the joints, and a decoction of willow bark.

Though much eased, the old lady was quite relieved to delegate some of her household duties. Laura welcomed the distraction.

Two days after Dr. McAllister's visit, a watery gleam of sunshine fought its way between the clouds. After her daily consultation with Mrs. Lloyd, Laura took the baby out onto the terrace for a breath of fresh air.

Priscilla was less easy to carry now, for she took an interest in everything she saw. A blackbird alighting on the stone balustrade elicited gurgles of delight and much waving of arms and legs. So Laura was definitely intrigued when Uncle Julius emerged from the Long Gallery pushing a sort of basket on wheels.

"My dear young lady, your push-cradle," he announced proudly. "It has rolled along quite smoothly all the way from the workshop. Except for the steps, of course, but as you just saw as I came out, it is possible to traverse a step or two without great difficulty."

"What a splendid invention," said Laura.

The old gentleman tried to look modest. "Do you think so? I have put a cushion inside for comfort, you see, and the hood will keep the sun out of the infant's eyes. Dear me, is this the child?" He leaned closer to peer. Priscilla gave him a big smile and hit him on the nose.

Laura apologized as he jerked back with a startled blink.

"No, no, no damage done. She has grown considerably, has she not? I must have taken longer to make the push-cradle than I intended. I had to learn basket-weaving as I had never tried before. She will be walking soon, I daresay," he added sadly.

"Not for ages yet," Laura assured him. "And even then, she will not walk far at first. The push-cradle will be very useful. Only, I promised Cousin Gareth to try it out with some sort of weight before I put

Priscilla in."

"Cautious chap, my nevvie. I shall find something."

He trotted off, to return a moment later with the mahogany weather-glass from the Long Gallery. Before Laura thought of a tactful way to say she doubted Gareth would be pleased if his weather-glass came to grief, Uncle Julius had stuffed it into the basket and trundled away across the terrace. Gazing after him, Priscilla cooed with joy, arms and legs windmilling.

When he returned, triumphant, and removed the weather-glass, now stuck at Stormy, Laura gingerly substituted her baby. Priscilla appeared to approve, staring up with wonder at the hood, so Laura pushed her to the other end of the terrace. Nothing tipped over, nothing collapsed. She turned back, to see Uncle Julius lost in contemplation of the weather-glass in his hands.

Knowing better than to disturb him to thank him — he probably would not even hear her — she continued to push Priscilla about. In no time the baby was asleep.

With the push-cradle close beside her, Laura stood at the balustrade, looking out towards the mountains where a patch of pale blue sky contradicted the weather-glass's threat. A movement caught her eye. Someone was coming up the steps from the English garden, a hatless figure, male, moving with a heavy weariness obvious from a distance.

He was half way across the upper garden, and she was about to take Priscilla into the house and send a footman to deal with the tramp, when she recognized Perry. His hair was plastered to his head, his face wan, smudged with dirt, his clothes sodden and filthy. He plodded along the gravel path as if on the point of exhaustion. But when he raised his head and saw Laura, he broke into a stumbling run.

She hurried to the gap in the balustrade and two steps down to the path. "Perry, what on earth — ?"

"Is she ill?" he gasped urgently. "She's not dead, is she? I haven't come too late?"

"My dear boy, your aunt is in some discomfort but not in any danger of dying."

"Not Aunt Antonia. Pris. Little Pris."

"Priscilla is as sound as a bell." Laura caught his arm as he tottered. "Sit down and put your head between your knees. That's it. Uncle Julius!" Her hand on Perry's slumped shoulder, she turned her head. Uncle Julius and the weather-glass had disappeared.

"But where is she?" Perry choked out through sobs. "Why isn't she with you, Cousin Laura?"

"She is. Just a moment. No, don't try to get up." Wheeling the push-cradle over, Laura took Priscilla out and sat down beside Perry on the step. For a moment the baby protested sleepily, then she caught sight of Perry. She waved her arms and chortled, her mouth open in a toothless beam. "You see?" said Laura. "She is very well, and very happy to see you."

Wordless, he reached out, then noticed the colour of his hands and quickly withdrew them. With one he brushed away tears, smearing the streaks down his cheeks and adding another layer of dirt.

"Which first," Laura asked, "a bath or a meal?" Now was not the time for more searching questions.

Perry managed a shaky grin. "A bath. This muck is because I only had enough of the ready to take the stage to Kidderminster so I had to walk most of the rest of the way, apart from a few miles in a farm wagon. I haven't eaten more than a crust in two days, but Aunt Antonia would rake me over the coals if I came to table like this. She'll have my guts for garters anyway, sooner or later," he went on gloomily, "if Gareth doesn't first. Oh, but you said she is ill? I'm sorry, I ought to have asked after her."

"She is abed with an attack of rheumatics."

"Don't tell her I am here," he begged, "nor Cornie. I'll have to give my head to Gareth for washing but —"

"It needs washing long before Gareth sees it," Laura said with a smile. "He is in London. I shall have to send for him, you know," she added gently as his face brightened.

"I suppose so. I'm really in the suds, aren't I? Lord knows what old Woffle's going to say — our headmaster. You see, Gareth wrote to me every week with news of Priscilla, so when a letter didn't come I thought . . . I thought she must be ill and he didn't want to worry me. It must have been because he was on the way to Town. I've made a real bumble-broth of it, haven't I?" He sank his head in his hands.

Laura put her arm around his shoulders. "Gareth will sort it out," she said comfortingly. "He will understand."

"Gareth's a great gun, isn't he? One couldn't ask for a better brother. I wish you had married him instead of Cousin Freddie."

So do I! Laura cried silently. *So do I, but*

272

when I met him he did not even notice me.

While Perry bathed, Laura wrote a quick letter to Gareth. A groom was sent off with instructions to ride straight through to London, pausing only to hire himself fresh mounts as needed.

Gareth reached Llys late on the third day. Laura, already in her nightdress and dressing-gown, had just fed Priscilla and was playing with her when he tapped on the door and in answer to her call came in. He was in riding clothes and looked deathly tired.

"Sit down," she said at once. "When did you last eat?"

"Midday." He reached for Priscilla. Laura put the baby in his arms and went to ring the bell to order a tray of food for him.

"You have not seen Perry yet?"

"No, that can best wait till morning. I want all you can tell me first." He gave her a wry grin. "Your letter was written in haste and therefore minimally informative. You should have heard the tale I spun to old Woffle about a family emergency."

"I take it 'old Woffle' was your headmaster, too. You came home via Rugby?"

"It seemed wisest to conciliate him in person. I daresay Perry will get six of the best for leaving without permission —"

"You mean he will be beaten?"

"He won't care for that, I promise you. You may be sure I shan't let him get away so easily. At least he will not be expelled, and no doubt he'll make a fine tale of it for his friends. It wouldn't do to tell them his real reason for decamping: He thought Priscilla was ill?" Gareth's voice rose in a question.

"You had been writing regularly with news of her, I gather, so when a letter did not arrive at the usual time, he feared the worst."

Gareth groaned. "I was on my way to Town on the day I usually wrote, and when I arrived it slipped my mind."

"Quite excusable," Laura soothed him, "and no lasting harm done. Indeed he now looks back on his travels as an adventure."

Her account of Perry's odyssey was interrupted by the arrival of the supper tray. At her command he started to eat while she changed Priscilla's napkin and put her to bed in the old cradle as she continued Perry's story.

"He was in a dreadful state when he arrived," she concluded, rocking the cradle. "Both physical and mental. I must admit I cannot quite understand why he was so desperate."

"My fault again." Gareth pushed away the tray, his supper half eaten. Bowing his head, he covered his face with his hands. "All my fault."

Laura's need to comfort him took the form of an overwhelming desire to stroke the back of his head. With a struggle, she confined herself to words. "You could not know that a missed letter would affect him so drastically."

"I might have guessed. I warned him that new babies are fragile creatures and it's wisest not to let oneself grow too attached."

"It did not work," said Laura, disturbed. "Perry dotes on Priscilla."

"I just wanted to preserve him from what I went through when. . . . I did not tell you, that day at Ludlow Castle. I didn't want to make you afraid for your own baby. But when Mama died, she left us a baby sister, and I . . . I suppose I turned to her for solace. I adored her."

"And she died."

He nodded, wordless. Laura's heart was too full for speech.

After a moment's silence, Gareth came to kneel beside the cradle, gazing down at Priscilla. In her sleep, she blew a bubble and smiled.

He broke the silence with a hollow laugh.

"Perry did not heed my warning," he said, "but neither did I. I confess, I adore her."

CHAPTER 17

Perry returned to school with a promise from Laura to notify him at once if Priscilla so much as sniffled. She didn't. She was the healthiest baby Mrs. Barley had ever seen, the nurse vowed.

A conspiracy between Laura, Gareth, and the sympathetic servants kept Perry's unauthorized visit from Aunt Antonia and Cornelius. Even George, Henry, and Arabella were sworn to secrecy. Uncle Julius was left out of the plot as Gareth considered it highly unlikely he had the least idea which of his nephews he had seen.

Gareth had mixed feelings about his uncle at present: he admired the push-cradle, but the weather-glass remained stuck at Stormy despite sunshine and heavy frosts.

Aunt Antonia took a turn for the better and left her bed. Laura knew she ought to be making plans for her return to Swaffham Bulbeck, but somehow the days slipped by. She could not leave before the boys came home for Christmas, she told herself. It would not be fair to them, especially Perry. Besides, they would all bring friends to add to those Gareth had already invited, and Aunt Antonia, still infirm, would need her help, especially with the Twelfth Night party.

Twelfth Night was second only to St. Wigbert's Day in the Llys calendar. The season precluding outdoor festivities, a supper and dance were held for servants and tenants in the Home Farm barn, for guests and neighbours in the Great Hall and Long Gallery. So that no servant need miss the party, the gentry's supper had to be set out beforehand for people to help themselves. It all took a great deal of organizing.

Laura was glad to hear that Lady Frobisher never attended since such informality did not suit her notions of consequence.

Rupert came home on leave, then Lance, then Perry. Their friends were all male, of course, but Gareth had somewhat redressed the balance by inviting three married friends with their wives and children.

Once again the manor was filled with noise and bustle. Holly and fir boughs sprouted from every wall-sconce, picture-frame, beam, and banister. The children, every age from two to twelve, practised Christmas carols. The kitchens smelled deliciously of cinnamon and ginger and orange peel.

With several new gowns — lilac and

willow green and pearl grey — to lend her confidence, Laura enjoyed the company, particularly that of the three married ladies. If not unaware of her scandalous history, they kindly refrained from mentioning it. In fact, they tended to treat her as their hostess, and several times she had to refer them to Aunt Antonia, whose position she had no intention of usurping.

Priscilla, now three months old, loved all the people and activity about her. She slept through the night and stayed awake most of the day now, apart from a long nap morning and afternoon, but when Laura was busy there was always someone ready and willing to entertain her. In spite of his friends' teasing, Perry often offered to play with her or hold her; and in spite of his duties as host, Gareth managed every evening to dress for dinner in time to amuse her after her feeding while Laura changed.

Christmas Day was a delight to Laura, from carols in church in the morning to a last uproarious game of charades before the ladies retired to bed. The Christmases she recalled from before her marriage had been schoolroom affairs kept strictly separate from her parents' house-parties. The last two years she had been allowed to join the adults, only to find their diversions so ruled by formal etiquette that she would rather have been back in the nursery. At Llys Manor, the children were part of the celebrations, and the grown-ups had almost as much fun.

She expected the same pleasure from the Twelfth Night party. The first hint that she had set her sights too high came after breakfast, when Perry stopped her on her way to the housekeeper's room and begged her to save the first dance for him.

"Oh no, Perry," she exclaimed.

"I may be young but I can dance, you know," he said, sounding injured. "At least, I've had a few lessons, even if I've not tried it in public. Actually, I was thinking, I wouldn't mind making a cake of myself with you, and then if I wasn't too dreadfully bad I could ask some of the others. But if you think I shall embarrass you —"

"My dear, you've forgotten I am still in mourning. I shan't stand up at all tonight."

Laura was slightly surprised to feel a pang of regret. She had hated balls during her Season, always feeling that her partner of the moment would rather be with her sister. In fact, they had almost always talked to her about Ceci, which did not make for an enjoyable dance. Then on St. Wigbert's Day, she had been not only in mourning but far too pregnant to wish to cavort about.

Now, among friends, she would have liked to take to the dance floor, and the only reason she could not was Freddie's stupidity in breaking his neck. On the other hand, had he not, she would never have come to Llys. Poor Freddie! Her feelings towards him were as ambivalent in death as they had ever been in life.

"Cheer up, Cousin Laura." It was Lance. "Is this puppy trying to bag the first set? You need not feel obliged to let him prance about the floor with you. If you will do me the honour, you and I will cut an elegant figure and show him how it should be done."

"Puppy!" said Perry, without heat. He was used to his brother's friendly insults. "I'd rather be a puppy than a popinjay, at all events. Why should Cousin Laura want to stand up with a man-milliner?"

"Boys! I was just reminding Perry, Lance, that I cannot dance because of being in mourning."

"Oh, shame!"

"What's a shame?" Now Rupert joined them.

"We both wanted to dance with Cousin Laura tonight," Perry explained.

"Stands to reason she don't want to stand

up with a couple of young scrubs." Rupert preened his moustache. "It's a scarlet coat all the ladies fancy. Beg the pleasure of the first dance, Cousin."

"You are old enough to know better, Rupert," Laura snapped, and flounced away, leaving the young officer staring after her, to be enlightened by his brothers.

Later she apologized to him. With his usual good-nature, he apologized in return. "You're quite right, I should have realized what's what," he said, then added with a grin, "and having to turn down a dance with a scarlet coat's enough to make any female cross as crabs."

Though glad he had not taken offence, Laura was still filled with remorse for her bad-tempered outburst, and with discontent for having to miss the dancing. Cornelius's well-meant sympathy made it no easier to bear.

"For unlike some of my, hm, brethren in the church, I consider dancing an innocent amusement," he said in his ponderous way. "Though this German dance, the waltz, which I observed in Town last summer, is certainly, hm, indecorous. Still, I see no harm in a, hm, man of the cloth taking part in a country dance now and then, do you, Cousin?"

Laura agreed, holding back with difficulty a screeched demand as to what was the harm in a woman nine-months widowed taking part in a country dance. The harm, as Aunt Antonia anxiously reminded her, was in the eyes and tongues of the beholders.

"I don't mean to stand up, Aunt," Laura reassured her, "though I should dearly love to."

The old lady patted her hand. "There will be other times, my dear," she said.

But there would be no other times. Laura's resolve to leave Llys was fed by dismay at her resentment over the dancing and her rudeness to Rupert. Once again she feared becoming as spoilt and petulant as Maria. Her hurt when Gareth neither asked her for a dance nor wished she might stand up with him made it plain she was growing much too dependent upon him emotionally. It was useless to tell herself he did not realize how much she wanted to be his partner . . .

And that, of course, was the crux of the matter. She would not mind missing a thousand glittering balls if Gareth were not there.

That evening, for the most part Laura managed not to watch the dancing. Though Aunt Antonia was officially Gareth's hostess, Laura found plenty to occupy her. She introduced guests to neighbours, found partners for young ladies, kept an eye on the supper tables and, in the absence of servants, called on the younger Wyckhams to remove emptied platters. In her moments of leisure there was always someone wanting to chat with her. Once she went up to the nursery to make sure the nurses who had gone first to the other party had returned to relieve their colleagues.

She was coming down again after this when from the gallery she saw Gareth whirl the pretty daughter of a neighbour into the Great Hall. The girl laughed up at him, he smiled down at her, and a shaft of pure jealousy struck Laura. The pain stopped her breath; her hands clenched white-knuckled on the banister rail.

There were others in the hall, of course. Gareth helped the young lady — he had known her all his life — to a plate of food, seated her with friends, and returned to the Long Gallery to find his next partner. He was just being a good host.

But Laura had recognized the dreadful, consuming emotion she had lived with in the days when Ceci had everything she had not. She could not live with it again. She had to go.

By the second day after Twelfth Night, all the guests were gone. Rupert had two days of leave remaining, Lance and Perry a week or two of their holidays. Laura decided the time had come to make her announcement.

Perhaps she ought to break the news individually to Gareth and Aunt Antonia, but the prospect made her quail. It would be easier to face everyone at once.

The moment she chose was tea-time, when the family all gathered in the drawing room. Gareth had Priscilla in his lap. Beside him Cornelius was making most unclerical grimaces at the baby, who chortled with glee. The children had come down from the nursery and George and Henry were helping Perry make toast at the fireside with the redesigned toasting fork — Uncle Julius, having turned up for once, was eating most of it.

Laura poured the tea, as she generally did these days, the large teapot being too heavy for Aunt Antonia's rheumatic hands. Lance distributed the cups. At Laura's side, Rupert mourned the end of his leave.

"Not that they're not dev . . . dashed good fellows in our mess," he said, "and London can't be beat for any amusement you fancy, but home is home, when all's said and done. It's always a wrench to go away."

Laura seized the opening. "I too shall be sorry to leave Llys," she said, "but it is past time I was going home to —"

"Leave Llys?" Lance put down a teacup with a clatter and gaped at her, aghast.

"Going home?" said Rupert. "Dam . . . dash it, Llys is your home!"

"Indeed it is, Cousin Laura," Cornelius weightily endorsed him. "You are one of the family."

Arabella flung herself into Laura's lap and clung to her. "Don't go 'way," she wailed. "I'll be good. I'll be ever so good."

"Is it because we were naughty?" Henry asked, horrified.

"Did we make too much noise and wake the baby?" George wanted to know. "We didn't mean to, honestly, Cousin Laura. If we promise to be quiet, will you stay?"

"I need you," his little sister insisted.

Perry, white-faced, swallowed visibly. "So do I. Please, please, don't go."

"I'm afraid," said Aunt Antonia, her usually measured tones uncertain, "I have been asking too much of you. I am quite well again now and quite as capable of running the household as ever I was."

"Dear Aunt, that is not my reason for leaving —"

"You cannot leave," exclaimed Uncle Julius. "I'm designing a baby-cage."

This extraordinary announcement at least had the merit of diverting Perry, who said incredulously, "A cage? You cannot put Pris in a cage, Uncle!"

Over Arabella's golden head, Laura's gaze met Gareth's. He said nothing, but it was the desperate plea in his eyes as he held Priscilla close which brought surrender.

"Well, after all," she said, despising herself for her weakness, "there is no great hurry. In three months, at Easter, I shall be out of mourning, and Priscilla will be bigger and stronger, and the roads will be better —"

If Gareth spoke, it was lost in the joyful clamour of the children. To them, three months was forever.

The following morning, when Laura was in her sitting room changing Priscilla's napkin before her nap, Cornelius knocked and came in. Laura was surprised. She did not doubt the vicar's fondness for the baby, but unlike Gareth and Perry, and even Lance and Rupert on occasion, he had never come especially to see her.

"She's sleepy and fussing a bit," Laura

told him. "Just before her nap is not a good time to play with her, I'm afraid."

"No, no, put her to bed by all means, Cousin. I hoped for a private word with you. If we talk quietly, shall we disturb the child?"

"Give her a minute or two to settle." She kissed Pris, and Cornelius gravely followed suit. Then she tucked her in, while he stood in silent contemplation of one of Arabella's drawings — a rose-red cow with horns longer than its legs. By the time the changing table was tidied and the wet napkin in a covered bucket set outside the door to be taken to the laundrymaid, Priscilla was fast asleep.

Laura invited Cornelius to sit down. Uncharacteristically unsure of himself, he hesitated before he took his seat. "What can I do for you, Cousin?" she asked encouragingly.

He cleared his throat. "Erhem. My dear Laura — if I may make so bold? — it is unthinkable that you should leave Llys and struggle alone to raise the child. I have come to the conclusion that she, hm, needs a father, and you a, erhem, hm, hm, a husband. It is my duty, my privilege, and my, hm, pleasure to offer you a home. And my hand, of course," he hastened to add, rather flushed. "When your mourning year is over, naturally. We would have to keep our agreement quiet until then."

After a dumfounded moment, Laura regained control of her tongue. "What a good, kind man you are, Cornelius. I am honoured and very grateful, but indeed it is impossible."

"The vicarage is really quite comfortable," he assured her anxiously. "Of course it is not so grand as the manor, but I daresay we might be cosy as three peas in a pod."

"It is much grander than my cottage in Cambridgeshire. I will not marry just for a larger establishment. I have the greatest respect for you, and no little fondness, but it is the fondness of a sister, and I suspect your feelings for me are those of a brother. One day you will find a woman you truly want to be your wife and helpmeet."

Cornie sighed. "Well, well, I shall not trouble you with arguments. But do believe, my dear, that I should be exceedingly sorry to see you leave Llys, as should we all. I hope you will reconsider that decision, and my offer of marriage remains open, should you change your mind. We can still be friends, can we not? There need be no awkwardness?"

"None at all. I shall always consider you

my friend." Deeply touched, Laura watched the worthy vicar's dignified retreat with tears in her eyes. What a dear man he was!

But she did not want to marry him. She would be as dissatisfied with him as Freddie had been with her, and one mistake of the kind was more than enough for a lifetime. Besides, to live in the vicarage as another man's wife, so near to Gareth and yet so far, would be even worse torture than to stay on as his pensioner.

That afternoon, Laura had just finished changing Priscilla after her second nap of the day when Rupert arrived.

"Halloa, little lady," he said jauntily, taking her from Laura. "Wide awake now, are we?" He sat down and, giving her two large fingers to grasp, raised her to stand on his knee. "Are you sure she's too young yet for 'Ride-a-cock-horse' or 'To market, to market,' Cousin Laura?"

"Quite sure. Give her a few months."

"All very well, but you're talking of — Ouch!" he yelped as Pris exchanged her grip on his finger for a grab at his moustache. She collapsed in his lap, gurgling as he tickled her tummy. "You're talking of going away in a few months," Rupert continued, "so I shan't be able to bounce her on my foot."

Laura smiled. "You will always be welcome in Swaffham Bulbeck for a game of 'Ride-a-cock-horse.' "

"Got a better notion. What d'you say we tie the knot? Then I'll be able to teach her to ride a real horse, when she's old enough."

"Tie the knot?" Laura was certain she had misunderstood. "You mean . . . ?"

"Get leg-shackled. Take the bull by the horns and hop into parson's mousetrap. We can't have you going off alone like that. I daresay I'm not the sort of husband you'd choose, but any husband's better than none, ain't it? Every female wishes to marry."

"Rupert, I'm a widow, remember?"

"Always had a soft spot for widows. Ask anyone. Not that there'd be any more of that, mind, if we get spliced! Tell you what, Laura," he said with an air of heroism, "I'll even sell out if you don't fancy being a soldier's wife. Daresay Gareth'll find me something to do about the place, so we can stay here at Llys. What d'you say?"

"I could not ask such a sacrifice of you!"

"You think you'll like to follow the drum? Not that it's going anywhere much but London, with Boney shut up on Elba. You'll like the colonel's wife, she's —"

"No, Rupert, I meant such a sacrifice as to find yourself caught in parson's mousetrap. I should hate to be responsible for the disappointment of goodness knows how many widows."

"No, really, Coz, you're roasting me. Daresay I shouldn't mind being a tenant for life a bit, once I got used to it. Deuced fond of you, you know, and of little Prissie."

"And I am fond of you, my dear, but it would not do." A year his elder, she felt infinitely older. "You have a few wild oats left to sow before you settle down."

"I'm not like Cousin Freddie," Rupert protested, injured. "Don't say I never sport a trifle on a game of cards, but I've better things to do with my blunt than to squander it on some knock-kneed nag. Gareth's never had to tow me out of the River Tick."

"I am excessively glad to hear it. However, I'm perfectly certain you have better things to do with your blunt than to support a wife and family."

"By Jove, there's that," he admitted, much struck. Somewhat abashed, he went on bravely, "I'll do it, though, demme if I won't, if you'll marry me."

Much relieved by her persistent refusal, Rupert departed whistling a merry air from The Beggar's Opera.

■ ■ ■ ■

Somehow Laura was only mildly surprised when Lance drew her aside after tea and begged for a private interview. She wondered if she could forestall a proposal, but it was impossible without showing she guessed what he was about. That would be unkind — and after all she might be wrong.

"Come up to my sitting room," she invited. "Priscilla is always in need of a quiet time after the excitement of being with the entire family."

With a thick towel draped over his impeccable Inexpressibles to guard against accidents, Lance took Priscilla on his knee. His gaze firmly fixed on her efforts to capture her own feet, he began, "Cousin Laura, you must be aware of my sincere respect for you."

"Why, thank you. I hope I may continue to earn it."

The tips of his ears turned pink. "Do you," he said in a low voice, "do you think you might ever come to respect me?"

"I do respect you, Lance. I greatly admire your resolve to become a physician."

"Do you?" he asked eagerly, looking up.

"You would not mind being a doctor's wife?"

"Not a bit, in theory, but I must remind you that you will not be qualified for a number of years yet — and I am not your wife."

"No, but I should like you to be." His face scarlet, he said wretchedly, "I'm making a dreadful mull of it. I ought to go down on one knee, only I cannot with Priscilla, but I could at least have used the right words, all about doing me the honour, and begging you to accept my hand. I practised."

"Consider it said." Laura sternly suppressed a twitch of the lips. "I cannot marry you, Lance, though I am deeply grateful for the honour you do me in offering."

"Why not? Because I'm younger? It's only four years and though it seems a great gulf at present, it will scarcely signify by the time I am forty. Forty!" he exclaimed, suddenly aghast at the prospect of some day reaching that great age.

"Your age must be a consideration, to be sure, and the years of training ahead of you. More important, I do not feel towards you as I should wish to feel towards my — my husband." She had married Freddie without loving him. Better to live the rest of her life alone than to cheat another man so.

"Though I hold you in great affection," she assured Lance, "it is a sisterly affection."

"I wish you were my sister, for then you would not doubt that you belong at Llys." He turned his eyes back to Pris, who gazed up at him with a serious look while she sucked contentedly on her toes. Blushing again, not glancing at Laura, Lance asked, "Cannot sisterly and brotherly affection ripen into something — warmer? By the time I qualify as a doctor, if you will just stay at Llys, perhaps we may find —"

"You will always be welcome to visit us in Cambridgeshire, Lance, and if, when you are qualified, you choose to renew your offer — why, then we shall think again."

"I shall see if I cannot study medicine at Cambridge," he cried, "though it will be a shocking thing for an Oxford man!"

What an amiable, generous adoptive family she had! On the whole, Laura considered she had brushed through the spate of proposals tolerably well, succeeding in refusing all three without offence. There would be no more. Perry was by far too young to give the remotest thought to marriage, and Gareth had vowed never to marry.

CHAPTER 18

"I know I'm too young," Perry conceded, gently patting Priscilla's back to bring up her wind, "so you need not tell me so. It's an awfully long time till I'm of age, but if you will only wait, I expect Gareth will let me marry you when I'm eighteen."

"He would be shockingly remiss in his duty as your guardian if he did," Laura exclaimed.

"He might, though. You and Pris can stay here till I finish at Rugby, and then if he says no it will only be three years more. Won't you wait? I do love Pris so, and — and you, too," he finished with shy dignity.

"And I love you, Perry dear, but as a mother loves her child."

"I'm not a child! And you are not old enough to be my mother. I worked it all out. You're only ten years older than me, and Cornie says my father was a good ten years older than my mother, though she died first. So it's no great matter."

"The world approves a man being older than his wife, but the reverse, by such a number of years, is cause for scandal. It may seem unreasonable and unjust, but thus it is."

"I don't care a fig for scandal," Perry

declared scornfully. Priscilla belched in apparent agreement. "Oh, clever girl. Shall I give her some more pap, Cousin Laura? Here, my pretty sweeting, let's try another spoonful."

Pris swiped at the little silver spoon, which, like the cradle, had served generations of Wyckhams. She missed, and Perry slipped it into her mouth. As she mumbled the soft, milky mixture, he said to Laura with a serious look, "I daresay to be the butt of scandal would be pretty dreadful for you, but I would take care of you. We all would, that's agreed."

"We?" she asked, startled.

"My brothers and I. It's a conspiracy. We put our heads together and decided the best way to get you to stay at Llys, to keep you and Pris in the family, was for one of us to marry you."

"Good gracious!"

"That's why you're leaving, isn't it? Because you are not really related to us, not by blood, so you don't feel entitled to live here? But if we were betrothed, even if it must be secret from everyone else for the present, then you need not be uneasy. Marry me, Cousin Laura," he urged. "Do say you will."

"Truly, my dear, it will not serve. I have

other reasons for going away, reasons I cannot discuss —"

At that moment, Priscilla puffed out her cheeks and, with every evidence of delight, blew her mouthful of pap into Perry's face. "Abadakaboo," she cooed, and giggled.

"Little monkey," he said tolerantly.

What a marvellous father he would make, if he did not change as he grew up, Laura thought, taking the laughing baby from him. His wife would be a lucky woman, but he was not for her. As he went off to wash, she hoped the subject was closed. Surely he would not ask her reasons, when she had plainly said she did not wish to give them.

She could not possibly tell Perry she loved Gareth, that only as Gareth's wife could she remain here.

Of the conspirators, only Gareth was left. If he had changed his mind about taking a wife, why had he let all his brothers try first? Hurt, she had to assume he hoped she would accept one of the others. If he forced himself to propose, it would be for Priscilla's sake anyway, she reminded herself. Could she bear to wed him for the baby's sake? Had she the fortitude to refuse if he asked?

But the days passed, and her fortitude was not put to the test.

The day before Perry returned to school, Gareth sent for him to the library to pick up his pocket-money, since he did not yet receive a regular quarterly allowance as did the others.

"Don't spend it all on cakes," he advised, handing over a pair of bank notes and a handful of guineas.

"As though I should!"

Gareth grinned. "I recall my own schooldays very clearly."

"There is one thing at least . . . I saw it in a shop just before Christmas and wanted to buy it, but my pockets were to let. I hope it is still there."

"What's that?"

"A jointed wooden doll, painted in bright colours, and it had a string you pulled to make it dance. Don't you think Pris would like it hanging over her bed?"

"I'm sure she'd love it, but pray do not run away again to bring it to her! Perry, you're not still afraid of her dying, are you?"

"Well of course, but only a little bit, not much more than of you or Lance or the others dying, or Cousin Laura, or the children." The boy leaned forward in his chair, his

298

hands linked in supplication. "But Cousin Laura means to go away. Can't you stop them going? Her and Priscilla?"

"As Cousin Laura made very plain to me when I went to fetch her to Llys," Gareth said wryly, "I have no authority over her whatsoever. Nor any desire to rule her, I may say. She is free to choose where she wishes to live."

"Oh, I know that. Only, if you were to marry her, then she'd stay. She might accept you, even though she won't have any of the rest of us."

"She what?"

Perry flushed guiltily. "I'm not supposed to tell. We knew you wouldn't like it."

"Like what? Perry, cut line this instant!"

"Swear you won't tell them I told you?" He reverted to schoolboy language: "Cross your heart and hope to die if you do."

"Upon my honour," Gareth said impatiently. "Now, what mischief have the four of you been up to?"

"Not mischief. It's just that none of us want them to leave, and we think Laura ought to have someone to look after her and the baby, so each of us in turn offered her his hand. Cornie went first, because he's eldest."

Stunned, for a moment Gareth could only

stare. "And you, I collect, went last because you are youngest."

"Yes, but she wouldn't —"

"Perry, you are fifteen years old!"

"Nearly sixteen. I explained she would have to wait, maybe even till I come of age."

"Good gad!" Gareth was furious. "Cornelius at least should know better than to plot such a crackbrained scheme behind my back. And when she is still in mourning! Did it occur to none of you that Laura might be distressed and offended?"

"It wasn't as if it was some sort of jape," Perry cried. "We all meant every word. And she wasn't offended, truly. But if it was wrong, punish me and don't tell the others. You promised."

"I cannot punish you for being misled by your elders. Don't worry, I shan't tell. Although, for all your secrecy, Laura might well have told me."

"She wouldn't. She is the kindest person in the world, and besides, Cornie said she has by far too much delicacy of mind to speak to a third party of proposals of marriage. Of course you'd have had to know if she accepted one of us, but she refused us all. You want them to stay, don't you? You must try your luck, Gareth, you must!"

"There is no 'must' about it," Gareth said

sternly, but his anger had died. Though he could not approve their collusion, in a way he was rather proud of his brothers. What had they done but what he would like to do himself?

What he would do, dammit! In any other sphere, to let fear hinder him would be to admit himself a coward. He could not let fear keep him from the woman he loved.

The thought that Laura might even now be betrothed to Cornelius or Rupert made him shudder. Thank heaven she had rejected his brothers' offers. He would speed at once to her side to lay his heart before her if it were not that he'd not for the world have her imagine he was a party to their plot. No, he owed it to her and to himself to observe the propriety they had ignored, to wait until her mourning year was over.

She had said she would stay until then. Only three months, but what a long three months they were going to be!

Yet the time passed quickly. Priscilla's hair darkened to match her mother's and her eyes turned grey. She outgrew the cradle and moved into a crib.

Dismissing Gareth's doubts, Laura took her outdoors in the push-cradle whenever the winter weather was not utterly foul. As strong-minded as her mother, Pris refused to sit still in the push-cradle. After a tumble — luckily onto soft, if muddy, grass — Uncle Julius hastily created a chair on wheels with a strap round her tummy to hold her in.

This delayed his production of the baby-cage, renamed a baby-pen at Perry's insistence. Before it was ready, Priscilla started to creep, lifting her little bottom in the air and shooting forward at a remarkable rate. An active and inquisitive child, she had to be watched constantly. Mrs. Barley at last began to earn her keep, and Gareth dared hope Laura was starting to realize the difficulties of bringing up her daughter on her own.

He spent as much time as possible with Priscilla, partly to demonstrate to Laura that he would be a good father, partly for the sheer pleasure of it. Her arms around his neck, her nose nuzzling his cheek, were ample rewards for endless games of peek-a-boo and pat-a-cake.

The long winter evenings also allowed more time spent with Laura. They played backgammon or discussed the estate, the political news of the day, the books he read aloud to her and Aunt Antonia while they plied their needles. Though Laura was quite willing to admit her ignorance of the world and to learn from him, once she understood matters she had strong opinions and no reticence about expressing them.

She often shocked Aunt Antonia, but Gareth found himself more and more in love.

Alas, his growing love not only increased his yearning to make her his wife, it magnified his dread of eventually being the cause of her death. A platonic marriage was out of the question. If she was his, he would not be able to resist making love to her. He sometimes found it difficult even now, when she was close to him, when he touched her hand by chance or lent her his arm, when she stood before a window, her figure outlined by the wintry light.

He did his best to conceal his desire and his torment from her. Whether she guessed or not, he could not tell, but she said nothing. However, Aunt Antonia's sharp eyes eventually detected something amiss.

One morning towards the middle of March, she requested his presence in her sitting room. "Sit down, Gareth," she said with unwonted gentleness. "You are troubled, I believe. Do you wish to tell me what is amiss? You know if there is the least thing I may do to help, nothing could give me more satisfaction."

He subsided into one of her flowered-chintz chairs, running his hand through his hair. "Laura will leave soon. Is that not trouble enough? At least, I assume she will, since she has not told me she will not."

"Yes, she speaks to me now and then of departure. She wishes to leave soon enough not to have to travel on Good Friday."

"When is that?"

"Easter Sunday is on the 26th of March, I believe."

"Two weeks! Shall you not be sorry to see her go, ma'am?" he cried, her composure irksome to his fretted nerves.

"Indeed I shall, more than you can guess. I also envy her, for being free to choose without the restraints of her family's expectations."

"As you never were?" Dismayed, he reached for her hand, a white, slender, elegant hand still despite the swollen knuckles and prominent veins. "Are you not satisfied here at Llys, Aunt Antonia? You know you have only to voice your wishes, for we all owe you more than can ever be paid."

"My dear, you owe me nothing." She patted his hand. "I am resigned to the past, and content with the present, though I was not always so. However, we were speaking of Laura, not of me. She is too young for resignation and too independent of spirit to bow to what most females would regard as the dictates of Fate."

"Still less the dictates of any man!"

"Did she seek my advice, I should beg her to stay, for my sake, for all our sakes. Whether for her own sake, I cannot tell. Only she can decide what is best for her."

"She cannot decide for the best," Gareth said in a low voice, "unless she is fully aware of the alternatives."

His aunt gave him a penetrating glance. "To live in a cottage in straitened but independent circumstances, or to reside at Llys Manor with every comfort and elegancy — as your dependent."

"As my wife."

She seemed unsurprised. "You have not asked her, I collect."

He jumped up and took an agitated turn about the room. The urge to open his budget was near irresistible, but how could he approach such a subject with his prim and proper, ever-decorous spinster aunt?

"You love her, do you not?" she said, a hint of disturbance ruffling her usual calm. "I have suspected it any time these several months. But you are thinking of your mama."

"Yes." Gareth rushed to her side and sank

to his knees, clasping both her hands. "Aunt Antonia, what shall I do? I love her to distraction. I should die if my passion were to blame for her death."

Colour tinged her thin cheeks. "Emily never blamed Wyckham for his . . . his claiming the rights of a husband."

"He blamed himself. I heard him." In a whisper he repeated the dreadful words: " 'Oh God, why could I not leave her alone?' If I married Laura, if she accepted me, I should not be able to leave her alone."

"Gareth, Laura is a healthy young woman. Your mama was always fragile, though a good deal tougher than she looked. She bore five surviving children, remember. It was not childbirth in itself which killed her, it was too frequently repeated childbirth." The old lady's pinkness deepened. "She . . . she conceived easily, which I believe is not the case with all women. Should it prove so with Laura . . . I am far from qualified to speak on the subject, but surely a . . . a little self-restraint would answer the purpose."

She did not understand. How could she? Of course self-restraint was the answer, but it was precisely what he feared he lacked. He envisaged years of sleeping alone and unsatisfied in his dressing room, aching for Laura while she lay lonely in the marital bed. Simple lust might be satisfied elsewhere, yet he could not imagine being unfaithful to Laura, though many men preserved their wives from constant demands and frequent pregnancies by taking a mistress.

"That's it!" He hugged his startled aunt, whose words had set him at last on the right track. "At least, I hope that's it. I shall have to go to Town."

"To Town!"

"To request Lord Medway's permission to address his daughter," Gareth invented airily, though now he came to consider it, it was not half a bad idea. "A mere formality, since he's unlikely to object to my suit and if he should I shall disregard it. Not a word to Laura."

"Naturally. But Gareth, while I am delighted that you see a way through your difficulties, I feel obliged to caution you not to let your spirits rise too high. I must reluctantly approve your disregard of Lord Medway's possible refusal — a most unnatural father! — yet there is one whose consent is both uncertain and indispensable."

"Laura," he said flatly. "Will she have me, Aunt?"

"My dear, only she can say."

■ ■ ■ ■

Laura smiled at Gareth as he came into the breakfast room at midday. She found it more and more difficult to smile as the time for her departure drew nearer, though fixed by her own choice. It was difficult to talk of indifferent matters, too, so she was glad to see he carried *The Times.*

"Any news worthy of note?"

"I have not yet had a chance to look." He unfolded the newspaper and glanced at the headline. "Good God, Bonaparte has escaped from Elba!"

The news, now a week old, that the ex-emperor had once again raised his standard on French soil naturally superseded every other topic. Gareth at once announced his intention of hurrying up to Town to find out what was going on.

"I shall go with you," declared Cornelius, who had dropped by for luncheon. "Renfrew can take the service on Sunday."

By mid afternoon they were gone.

Laura tried not to feel hurt that Gareth should go away when she had so little time left at Llys. He might even have forgotten, she told herself. She had not mentioned the painful subject to him for some weeks.

In some ways, his absence was actually a relief. She had prepared herself for arguments, which she knew she would find difficult to resist. She had come to think of Llys Manor as her home, of its inhabitants as her family, and she knew she would miss them desperately.

Her vaunted independence was ashes in her mouth. If she could not bear the prospect of remaining at Llys as Gareth's pensioner, it was only because she wanted to be his wife. Yet even that would not be enough.

She wanted him to marry her because he loved her, not because Priscilla needed a father.

CHAPTER 19

Laura began to sort her belongings for packing. Myfanwy was dismayed.

"If it's go you must, my lady," she said, "then I go with you."

"I shall have no need of an abigail," Laura explained. "The cottage is too small, and I have not means to pay, nor shall I have occasion to dress fine. If Sally cannot return to me, I must hire a new maid-of-all-work."

"When you are gone, my lady, no need of an abigail there'll be here at the manor, look you. A housemaid I was afore you came, and a housemaid I'll be again. Scrub floors for you I will, and help care for Miss Pris, and I can cook a bit, too. 'Sides, on the journey there's help you'll be wanting."

"Oh, Myfanwy, I should like to have you with me, but you would miss your family and your home. Cambridgeshire is very different from Shropshire."

"Then let's give it a try, my lady," said the maid practically. "If it's terrible homesick I am, you can look about for another girl and home I'll come. Leastways you won't be on your ownsome to start off."

Laura gratefully accepted.

Aunt Antonia did not attempt to persuade her to change her mind, though making it plain Laura's decision distressed her. On two points, however, she was adamant: first, Laura must not leave before Gareth returned; and second, she must take the Wyckham carriage and not even contemplate travelling with the baby by stage or mail.

The first stipulation Laura acceded to with mixed feelings. Common courtesy demanded that she not sneak away like a thief in the night, though a farewell meeting promised to be as painful as never to see Gareth again.

As for the travelling carriage, which he

had left behind, taking only his curricle, she had to acknowledge it would make the journey a hundred times easier. Yet to plan in Gareth's absence to make use of his equipage and his coachman seemed highly improper, not to say encroaching — especially as he disapproved of her departure, and although she knew he would offer the coach were he present.

But he was not present, so perhaps he did not care about her leaving after all.

None of this could she say to Aunt Antonia, but she did bring forward a practical objection. "I cannot afford to hire horses, ma'am, nor to stay at inns as often as would be necessary if we travelled slowly enough to take Cousin Gareth's team all the way."

"My dear, I shall defray your expenses. Gareth, and his father before him, have always made me a generous allowance which I have had no reason to spend. I have a nice little nest egg saved up and it would give me great pleasure to open my purse to ease your way. Indeed, it will only be to anticipate the future, for one day the whole will be yours."

"Mine!"

"I have not mentioned it before, but last time we went into Ludlow I called on my lawyer and changed my Will in your favour."

Tears in her eyes, choked with emotion, Laura embraced the old lady.

Her last qualm about taking the carriage vanished when Cornelius came home and seconded his aunt. "I am Gareth's heir," he pointed out, "and in his absence his, hm, representative. What is more, I'm dashed if I'd know how to face him if I let you plan to take Priscilla on the stage! Must you go, Cousin?"

"Yes," Laura said firmly. "What news of France?"

Cornelius reported that Napoleon was gathering troops in the south. "Rupert is cock-a-hoop at getting a chance to grapple with Boney. He missed the Peninsula, you know. Gareth has been in and out of the Foreign Office. With so many of our people in Vienna, anyone with an intelligent opinion is much in demand. He has other business in Town, also, but he intends to be home before Easter."

With everything prepared for Laura's departure, all she could do now was wait till Gareth deigned to put in an appearance.

The news from France was bad. As soldiers flocked to Napoleon's banner, despatches flew between Paris, Vienna, and London. While the British Government urged the

Congress to appoint the Duke of Wellington as supreme commander of the Allies, King Louis shivered on his shaky throne. Marshal Ney, who had promised the stout monarch to deliver Bonaparte to Paris in a cage, went over to the usurper's side.

Gareth, having used Boney's escape as an excuse to come up to Town, found himself caught up in meetings and consultations. He had neglected his Parliamentary duties for some months — since Laura's arrival at Llys, in fact — but he was known to be knowledgeable about foreign affairs. After a week in London, he was no nearer completing his personal business.

All too clearly he recalled Aunt Antonia saying Laura meant to leave Llys in time to reach her cottage the day before Good Friday. Surely she would not run off without a farewell?

He sent Cornie home with orders to delay her departure, if necessary, without appearing to command her, without annoying or distressing her.

No easy task. Gareth had to be there himself to stop her. He wrote a note to his aunt: He would reach home by Monday morning come fire, flood, or famine — and he humbly begged her forgiveness in advance for travelling on Sunday.

One last time he went to Downing Street to urge subsidies for Britain's irresolute allies, even if the money must be borrowed from Nathan Rothschild. Then he bought a box of bonbons and drove out to Chelsea to call upon Eulalie.

In spite of her name, Eulalie was as English as roast mutton, having started life as Nellie Potter of Islington. After a brief career as an opera dancer, she had gone on to become one of the most expensive Birds of Paradise on the town. Unlike so many of the sisterhood, she had salted away the wages of sin, and when her charms began to fade, she was decidedly plump in the pocket. For a while she specialized in initiating youthful gentlemen into the arts of love, more to keep her hand in, she said, than from want of the ready. Now retired and growing stout, she retained the affection of many of her initiates, including Gareth.

"Why, Lord Wyckham, what an unexpected pleasure," she said, beaming, as her maidservant showed him into the cosy parlour of her small villa. "Bring the madeira, Dolly."

He gave her the bonbons and bent to kiss her heavily powdered, rose-scented cheek. "Beautiful as ever, ma'am," he declared.

She chuckled. "If I was, you'd be calling

me darling, not ma'am. No need to upset the butter-boat. Here, take a glass and let's drink to old times."

"Old times!" He sipped the wine in silence, wondering how to broach the subject on his mind.

As if she read his mind, Eulalie asked shrewdly, "Not married yet, Wyckham?"

"No." He gave her a faint smile. "But on the verge. I wanted to consult you before I pop the question."

"Very wise, but I can't believe you have forgot my lessons. From what I've heard there's a string of High Flyers fighting for your attentions and it ain't just because of the depth of your purse."

Gareth grinned. "There was," he admitted. "Not since I met the lady I wish to marry."

"What's the trouble then, dearie? Come on, let's hear it."

"Lalie, did you ever have a child?"

"What, me get caught with a bun in the oven? Not bloody likely, if you'll pardon the expression. I won't say there ain't some luck to it, but there's precautions a girl can take if she's got the sense the good Lord gave her."

"That's what I want to know about," Gareth said thankfully.

Eulalie frowned. "You don't want children?"

"I don't want my wife worn out with child-bearing."

Her face cleared. "Aha, besotted are you? Well, I hope she deserves you, dearie. Now this is the way of it. You take a piece of sponge, about this big, and tie a thread around it. Then you soak it well in brandy."

"Brandy? Not eye of newt and toe of frog?"

"It needn't be the best cognac," she said tolerantly. "I've heard of using gin instead, or even vinegar, but brandy's what I always used. It's not you needs to worry about the expense, after all. You take this sponge and push it up inside as far as it will go."

"Inside? Oh, you mean . . . ?" Gareth's face flamed as he imagined discussing the wretched sponge with Laura rather than an old whore. He'd do it, though, bedamned if he wouldn't.

"Yes, that's what I mean," she agreed with surprising delicacy. "Just make sure the end of the thread's dangling, though it's not the end of the world if it gets lost. When you've had your fun, you pull on the thread and out it pops." She gave him a stern look. "And don't you go believing you can't have a bit of fun with your wife same as with the muslin company. There'd be a lot fewer girls in my old business if gentlemen wasn't to take that sort of nonsense into their heads."

"I shan't," he promised, his heart light as air.

"It's not infallible, mind," she warned, "but at least she won't be confined every time you look at her. I'd like to send my compliments, but I don't suppose she'd appreciate the thought. She's a lucky lady, she is. Off you go now, my lord, and lay in a good supply of sponges!"

"Bless you, Eulalie." Gareth kissed her again and departed with a spring in his step. Laura had let him stay at her side while her child was born: She was not likely to prove so prudish as to reject the use of the sponges.

It was too soon, however, to lay in a supply. She might reject him. He believed she was fond of him, but she was fond of his brothers and had refused one and all. It was not as if she had to marry him to remain at Llys. That day at Swaffham Bulbeck, under the apple tree, he had offered her a home not a temporary refuge.

Could she have forgotten, or misunderstood? Could she possibly imagine she had outstayed her welcome? Before he proposed he must make quite sure she realized she belonged at Llys whatever her answer. But suppose she did realize and had already changed her mind about leaving. Then, if he proposed and she chose to refuse his hand, her sense of delicacy might make her leave after all.

Devil take it, he was going to have to phrase his offer with all the diplomacy at his command!

Gareth drove back to Mayfair and stopped in Grafton Street, outside the Earl of Medway's town house. Diplomacy was going to be needed here, too, if Laura was to meet with her family on civil — if not cordial — terms. He did not know the full story of her elopement, but Aunt Antonia had accepted Laura and stigmatized Medway as an unnatural father, so obviously Laura had been as much sinned against as sinning.

Cast off by her family, tied to a heedless here-and-thereian like Cousin Freddie, the poor girl had suffered enough for her mistakes. Gareth vowed her future happiness should make up for her past suffering, if he had any say in the matter.

Knocking on the door, he intended to leave a note requesting an interview at Medway's earliest convenience. The butler said his lordship was at home, so Gareth asked to see him at once.

"On business."

"If you would not mind waiting here for a moment, my lord."

He was distantly acquainted with the earl. He had met him at his clubs, on social occasions, and in the House of Lords, where Medway's chief preoccupation was increasing the number of offences for which hanging was the penalty. A short, heavy-set man with a thick neck, he had an unattractive manner at once pompous and belligerent.

The countess Gareth knew chiefly from the days when he had joined the court of the ravishing Lady Cecilia — before he discovered she had not an idea in her head beyond what her mother or her governess had put there. Since those ideas revolved around her own beauty and the importance of making a splendid match, Gareth's opinion of the haughty Lady Medway was not high. Nor did he care for the heir to the earldom, an arrogant puppy the same age as Lance but with half the sense.

How had his Laura sprung from such stock? Though Gareth wished for a reconciliation for her sake, he hoped she would not be restored to the bosom of her family to such an extent that he'd have to see much of them.

"His lordship will see you now, my lord."

The small study Gareth was shown to seemed designed to establish its owner's importance. The walls were hung with charts, tables, and maps stuck with varicoloured pins, one showing Napoleon's present progress across France. The desk was piled high with finically neat stacks of papers, many displaying the red tapes of official or legal documents.

Lord Medway rose from his seat behind the desk, but confined himself to a minimal bow rather than coming around to shake Gareth's hand. "I suppose you mean to dun me for the jade's expenses," he said unpleasantly, leaning on the desk, his head thrust forward between his shoulders.

Gareth swallowed his anger. "If, as I must suppose, you are referring to Lady Laura," he said coldly, "nothing could be further from my mind. As my cousin's widow she has a claim upon me, though she has never presumed upon it. On the contrary, she would be the first to deny it. She is at Llys — as I collect you have discovered — at my invitation."

"And willing enough to grant her favours in return, no doubt."

How could the man speak so of his own daughter? With an effort, Gareth overlooked the salacious implications. "Lady Laura is indeed a most obliging person. She is an amiable and helpful companion to my aunt, and a friend to my brothers, besides being of signal service to my cousin's young children, who live with me. We are all very fond of her, and of your granddaughter."

"My granddaughter, hey?" There was no sign of softening in the bulldog face. "It's for the brat you've come to beg?"

Through gritted teeth, Gareth spat out, "Lord Medway, pray disabuse yourself of the fancy that I have any desire whatsoever to prey on your purse. I am come to request your permission to pay my addresses to your daughter."

Medway stared. "No business of mine if you want to make a cake of . . . to wed the chit," he amended hastily as Gareth took a step forward. "Washed my hands of her years ago. You needn't think I shall make any new settlements this time around, either. Gave her more than she deserved when she married Chamberlain, to get her off my hands."

"Forty pounds a year!"

"So she's complained, has she?" the earl sneered.

"Never. She told me to prove her independence, her lack of need for charity."

"The forty pounds is pure charity. Chamberlain was too much of a fool to ask for anything at all."

"So am I," Gareth informed him coolly, thinking more kindly of poor Freddie than he had in years. At least his cousin had not run off with Laura in hopes of a fortune. "Well, I have informed you of my intentions, sir. It remains only to say that I assume you will receive Lady Laura with decent complaisance when she comes to Town as the Baroness Wyckham —"

"Hah," Medway grunted, but ungraciously conceded, "Shan't cut her, at least."

". . . If she accepts my hand."

"If?" He guffawed. "Daresay she's learned to tell which side her bread is buttered!"

Seething, Gareth bowed and departed without another word. It was that or strangle the earl, and he could not bear the thought of touching him.

No wonder she had eloped with Freddie! For all his improvidence, his careless charm must have seemed inducement enough to flee such a family. All the same, Gareth was glad to recall that whatever her original feelings for her husband, his frequent absences had ceased to distress her long before his death.

Gareth wanted her love, but he would take her without and hope in time to earn it. The question was, should he declare his love for her, or might it make her refuse him because she could not reciprocate?

Dammit, never had a man so many considerations to bear in mind when he planned his proposal!

Next morning he left early for Llys. He had time enough to reach home by Sunday evening but, pondering how best to offer his hand and his heart to Laura, he drove into a ditch. Though he, his groom, and the horses were unhurt, a spoke of the curricle's wheel snapped. It was past noon on Monday by the time he turned up the drive to the manor.

His travelling carriage stood before the door. The baby's wheeled chair tied on behind made it all too obvious for whom it waited. Flinging the reins to the groom, Gareth dashed into the house.

"Here he is," cried Perry — Gareth had forgotten the boys were due home Saturday for their Easter holiday. "I told you he would come when he promised."

Perry, Lance, Cornelius, Aunt Antonia; to one side Myfanwy, cloaked for travelling, and the coachman; George and Henry, and Arabella clinging to the skirts of Laura's carriage dress; all wore long faces.

Laura turned. Beneath the midnight-blue

bonnet, her cheeks were pale, her eyes red-rimmed. "I waited . . ." she said.

Gareth wanted to pull her into his arms and beg her to be his wife, but she was carrying Priscilla. Pris reached out to him with a crow of delight, so he took her. She gave him a damp slobber, because she had not yet quite worked out kisses. He wanted to suggest to her mother that they give a demonstration, but Aunt Antonia was there, and Cornie, and the boys and the children and the servants.

He kissed Priscilla, and holding her tight enough to make her squirm, he looked over her dark curls at Laura. "Stay," he blurted out, diplomacy and oft-practised pretty speeches forgotten. As she started to speak, he interrupted, softly but urgently, "Marry me!"

"I cannot," she said, agitated. "I must go. We must go if we are to make any distance today. I only waited to say good-bye and to thank you . . . for everything. Myfanwy!"

With a curtsy and an "If you please, my lord," the abigail took Priscilla from him and started towards the front door.

Everyone followed. Amidst the press of last minute farewells, kisses and embraces and promises to visit, Gareth had no chance to explain himself further. Cornelius handed

Laura into the carriage, Myfanwy climbed after with the child, the coachman mounted the box, and they were off.

How could he stand with the others waving good-bye to all his hopes? Alone, Gareth went into the house.

CHAPTER 20

With burning eyes, Laura stared blindly out of the carriage window as the carriage rolled through Llys village. On the seat beside her Priscilla slept already, exhausted after exchanging her morning nap for an endlessly protracted leave-taking. Opposite, Myfanwy sniffled.

Laura forced herself to speak. "My dear, it is not too late to change your mind."

The little abigail shook her head. "Not me, my lady," she said determinedly. "There's mopish I felt just for a moment to be leaving home, but 'tis over now. An adventure it is to be going so far off, look you."

An adventure? If only Laura could so regard the journey, but she did not even feel she was going home. She had left her heart behind her at Llys Manor.

Her chagrin at Gareth's absence during her last fortnight in his house had vanished.

Her anger at his all too public proposal had never been more than a flash in the pan. Somehow he had overcome his reluctance to wed. When he held Priscilla for the last time, he had suddenly realized that he could not bear to lose her.

Or perhaps his offer had simply been another instance of his generosity, stretched to the utmost, the only way he could think of to allow Laura to stay at Llys without living on charity.

Should she feel grateful, or should she feel selfish for depriving him of the child he loved? She was also depriving Priscilla of all the advantages of an upbringing at Llys, she thought with a pang. If it had been pride alone which prevented her accepting Gareth . . . But it was fear, too, fear that she might come to hate him for not loving her as she loved him, for not wanting her as she wanted him.

For what else could explain his victory over his fear of marriage? It must mean he did not desire her, so he would not make love to her, so she would never conceive another child, to terrify him with memories.

She could not marry him on such a basis! Not that she had the choice now, after publicly rejecting him. Never mind her pride; his would rebel against a renewal of his suit.

He would thank her in the end, Laura persuaded herself. He had proposed on an instant's impulse, without reflection. When he came to consider the consequences of marrying a widow with a scandalous past, he would realize her refusal was a lucky escape. She would not be a wife he could take to London and present with pride to the Ton. Those who had forgotten her elopement would soon remember when her parents, his Aunt Sybil, and the Chamberlains declined to receive her.

It was best for both of them that she should go back to the quiet contentment of her cottage, with the added joy of her child.

Changing horses at the Feathers in Ludlow was painful. Every turn of the street in the little market town reminded Laura of Gareth. Every glimpse of the castle recalled his explanation of his fears and the brief embrace which had shaken her world.

The change was quickly accomplished and they drove on. After that, Laura and Myfanwy were kept too busy entertaining Priscilla for regrets. The miles and the days passed, until at last they reached Cambridge, where they spent the last night on the road.

"I do not want to arrive at the cottage in the evening," she told Myfanwy. "It has stood uninhabited for ten months so I daresay it will take a day or two to set all to rights. At the very least the sheets will need airing."

The first sight of the cottage was dispiriting. The beech hedge was so overgrown, the gate was barely passable. In the tiny front garden, violets, primroses, crocuses, and daffodils struggled through a mat of last year's dead weeds and this year's already thriving dandelions and goosegrass. The latch on the front door was so rusty with disuse it took the coachman's strength to budge it.

Inside was worse. The dust Laura had expected — the money she left for Sally had run out long since, and she could not expect the girl to go on cleaning for no wages, especially with no notion when Laura might return. The dank chill and the cobwebs were unpleasant but inevitable. But upon opening the parlour door, she found the floor and furniture nearest the fireplace covered with soot.

"A bird in the chimbley that'll be," said Myfanwy, peeping around her, "or a squirrel, mayhap."

"Let us hope whatever it was is not stuck

in the chimney," Laura exclaimed. "The rug and the chairs will never be the same again."

Whatever it was in the chimney, the cause of the chaos in the kitchen was plain. A very dead squirrel lay under the stone sink. The smell was indescribable. Pots and pans and broken china littered the floor, the flowered chintz curtains were shredded, and gnaw-marks on the window frame showed where the poor creature had tried to escape. How it had entered was a mystery.

No mystery about how the rain had entered the back bedroom, producing a flourishing crop of mildew: a falling branch had broken a windowpane. It had then fallen on the woodshed and crashed through the roof. Practically all the firewood was damp.

Laura and Myfanwy looked at each other and laughed, because the only alternative was to cry. "At the very least," Laura ironically repeated her own words, "the sheets will need airing."

"A day or two to set all to rights," the maid quoted. "Well, my lady, longer'n that it'll take us, seemingly, but the sooner 'tis begun, the sooner 'tis done."

During Gareth's absence, a stack of letters had accumulated on his desk in the library. They promised distraction from his misery, so he resolutely ploughed through them.

All but one were easily dealt with, or set aside to be answered later. The one he took to Aunt Antonia's sitting room.

He found the old lady seated at her bureau. Writing paper, blotting paper, inkstand, quills, sealing wafers lay before her, but the writing paper was blank, the pen in her hand undipped.

She set down the pen as he entered, and passed a hand across her eyes. The gesture wiped out the melancholy expression on her face, but not before Gareth had seen it. Her smile was an obvious effort.

"What can I do for you, Gareth?"

"I've a letter from Maria. She is engaged to be married — and I am not." The last four words were reft from him against his will.

His aunt's face crumpled. "I miss her already." She was not talking of Maria.

Gareth slumped into the nearest chair. "I've lost her. I did everything wrong. You heard me ask her to marry me?"

"No, but I guessed. No doubt it was unwise to toss so momentous a question at her so abruptly, and so publicly."

"I ought to have demanded a word with her in private, but I lost my head when I saw she waited only upon my arrival to depart. Why was she in such a hurry to go? After all these months, did I not deserve a proper leave-taking?"

"I believe she was hurt that you absented yourself when she had so little time remaining at Llys. I could not take it upon myself to tell her you had gone to Town to speak to her father. With what success?"

"What does it matter since she won't have me?" he mourned, burying his face in his hands.

"My dear Gareth," Aunt Antonia said in a caustic tone she had rarely used towards him since boyhood, "surely you do not mean to give up so easily? I had thought better of you. A momentary despair is excusable. Indeed, I shared it myself. But —"

"Where's young what's'ername?" Uncle Julius invaded the sitting room with his usual lack of ceremony. "You know the one I mean, the pretty chit with the baby. Can't put my finger on her name. Hazel? Heather? Ivy? Lilian?"

"Laura," Gareth and his aunt said as one.

"That's the one. I knew it had something to do with plants. I've finished the baby-pen. Where is she?"

"Laura has gone back to Cambridgeshire, Julius."

The inventor gaped at her in consternation. "Gone? And taken the baby?"

"Yes, Uncle." Gareth jumped up, shaken by a sudden hope. "But never fear, I shall take the baby-pen to her. Don't you see, Aunt, it will give me an excuse to follow her, so she doesn't feel persecuted. I shall let a few days lapse, to give her time to settle into her cottage. And when I get there, I shall tell her about Maria, and explain that I should have better grounds for keeping George and Henry and Arabella if I were married —"

"No! Do not, for heaven's sake, Gareth, confuse the issue any further. Tell her you love her!"

Gareth grinned. "Yes, ma'am. Aunt Antonia always knows best."

"Priscilla, no!" Laura caught the baby's hand just as the celandine was about to disappear into her mouth.

Pris screeched in annoyance as her hand was pried open. Just a moment ago she had been lying quietly on the rug on the lawn, playing happily with her own feet. Laura had turned from wrestling with a particularly stubborn dandelion to find her daughter ten feet from where she had been laid. Oh, for Uncle Rupert's baby-pen!

The mild March day slipped towards evening. The air was growing chilly. Pris in her arms, Laura turned back to gaze at the patch of vegetable bed she had cleared of weeds. The expected sense of accomplishment was missing. She did not seem to be able to feel anything these days other than the hollow ache in her heart.

"Time to go in, lovie, Myfanwy will be back from the farm soon with a nice fresh egg for your supper."

"Ma-ma-ma-ga-ga," said Priscilla.

Was she saying Mama on purpose? Surely she was too young to be trying to say Gareth. She missed him, and all her friends at Llys, Laura was certain, though Myfanwy ascribed her increased fussiness to teething.

They went into the cottage, clean again and neat as a new pin except for the parlour fireside chairs, for which new covers would have to be made. The sweep had come that morning and swept a rook's nest out of the chimney. In the kitchen, wood was stacked by the fireplace to dry out. Laura noticed the fire was low. She might as well mend it before she cleaned off the garden dirt.

Pris started her wet-napkin whimper just as Laura heard the front door open and close. Myfanwy came into the kitchen and set down a can of milk and a basket of eggs, butter, and cheese on the table.

"Take her upstairs and change her please," said Laura. "Just her napkin, not her clothes, which will be all over food in no time. I must wash my hands."

"There's your face could do with a scrub, too, my lady," Myfanwy said with a smile. "Pushed your hair out of your eyes with a muddy hand you did, I 'spect. Come on then, Miss Pris."

Priscilla decided to take exception to the transfer. She bawled as the maid carried her upstairs, and furious screams came from above. Tears stung Laura's eyes as she turned to the fireplace. The silliest things made her want to cry nowadays, though so far she had managed not to weep until she was alone in her bed at night.

Her eyes were soon stinging in earnest. Inattentive, she had put a damp log on the fire and choking smoke billowed out. The tears that poured down her face were not all smoke-caused, however, as spluttering she groped for the fire-tongs.

Then through the haze strode a familiar figure. Gareth removed the tongs from her grasp and the offending log from the fire. His arm around her waist, he propelled her out to the tiny hall at the foot of the stairs.

Priscilla's wails resounded, but Gareth paid them no heed as he folded Laura in an irresistible embrace and kissed her thoroughly.

Clinging to him, she kissed him back. She had never known a kiss could set her blood on fire and make the rest of the world vanish.

"My darling, I love you," he said at last in a shaky voice. "Will you be my wife?"

"But I have mud on my face," she protested weakly.

He held her away from him and studied her with care. "Not much. I expect most of it is on mine by now. Laura, my dearest girl, you cannot kiss me like that and then refuse to marry me."

Laura flushed and lowered her gaze to his mud-smeared cravat. After hiding her love for so long, she had given away the secret. To deny it now was to proclaim herself a slut. Was it possible he truly loved her too? Or was it only words, to persuade her to take Priscilla back to Llys?

But he had ignored the baby's howls — was ignoring them as they grew suddenly louder —

"Beg pardon, my lady, my lord, but it's her supper Miss Pris wants, and right this minute."

Her cheeks aflame, Laura escaped into the parlour. She crossed to the window and stood fiddling nervously with the cord tying back the curtain. A moment later, scarce long enough for Gareth to greet Myfanwy and kiss Priscilla, whose yells instantly changed to coos, the door thudded shut behind Laura with a click of the latch.

His firm footsteps sounded on the brick floor. His arms closed around her and he nuzzled her neck, sending a tremor through her body.

"Well?"

"Gareth, it is not . . . it's not that you want Priscilla so badly you are prepared to marry me to get her?"

He laughed, the wretch! "Beloved, much as I love Pris, the one I want badly is you, and not at all in the manner in which I want Pris!"

"Truly?" She turned in his arms, her gaze searching his face. "But I know I'm not attractive in that . . . that way."

"What the deuce makes you think not?" he exclaimed, his clasp tightening.

Laura hid her face in his shoulder. "Freddie," she said in a muffled voice.

"Damn Freddie! He told you so? He was a sad rattle but I had not thought him cruel."

"Oh no, he was never deliberately cruel. He just never . . . that is, he hardly ever . . ." She took a deep breath. "He eloped with me out of kindness, because I was so unhappy at home, but he never touched me, not before we were married. He was too busy gambling with his friends. And afterwards, he was rarely at home, and when he was, generally in his cups."

"Good gad! Yet, having known Freddie for a baconbrained clunch any time these twenty years, why should I be surprised to learn he was blind to the charms of the most desirable woman in the world?" With one finger Gareth raised her chin till she was forced to look up at him, to see the sincerity in his deep blue eyes. Then he bent his head and kissed her lips very gently. "You are, you know, to me. Why else should I break my vow never to wed?"

"Gareth, you don't . . . You say I'm the most . . . You don't want a marriage in name only, do you? Because I don't think I could bear it."

"Confound it, no! Have you not understood a word I've been saying, little goose? Not to mention actions, which are supposed to speak louder than words."

"They do," Laura said pertly, reassured at last, pressing herself against him. "But I shall not let you wrap me in cotton-wool when I am in the family way."

"I know it," he said with a rueful smile, which swiftly gave way to the pleading look she knew so well. "Laura, you don't object to preventing conception by artificial means, do you?"

"Is it possible?" she asked in astonishment.

"Quite possible. I have made it my business to find out — That's why I went to London, incidentally. You see why I could not explain my absence! The method I learned about, though not infallible, is not difficult when you know how."

"I have no religious objection, if that is what you mean. But I want your children!"

"And I yours. A few. What I don't want is for you to be worn out by child-bearing, like Mama. I love you too much."

"Enough not to care if you are ostracized for marrying me?"

"Quite enough, but it is not a fate I expect." Raising his determined chin, Gareth looked down his aristocratic nose at her. "Much as it grieves me to boast, I must inform you that my consequence is sufficient for both of us."

"Hoity-toity!"

"Not that it will be needed. Aunt Antonia

is all agog to welcome you as my bride, and when people see both her and your family accepting you —"

"Truly?"

"Truly. Another reason I went up to Town was to speak to your father. Oh, I've just had a simply splendid notion." His eyes gleamed. "I shall make Aunt Sybil hold a betrothal party for us."

"No, Gareth, you must not!"

"Your wish is my command," he said mournfully. "But you will marry me, won't you?"

"Yes, my dearest, I will."

A highly satisfactory embrace followed, cut short — but not very short — by a piercing shriek from the kitchen.

"Oh dear," Laura sighed, "I'm afraid that means Priscilla wants me to give her supper. She lets Myfanwy do everything else, but not feed her."

"A female of decided opinions, like her mama." Gareth released Laura and looked her over by the last of the evening light. He grinned. "Not much worse than when I arrived. I daresay Pris won't mind tousled hair and a dirty face if I don't."

"Heavens, I forgot." A warm happiness filled her from tip to toe: He loved her even in her present state. "You are not much better yourself. Come on." She took his hand and led the way out to the hall, where another shriek greeted them. "Do you know, Pris said ga-ga today and I was sure she was trying to say Gareth."

"She will have to learn to say Dada or Papa now." He held Laura back for a moment and kissed the nape of her neck before they entered the kitchen.

Yet another shriek cut off abruptly at their appearance. Priscilla beamed. "Da-da-da-da," she said obligingly.

We hope you have enjoyed this Large Print book. Other Thorndike, Wheeler, Kennebec, and Chivers Press Large Print books are available at your library or directly from the publishers.

For information about current and upcoming titles, please call or write, without obligation, to:

Publisher
Thorndike Press
10 Water St., Suite 310
Waterville, ME 04901
Tel. (800) 223-1244

or visit our Web site at:

http://gale.cengage.com/thorndike

OR

Chivers Large Print
published by AudioGO Ltd
St James House, The Square
Lower Bristol Road
Bath BA2 3BH
England
Tel. +44(0) 800 136919
info@audiogo.co.uk
www.audiogo.co.uk

All our Large Print titles are designed for easy reading, and all our books are made to last.